D1359849

A
FAITH
of
HER OWN

Center Point
Large Print

Also by Kathleen Fuller and available from
Center Point Large Print:

Letters to Katie

**This Large Print Book carries the
Seal of Approval of N.A.V.H.**

A
FAITH
of
HER OWN

KATHLEEN
FULLER

CENTER POINT LARGE PRINT
THORNDIKE, MAINE

This Center Point Large Print edition is published
in the year 2015 by arrangement with Thomas Nelson.

The text of this Large Print edition is unabridged.
In other aspects, this book may vary
from the original edition.
Printed in the United States of America
on permanent paper.
Set in 16-point Times New Roman type.

ISBN: 978-1-62899-550-3

Library of Congress Cataloging-in-Publication Data

Fuller, Kathleen.
  A faith of her own / Kathleen Fuller. — Center Point Large Print
edition.
    pages cm
  Summary: "Having left the Amish community to pursue his dream of
becoming a veterinarian, Jeremiah now returns to Middlefield to work
in a practice there. As he rekindles a friendship with Anna Mae, both of
them are torn between loyalty to their loved ones and being pulled in
different directions"—Provided by publisher.
  ISBN 978-1-62899-550-3 (library binding : alk. paper)
  1. Amish Country (Ohio)—Fiction.
    2. Amish—Social life and customs—Fiction. 3. Large type books.
    I. Title.
PS3606.U553F85 2015b
813'.6—dc23

                                                    2015003354

To James Fuller
Thank you for going on this journey with me

GLOSSARY

Ab im kopp: crazy

Aenti: aunt

Amisch: Amish

Amisch mann: Amish man

Appeditlich: delicious

Boppli/bopplis: baby/babies

Bruder: brother

Buwe: boys

Daed: dad

Danki: thank you

Deitsch: language spoken by the Amish

Dochder: daughter

Dummkopf: dummy

Dumm: dumb

Englisch: non-Amish person

Familye: family

Frau: wife/Mrs.

Geh: go

Grienhaus: greenhouse

Grossmammi/grossmutter: grandmother

Grossvatter: grandfather

Gut: good

Gut nacht: good night

Haus: house

Herr: mister/Mr.

Kapp: Amish woman's head covering

Kaffee: coffee
Kinn: child
Kinner: children
Kumme: come
Lieb: love
Maed: girls
Mamm: mom
Mein Gott: my God
Mudder: mother
Nix: nothing
Nee: no
Onkel: uncle
Schwester: sister
Schee: pretty/handsome
Sohn: son
Vatter: father
Ya: yes
Yankee: non-Amish (Middlefield only)
Yer: your

PROLOGUE

Nine Years Earlier

Anna Mae Shetler walked the short length of the tree house, growing more impatient with every step. Where were they? It wasn't like Jeremiah and Amos Mullet to keep her waiting. Sure, her mother had said more than once since she'd turned thirteen that she needed to learn patience. And humility and steadfastness and all those other things the Bible said she had to have. She'd have time for that, though. Later. Right now she was eager to see Jeremiah and Amos.

When she heard the rustling of leaves down below, she stuck her head out the window and grinned at them. "About time. I thought you two would never get here."

Amos climbed up first. Stocky and slow, he took a lot longer to get up to the tree house. Jeremiah, although a year younger at thirteen, was leaner, taller, and faster. But he waited without complaint while his brother made his way up the new steps Daniel Beiler had nailed to the tree. His father had made him replace the old ones, which he had removed when he had tried not to get caught stealing money from the tree house.

Once Amos was near the opening of the tree

house, Jeremiah climbed up. Anna Mae smirked. She was sure her mother would approve of Jeremiah's patience.

Soon the three of them were sitting cross-legged on the slat wood floor.

"Look, Anna Mae," Amos said. "*Grossmammi* gave me a new art set. A real set, like real artists use. Charcoal and watercolors and a sketchbook." He pulled the set out of his bag and spread the treasures out on the floor. "I'm going to be a farmer-artist." He picked up the sketchbook. "I'll work as a farmer. I'll be an artist for fun."

Jeremiah smiled at her over Amos's head.

"*Grossmammi* said I could make pictures for you and Jeremiah," Amos went on. "I'll send them to Jeremiah at Dr. Miller's."

A panicked look filled Jeremiah's eyes. Anna Mae took hold of his hand and squeezed. "We'll see you all the time, remember? It will be like you're here with us."

But somehow she knew it wouldn't be the same. Although Jeremiah was going to live and apprentice with Dr. Miller, the local vet, she and Amos wouldn't see him as much as they did now. Deep inside she hoped that maybe he would change his mind about becoming a veterinarian. If he didn't, he would have to leave the *Amisch* to pursue his dream. More than anything she wanted him to be happy, but the selfish part of her didn't want him to go. And if he did leave her and the

Amisch behind . . . she didn't know if she could handle that.

She shoved the thoughts out of her mind, released Amos's hand, and glanced around the tree house. The space felt smaller, more confined, almost claustrophobic. It wasn't theirs anymore. Everything was changing. They were getting older and about to go their separate ways. Jeremiah would be gone as soon as he finished eighth grade. Amos would be busy helping his father with their farm. When she completed school she would . . .

She had no idea what she would do. Unlike Jeremiah and Amos, Anna Mae was uncertain about her future. Yet she knew whatever the future held, Jeremiah and Amos would always be her best friends.

She let out a quick breath. "I think we all know we won't be coming back here again."

"*Ya*," Jeremiah sighed. Amos nodded.

"Let's make a pact."

Jeremiah cocked his head. "A pact?"

A pact was a promise. Anna Mae felt the rightness of the words. "We'll make a pact that we'll let nothing come between us. That we'll always be the best of friends, no matter what."

Jeremiah grinned and stuck his hand in the middle of the circle. "To friendship," he said. "*Nix* will come between us."

Amos slapped his hand on top of his brother's. "Not even work and art will come between us."

Anna Mae smiled and laid her hand on Amos's.

"Not even our dreams will come between us." Jeremiah placed his other hand on top of hers.

Amos put his other hand on Jeremiah's.

Anna Mae put her other hand atop the pile. "We promise to always be best friends."

And Anna Mae knew that the promise was true. No matter how life changed, no matter what path they traveled, she knew they would always have this friendship.

That, she could count on.

Forever.

CHAPTER 1

Nine Years Later

Anna Mae folded her hands in her lap as the buggy rolled past the lush grove of oak and maple trees. She sat in the back behind her parents, tilting her face to let the warm June air flow over her, perfumed with the scent of fresh-mown hay, clover, and timothy grass.

"It's been awhile since we've all gotten together," her mother said from the front seat of the buggy. She glanced at Anna Mae over her shoulder. "Other than church, of course. But it's nice to have time with just the family, especially since it's growing so fast."

"*Ya.*"

"It's hard to believe Mary Beth and Christopher have been married for nearly nine years," *Mamm* said, referring to Anna Mae's brother and his wife. "I just wish Rachel could be here. Then we'd all be together." She turned around in her seat. "You're very quiet this afternoon, Anna Mae."

"Unlike some people," her father muttered good-naturedly.

Mamm lightly smacked him on the arm with the palm of her hand before turning her full attention back to Anna Mae. "Is something wrong?"

Anna Mae turned from the fresh air and looked at her mother's wide eyes, filled with feigned innocence. Something was wrong and they both knew it. But Anna Mae wasn't in the mood for a lecture, discussion, or argument. Not today. "*Nee,*" she said, mustering up her sweetest voice. "Everything is fine."

"*Gut,*" her father said, turning into her brother's driveway. "Because we're here. And I'm starving."

Mamm's eyes narrowed slightly as she gave Anna Mae one last look before facing front.

When the buggy stopped, Anna Mae scrambled out, glad to be free of the tight thread of tension that had connected her and her mother for the past several months. That her father was oblivious to it was a testament to the effort both she and her mother expended in hiding their true feelings around him. But it was getting harder for Anna

13

Mae to keep silent, to pretend everything was okay when it wasn't. She suspected it was becoming difficult for her mother too.

Anna Mae looked around, noting all the buggies parked neatly in a row by the side of the driveway. The horses must have all been stabled in the barn. Her father was leading their horse, Licorice, there already. She smiled, remembering when her father let her name the horse after her favorite candy.

Her thoughts turned bittersweet. Life had been so much easier when she was a child.

"Anna Mae!"

She turned to see one of her relatives by marriage, Bekah Yoder, striding toward her. She was twenty-five, three years older than Anna Mae. They weren't particularly close, but Anna Mae liked her. She was different from a lot of the friends Anna Mae had—in her mid-twenties and still not married. She had joined the church as soon as she could, yet she managed to remain independent and happy—the opposite of Anna Mae.

"We need more hands in the kitchen," Bekah said, linking her arm with Anna Mae's. "Actually, we need more competent hands in the kitchen."

"You've been kicked out?"

"Voluntarily removed." Bekah laughed. "I didn't want to spend the afternoon cooped up in there anyway."

Anna Mae grinned. Bekah was notorious among

their family not only for her independent spirit but for her complete lack of cooking skills.

"I offered to help man the grills, but *nee.*" The smoky scent of smoldering charcoal filtered through the air. They stopped on the front porch. "Apparently only men are allowed to do that job." She sighed, her pale-brown brows knitting together. "I guess I'll set the tables. And they'll be the best set tables you'll ever see." Bekah released her arm and headed for the backyard, where Anna Mae knew there were at least two long tables and over a dozen chairs to accommodate the family.

Anna Mae went inside and proceeded to the kitchen, where there were indeed many good cooks—her sister-in-law, Mary Beth; Mary Beth's mother, Margaret Mullet; Bekah's sister Katherine, who was married to Mary Beth's twin brother, Johnny Mullet; and Anna Mae's mother, Caroline, who must have gotten to the kitchen through the back door while Anna Mae was talking with Bekah.

She hung back and stood in the doorway, watching them finish up the final preparations for a meal that included a bounty of food to accompany whatever grilled meat was cooking outside. Anna Mae saw a plate of deviled eggs, a bowl of pickles, two platters filled with Swiss, cheddar, and American sliced cheese, three huge bowls of red-skinned potato salad, two jars of chowchow, a fruit salad, a plate of cookies, and four pies.

Her stomach growled as she kept observing the bustle in the kitchen, each woman wearing a different colored dress but with the same white prayer *kapps* secured to their heads. They spoke to each other in Pennsylvania *Deitsch*, only stopping the conversation with a smile or a chuckle. They all seemed happy. They all seemed at peace.

All but Anna Mae.

"Anna Mae," her mother said, motioning her to come inside the kitchen. "Put out these yeast rolls Katherine made." She lifted the lid to the plastic container and sniffed. "They smell *appeditlich*. Reminds me of the ones your *grossmammi* Bertha used to make."

She took the rolls from her mother with a small smile. *Grossmammi* had passed away two years ago, and she still missed her. She could be tough, especially when it came to Anna Mae learning how to cook, take care of the house, and be a *gut Amisch* woman. But as Anna Mae grew up and her grandmother grew more frail, she'd learned to appreciate *Grossmammi* more. Maybe if she were here, Anna Mae could confide in her.

Then again, she probably wouldn't have understood. No one did.

A blast of warm air hit her when she went outside, her nose detecting the grilled pork chops that were on the menu for the Saturday supper meal. The sun still gleamed brightly in the late-afternoon sky, with only a few dainty puffs of clouds dotting the brilliant blue expanse above.

"I see you finally have a job you can handle."

Anna Mae glanced at Caleb Mullet, her sister-in-law's younger brother, who was behind one of the grills flipping over a pork chop with a metal spatula. His words were aimed at Bekah, who was putting the last fork on the table.

"At least I'm not burning supper," Bekah said sweetly.

A quick look of panic crossed Caleb's face, disappearing when he realized the chops were fine. "They're not burned."

"I'm sure they will be."

"What they will be are the best chops you've ever tasted."

"A little full of yourself, *ya*?" Bekah straightened one of the chairs.

"More like confident."

Anna Mae kept her head down as she placed the rolls on the table. She'd seen them go at it like this since Christopher had married Mary Beth. Always sniping, always trying to one-up each other with the sarcastic comments and veiled insults. She wondered when they'd figure out they were meant for each other.

When the meat was done and the rest of the food laid out, everyone found their places at the table. The only ones missing were Mary Beth's younger brothers, Micah and Eli. Anna Mae had overheard Caleb mention that they were spending the day fishing on Lake Erie with a few of their friends.

Her parents sat at one end, Mary Beth's at the other. In between were the couples, Mary Beth and Christopher, Johnny and Katherine. Bekah and Caleb sat across from each other, both pretending to ignore the other, and Mary Beth and Christopher's two children sat by their parents. The table was crowded, and Anna Mae sat on the corner edge next to her mother, her plate barely fitting on the table.

Everyone had a place. Everyone fit. Everyone belonged.

Everyone but Anna Mae.

Jeremiah Mullet turned off the engine and gripped the steering wheel of his car. He looked at the veterinarian clinic in front of him and the modest house connected to it. For the hundredth time since he'd started the drive from Columbus, he questioned his decision to come here. But he owed Doc Miller, and after he received the call for help from his former mentor yesterday, Jeremiah threw some clothes in his beat-up two-door early this morning and hurried here before he could change his mind.

He checked his watch. Although the sun had

risen only an hour ago, he knew Doc would be up. He remembered how, when he was Doc's apprentice years ago, Doc would wake him up at four in the morning, ready to get a start on the day. Jeremiah was still an early riser, which had annoyed his roommate at Ohio State, who was often just stumbling into bed when Jeremiah was getting up.

His college and vet school years had been so different from his former Amish life. He hadn't been to Middlefield since he was sixteen and left for school. That same year he'd gotten his GED and continued on to college. He took accelerated courses, then sped through vet school. It had taken a lot of work and sacrifice, even though school had always come easy to him. Staying focused on the goal had gotten him through, and he'd been the youngest in his graduating class. Now he was back, and he could see the area had pretty much stayed the same.

But he had changed. For the better, he thought. Until now, as he sat in Doc's driveway dealing with the assault of the past. The guilt for leaving his family the way he did.

For not telling Anna Mae good-bye.

He drew in a deep breath, steadying his thoughts. He was here to help Doc Miller for a short time, but that was it. Then he'd hightail it back to his life in Columbus, where he had been applying for jobs at clinics around the area. Sure, he lived in a dump and could barely pay his bills with the part-time convenience store job he quit yesterday to come back here. But as his grandmother Ella had said, he had to follow his heart and his dreams. Which he had, by graduating last month from vet school.

Another wave of guilt flowed over him at the thought of his grandmother. He shoved it away and got out of the car. His worn work boots scraped against the black asphalt driveway. Two giant bumblebees hovered over a basket of purple flowers hanging from a hook under the front porch awning. He knocked on the door.

"Jeremiah Mullet." Amy Miller grinned as she opened the door and motioned for him to come in. "I'm so glad you're here." She opened her arms for a hug, and Jeremiah embraced her. During the three years he apprenticed with Doc, the Millers had been like family to him.

She released him. "Did you have breakfast?"

"Not yet."

Amy headed for the kitchen and Jeremiah followed. "I can whip up some eggs and bacon real quick, if you want."

"That's okay. I'm not really hungry."

"How about some coffee, then?" She went to the counter and picked up the black coffeepot. She poured the dark brew into a cup that said *Got Fleas?* along with an advertisement for flea-prevention medication. She handed it to him. "Doc will be down in a few minutes."

"How's he doing?"

"He was able to start with the crutches yesterday, but he's still having trouble with them. I offered to help him down the stairs, but you know Doc. Stubborn as the day is long. You wouldn't believe how hard it was to convince him to call you for help." She lowered her voice, her mouth tightening with worry. "It isn't just the broken leg, Jeremiah. He's been moving a little slower lately. His arthritis is getting to him."

"Is he taking anything for it?" Jeremiah sat down on the tufted cushion tied to one of the white kitchen table chairs. The sun streamed through the window, brightening the already cheery room.

"A couple of prescriptions, but they don't seem to help too much. Don't tell him I told you. He wouldn't be happy with me." She lifted a flowered mug to her lips and sipped.

"No problem. I won't say anything."

"Say what?"

Jeremiah turned as Doc walked into the kitchen. He tried to hold back the surprise at the man's appearance. He'd changed a lot in the last six years—thicker in the middle, and what little hair he had on his head was more gray than brown. He seemed to be doing okay with the crutches, though. Yet when he plopped down next to Jeremiah and placed his hands on the table, that's where the real effects of the arthritis were most noticeable. His fingers were bent slightly to the side and his knuckles were swollen, the blue veins under his skin bulging and prominent.

Jeremiah closed his hands underneath the table. His hands were his most important tools. Performing surgeries; delivering colts, calves, ewes, and a variety of other animals; administering shots and IVs; and so many more manual tasks—he couldn't imagine doing all that with painful, misshapen hands.

When Doc had called him, he hadn't given a hint of how important it was that Jeremiah return to help, only that he'd broken his leg and would be laid up for a few weeks. But it was clear the man was in pain.

"I was just saying," Jeremiah said, glancing at Amy before picking up his coffee cup, "that your wife makes the best coffee I've ever had."

"Yes, she does." Doc looked up at her and smiled. His formerly brown beard was completely gray.

"I also make pretty good oatmeal." Amy set a bowl in front of Doc. "Now eat up."

Doc picked up the spoon out of the bowl and frowned at the big clump of warm cereal. "My breakfast for the last year," he mumbled.

"Doesn't look so bad," Jeremiah said.

"That's because you don't have to eat it."

Jeremiah chuckled. "I've eaten worse."

"Ah, yes. The glamorous life of a starving

veterinarian student." He looked at Jeremiah. "I am now thankful for my oatmeal."

While Doc ate, he and Jeremiah chatted about school, some of Doc's patients, and how Doc had broken his leg—he was examining a horse and it kicked him in the shin. "Didn't move fast enough," Doc said, scraping the last bite out of his bowl.

Jeremiah met Amy's worried gaze, then quickly focused his attention on Doc.

"Oh well. Stuff like that happens." Doc grabbed his crutches. "Ready to go?"

Jeremiah nodded. "Thanks for the coffee, Amy."

"Anytime." She took the cup from him and put it in the sink.

They walked next door to the clinic. The bell above the door rang as Jeremiah opened it, holding the glass door so Doc could limp inside. Jeremiah looked around the waiting room, which had remained the same since he'd left. He was relieved. Everything else in his life had changed so much it was disorienting. More memories came flooding back from when he was younger and helping Doc with the various animals both Amish and Yankee clients had brought to the clinic.

"I've been spending most of my time here the past year or so," Doc said. When Jeremiah didn't say anything, he added, "Thought you'd ask me why."

"It's not any of my business. It's your practice. You need to do what's best."

"That's what I keep telling my wife." Doc leaned against the front counter, holding on to the top of his crutches with his hand. "She kept wanting me to give up the large-animal part of the practice." He looked down at the cast on his leg. "When this happened she thought she'd been proven right." He chuckled. "Maybe she was. Like I said with how I broke my leg, I don't move as fast as I used to." He looked up. "I've finally given in. I think I could manage if I only had the small critters to take care of. But I still have a lot of people with livestock asking if I can help them out." He looked at Jeremiah. "That's why I called you."

Jeremiah didn't let on that he knew crippling arthritis was the real reason Doc needed to stop working with livestock—and probably needed to stop practicing altogether. "I'm glad you did."

"Are you?" He pushed up his glasses. "I was kind of worried how your dad might feel about you coming back."

"I wouldn't know. I haven't seen him yet."

Doc lifted a bushy brow. "You came here first?"

Jeremiah nodded. "I wanted to come and check on you. Your call seemed so urgent and all."

"It wasn't that urgent." Doc paused. "But I understand why you're putting off going home."

Home. Jeremiah hadn't had a real home in

years, and where he grew up wasn't home to him anymore. But he nodded. "Yeah."

Doc took up his crutches and limped over to the coat tree in the corner of the waiting room. He took a white lab coat off one of the hooks and awkwardly put it on. Jeremiah was going to ask him if he needed help, but he held back. When Doc was finished putting on the coat, he turned to Jeremiah. "I guess I was kind of hoping . . ."

"Hoping for what?" Jeremiah asked.

Doc shook his head. "Never mind. So when are you ready to get started?"

"Right now."

"Sure you don't have any business to take care of first?"

Jeremiah met the vet's questioning gaze with a stern one of his own. "Positive."

"All right, then. Let's go in the back."

They went to one of the exam rooms. Doc moved to the counter and opened one of the drawers. He pulled out a card and handed it to Jeremiah. "I ran into Bud last week, before this happened." He gestured to his leg. "He told me one of his alpacas was acting funny."

Jeremiah read the card aloud. " 'Bud Turner's Alpacas. Once you Alpaca, you never go backa.' "

"Like we've never heard that one before." Doc smirked. "But Bud's a good friend of mine, so I went to Orwell and checked it out. Sure enough, one of his alpacas had an inner-ear infection.

Gave her some Banamine and Baytril and told Bud to keep treating her twice a day with the Banamine. I called him yesterday to find out how the girl was doing. He said she was 'sorta kinda looking a little better.'"

"I have no idea what that means." Jeremiah chuckled.

"Me either. So I'd like you to follow up. Everything you need is in the back. Do you remember?"

Jeremiah nodded. "Yep. It's almost like I never left."

Doc clapped him on the shoulder. "I'm just glad you came back."

He looked at Doc and smiled but didn't say anything. The strain he'd felt while driving to Middlefield had nearly disappeared. Working with Doc again was a good thing. As a vet, Jeremiah was firmly in his comfort zone. He could help animals—cure their illnesses, keep them healthy, educate their owners, and when necessary, comfort them.

He was in control and confident in his job—the exact opposite of how he felt in every other aspect of his life. Because when it came to his own family, he was at a loss.

CHAPTER 2

Anna Mae placed her hand on the warm window-pane, staring outside the kitchen window. The sunshine and blue skies beckoned her, making her wish she could strip off her *kapp* and run through the tall grass in the field across the road. She longed for just a tiny taste of freedom. Any possible way to escape her thoughts . . . and her life.

"Anna Mae? Help me pin the hem on the rest of these curtains."

She took one last look at the gorgeous field, turning away from the sun's warmth and joining her *mamm* at the table. *Mamm* slid the pin-cushion toward her. "Please make sure the hem is straight this time." She sighed. "You've been very dis-tracted lately."

She pulled one of the silver pins out of the cushion and slid it between two layers of light-blue cotton fabric. Normally she was an excellent seamstress. Yet *Mamm* was right; she had been distracted. And anxious, confused . . . so many thoughts and emotions whirled through her head nowadays that she could barely contain them all.

Her mother smiled as she smoothed out the fabric. "Your *schwester*, Rachel, will be so surprised to get these curtains for her birthday. I wish we could visit her," *Mamm* said. "I miss her so much since she and her *familye* moved to Colorado. I thought about her a lot at the supper at Christopher's last Saturday."

Anna Mae wished she could visit her sister, too, but not for the same reasons. Of course she wanted to see Rachel, who was ten years older than Anna Mae and had moved away with her husband three years ago. But the thought of visiting another place, especially somewhere as beautiful as the West, appealed to Anna Mae. She had seen pictures of the Rocky Mountains in books from the library. But Rachel's letters didn't do the images justice. She wrote about the children, about her garden, about new recipes she had tried. Topics her mother loved to read about. But when Anna Mae read them, she felt like a noose was tightening around her neck.

"I wrote to her the other day," *Mamm* said, interrupting her thoughts. "I asked her for the recipe for those monster cookies. The ones she sent us melted in your mouth, *ya*?"

"They were *gut*." Anna Mae focused on her stitching.

"Perhaps you could make them when she sends the recipe. You could practice some of your cooking skills. You know, for when you . . ."

Anna Mae didn't look up. Her mother's words were leading to a common discussion between them—Anna Mae's future marriage. Cooking, sewing, canning, gardening—once she turned thirteen her *grossmutter* Bertha had taught her the skills she needed to be a capable *Amisch* woman. Her mother had joined in, admonishing her to be meek, to be humble, to recognize that her husband would be the head of the home when she got married.

When Anna Mae didn't say anything, *Mamm* asked, "What are your plans for today?"

She threaded her needle. "I'm going to see Amos this afternoon. I noticed the other day his pants were getting too short, so I'm going to take some measurements and make new ones."

"That's nice of you." *Mamm* began stitching, her hand practically flying as she whipped the needle and thread through the fabric. "And the right thing to do, helping David take care of Amos."

"I don't take care of Amos because it's right." She started to sew. "He's my friend and he needs new pants."

"He needs a lot of things," her mother said under her breath.

Anna Mae pressed her lips together. She glanced at her mother, who put two pins in her mouth but kept on talking.

"I mean, I'm just saying that I think it's wonderful that you are there for him. It's the kind of thing we are supposed to do as *members* of our church."

Anna Mae winced as the needle slipped in her hand and dug into the pad of her finger. She knew they would eventually find their way to this topic—Anna Mae joining the church. But she didn't respond, just wiped away the spot of blood on her finger and kept sewing.

"Considering all the hardship he's gone through, Amos needs the support of the community."

Anna Mae remained silent.

"And David, poor *mann*." *Mamm* took out the pins and clucked her tongue. "With Ella passing away two years ago . . ." She looked at Anna Mae, her eyes filling with sadness. "I can't believe she and Bertha died within a month of each other."

Nodding, Anna Mae swallowed. She missed her grandmother, just like Amos missed his. The two women had been best friends when they were young. A rift had separated them for years, but they had made amends when Anna Mae was a teenager. Until their deaths, they had remained very close.

"So much loss," her mother continued, apparently determined to put a damper on the sunny morning. "David losing his mother, and before that Marie leaving him and the *buwe*—"

Anna Mae lowered her head, pretending to be engrossed in her sewing and trying to ignore *Mamm*'s prattling, wishing she would talk about something else. Amos's mother leaving him had happened years ago. He never talked about it, and David had never mentioned it—ever—in Anna Mae's presence. They had moved on from the past, but her mother didn't have a problem dredging it up on occasion.

"Then after all that, Jeremiah walking out on them . . ."

Anna Mae froze, needle in midair. *Mamm* never brought up Jeremiah, not since he'd left Middlefield six years ago.

"*Mamm*, I don't want to talk about him—"

"You'd think he would have been more sensitive to his brother and father, after what his mother had done to them."

"She abandoned Jeremiah too." Anna Mae couldn't believe she was defending him. But it was true, and like Amos and David, he had never talked about it. At least while he was still in Middlefield. She had no idea what he was doing now, other than attending veterinarian school in Columbus. Her mind went back to the promise he had made, along with her and Amos—back when they were teenagers in the tree house. *Nix will come between us.*

She'd been a fool to believe he'd keep that promise as an adult.

"*That* should have made him think twice about leaving the *Amisch*. About how much he hurt his *familye*. His community."

A sick feeling roiled in the pit of Anna Mae's stomach. Jeremiah had hurt the people he

31

claimed to care for when he left Middlefield. Yet she knew better than anyone how deeply he desired to be a vet. He'd had to make a difficult choice, one with far-reaching consequences. Although she considered him a coward for the way he left, she grudgingly admired the courage it took to leave.

Courage she didn't have . . . and wondered if she ever would.

But she didn't want to think about Jeremiah, especially in a positive light. She also didn't want to talk about the community or the church. Not with her mother, who wouldn't understand Anna Mae's conflicted emotions.

Fortunately, her mother decided to stop talking. They sewed in silence for a while before her mother said, "Don't stay too long at Amos's. I'd like you home in time to help with supper."

"All right." She tied a knot at the end of her thread.

"I'm serious, Anna Mae."

She glanced up to see her mother giving her a pointed look.

"Don't be late."

"I won't. I promise." Strange. She helped her mother with supper almost every evening. Why was tonight such a big deal? She opened her mouth to ask, only to clamp it shut again. It didn't matter what her mother had up her sleeve—she'd find out soon enough.

●●●

Caleb pulled his buggy into the driveway in front of his house. Well, it wasn't exactly his house. Technically it belonged to Johnny and Katie, but Caleb had moved in and paid rent ever since Johnny made him partner in the horse farm five years ago. He'd been surprised by the offer, considering he was only twenty at the time. But he knew horses and had been working with Johnny almost since the day he'd bought the farm six years ago. Moving in when he became partner had made sense. He'd helped Johnny renovate the ramshackle house, adding on so it now had four bedrooms plus a guest room.

He parked his buggy under the barn awning and unhitched his horse, Soda Bread. He'd had Soda for years, since he was fifteen, and there wasn't a finer horse. He patted the horse's flank as he led him to the stable and settled him in his stall. He started back to his buggy to retrieve his hardware store purchases, but when he walked around the barn, he had to pause.

As he looked around the farm, taking in the custom, sturdy fencing that surrounded two corrals, the second barn he and Johnny had added last year, and the acres of sweet pasture grass that provided plenty of grazing for their horses, his heart swelled with pride. He couldn't help it. It was hard to believe this was the same place Johnny had unwisely purchased seven years ago, when he was barely twenty and had just lost his job. The place had been a dump, pure and simple. In the end he'd sold it, not knowing his best friend Sawyer's Yankee grandmother had bought it as investment property. Only when Johnny had told Sawyer he was financially ready to start over again did he learn that Cora Easely, the fancy, rich Yankee woman who had found a new home in peaceful Middlefield, now owned the property.

Since buying and improving the farm, Cora had come to visit a few times. She had invested a bit of money into the farm, but not too much. Johnny hadn't let her. He had wanted to sink or swim on this venture on his own, and eventually he shared ownership with Cora. Now with Parkinson's slowing her down, she only came out with Sawyer for short visits. But the woman seemed at peace when she was here, happy to sit and watch the horses graze every time she came.

Caleb smiled and put his hands on his hips. Who wouldn't love this place? It was everything Johnny—and Caleb—had dreamed of. A lot of sweat was represented here, plus a lot of prayers. Mullet Horse Farm was a success. He and Johnny had worked hard to make it one. Until he worked at the farm, he'd struggled to keep jobs since he finished school at fifteen. It was never because of his work ethic, all his bosses had told him. It was always other circumstances. Layoffs.

Businesses closing. Seasonal construction work that never turned into full time.

But now he finally had something permanent. Something he'd helped create from the ground up. Nothing was better than that.

He went to his buggy and retrieved the bag of nails and wood glue from the backseat. When he turned toward the house, he frowned at the sight of Bekah hanging clothes on the line. She was here again? He looked away as he walked. Since she left her job as a waitress at Mary Yoder's, she'd been spending more and more time here, mostly with Katie. But every once in a while he'd find her in the barn, looking at the horses, and he'd have to chase her out. They weren't pets and they weren't hers. He needed to protect his investment from whatever trouble she could cause.

Because trouble seemed to follow Bekah like a horse after sugar cubes.

Despite his almost constant annoyance with her, he couldn't resist looking at her again as she hung the laundry. She wore a light-blue kerchief instead of her white *kapp*, and her lips were pursed, as if she were whistling. Her movements were quick and light, like a hummingbird flitting from flower to flower.

He pulled his gaze away, reminding himself that Bekah was nothing more than an irritant, like a pesky fly. She was a person he had to put up with since her sister was married to his brother. He lowered his head and went inside the house, determined to focus on anything but her.

Katie and Johnny were seated at the kitchen table, finishing up breakfast. "*Gut* morning," Caleb said as he walked to the stove and helped himself to coffee.

"Find what you need at the hardware store?" Johnny downed the last gulp of coffee from his mug. Caleb glanced at them. They seemed to be having a leisurely morning, considering there was so much work to be done. But he didn't say anything.

"*Ya*. I'm ready to get started on that storage bin." He added a splash of milk to the mug.

Katie rose. "I should get started on my morning too." She yawned. "I don't know why I've been so tired lately. I didn't even hear you and Johnny get up."

Caleb looked at her. She did seem tired, which was unusual for Katie. Normally she was up first and had breakfast ready for him and Johnny in the mornings. But this morning they ate leftovers from the night before. Which he didn't mind, but it made him appreciate Katie's good cooking even more.

"I'm glad Bekah is here," Katie continued as she cleared up the kitchen dishes. "I appreciated her giving me a hand with the laundry."

"I have some upstairs in my room that needs to be washed," Caleb said, setting down his coffee mug. He didn't like the idea of Bekah doing his laundry, but he didn't exactly want to do it himself either. "I'll bring it down."

"Then I'll meet you behind the barn," Johnny said. "I'll start measuring the wood for the bin."

Caleb nodded in reply and left the kitchen, but then tripped over the loose board on the threshold. He'd have to fix that later today. As he regained his balance, he caught movement out of the corner of his eye—a kiss between Johnny and Katie he wasn't supposed to see.

He hurried upstairs, a little embarrassed at catching the tender moment. That was really the only downside to living in this house. Sometimes he felt like he was in the way. Johnny and Katie had never purposely made him feel that way, but he still did. He could imagine it would be worse when they had children.

Lately he'd been noodling on the idea of building a small bachelor house next door to the main one, since he wasn't in any hurry to get married. Sure, he was one of the few single men around his age in the district, but that didn't bother him. Marriage was for life, and if he made a mistake and married the wrong woman, he'd have to live with it. He wasn't going to take that chance until he felt absolutely sure. Even Johnny and Katie had a four-year engagement because they had waited on the Lord to tell them the right time to get married. Caleb was of the same mind.

God would lead him to the perfect woman, and if he had to wait for her, he would.

Besides, he had plenty to do without worrying about romance. He hadn't dated much, with his longest girlfriend being Bekah's friend Miriam when he was seventeen, and that hadn't lasted very long.

He entered his room and gathered up the laundry from off the end of the bed. The living quarters were sparse, but enough for him. At least he had thought so until lately. He frowned. It would be nice having his own place, not having to be con-cerned with intruding on a private moment or paying rent to his brother. He'd talk to Johnny about it later. Surely they could work out some-thing.

He spied a black sock on his small desk beneath the window. How did that get there? He picked up the sock and looked outside, pausing when he saw Bekah again. Instead of pinning clothes to the line, she was staring up at the tree limbs swaying in the summer breeze. Figured. Bekah was an expert at wasting time. Katie would have had the laundry already hung by now. He shook his head. At least if he had his own place he'd have less of a chance of running into her. Maybe he'd talk to Johnny about that sooner rather than later.

Katie pulled away from her husband's embrace. "I think Caleb caught us," she whispered.

"So?" Johnny grabbed her hand and put it at his waist. He slid his fingers down one of the ribbons on her *kapp*. "Just because my brother is here doesn't mean I can't let *mei frau* know how much I love her." He kissed her again.

Katie put her hand on his chest but let him finish the kiss. She didn't want it to end either. After four years of marriage, the spark between them hadn't waned. She'd loved Johnny most of her life, but it wasn't until she married him that she realized how romantic he was. But she wasn't comfortable with public displays, even in front of his brother. "We need to be respectful of Caleb."

"Kissing you in our kitchen is disrespectful?"

"You know what I mean." She turned away to finish the breakfast dishes. "We should be more . . . discreet."

Johnny put his hand on her arm, stilling her movements. "Wait. Katie, Caleb has lived here for a long time. Is this about him? Or something else?"

She knew what he meant. She leaned over and kissed him lightly on the lips. "I'm not saying I want to stop trying."

"*Gut*, because I don't want to stop trying either." The playfulness in Johnny's expression disappeared. "I really believe you're not pregnant because God has a different plan for us right now. Katie, we've been able to save up enough money to have this dream." He gestured around him. "Instead of raising a *familye* in a teeny tiny home, we have a house large enough for a passel of *kinner*. They'll grow up on a beautiful horse farm."

"The size of the *haus* doesn't matter to me, Johnny."

"I know. And maybe that's a bad example, but *mei* point is still the same. God is in control. We both know that." He ran the back of his hand over her cheek. "We're used to waiting, *ya*? We waited to date. We waited to marry. And now we wait for a *boppli*." His voice lowered. "When the time is right, we'll have *kinner*."

Katie turned away, not wanting her husband to see her desperation.

But he tilted her head so she had to look at him. "Katie," he whispered.

She met his loving gaze. She could never keep anything from him. When it came to Johnny, she couldn't hide.

He smiled. "I've told you this before, and I'll tell you a thousand times more if you need me to. Even if God doesn't bless us with children, I will still love you. I love you more each day. That's not going to change, *nee* matter what happens."

"I know," she said. "And I don't have to tell you how much I love you."

He winked. "It's nice to hear, though."

She gazed at him. "I love you, more than anything. I just don't want you to be dis—"

"That will never happen." He kissed her. "Now,

if we need to we can talk about this later, but right now I have to go or Caleb really will wonder what we're doing if I'm still here." He gave her one last look before leaving the kitchen and heading out-side.

Katie sat down at the table, her head falling into her hands, fatigue seeping into her bones. Why was she so tired? Could it be from the strain of trying to keep up her spirits when she was with Johnny? She wished she had as much confidence in God's plan as he did. But they were twenty-eight years old, and after four years of trying she thought she would have had one or two children by now. Mary Beth had two. Katie's sister Hannah had five. Their friends Laura and Sawyer Thompson were expecting their second.

There was something wrong with her, and she knew it.

She'd read about women in the Bible who didn't have children, only to miraculously become pregnant in old age. There was Sarah, Abraham's wife. Elizabeth, mother of John the Baptist. Hannah, mother of Samuel, who was so grateful to finally have a child that she dedicated him solely to the Lord.

Maybe she hadn't prayed hard enough. Or had enough faith, like Johnny. She had to believe miracles still happened. If only it wasn't becoming harder and harder to hang on to hope.

She sat up and took in a deep breath. It

wouldn't do to wallow in self-pity. She'd be better off following her husband's example and putting all her faith in God. She stood and went to finish the dishes.

"Where do you want this?"

She turned and looked at Caleb, who was holding a small bundle of his clothes in his arms. "Downstairs by the washer. I'll get to them in a bit."

"So Bekah won't be washing them?"

Katie faced her brother-in-law, noting the slight pink tinge of his cheeks. Inside, she was smiling to herself. She never knew two people who were so bent on being in denial about their feelings for each other as Caleb and Bekah were. "*Nee*, I'll take care of it."

"*Gut*," he said, heading for the basement where the washer was located. "She'd probably ruin them." He went down the stairs only to call out, "On purpose!"

Katie chuckled and shook her head.

If he only knew . . .

CHAPTER 3

Outside, Bekah dawdled a little more than usual, hoping to avoid Caleb. She shouldn't be here as much as she had been lately, but she couldn't help herself. After leaving her job, she would rather be here than at home. The farm was beautiful, and the house was comfortable and welcoming. Everything here was so peaceful, so lovely, so perfect . . .

Except when Caleb was around.

She picked up the empty laundry basket and stared at Katie's light-green dress on the line, the skirt lifting in the summer breeze. She looked up to see Katie walking toward her, carrying another basket. Funny how she and her family had called her Katherine her entire life, but now everyone called her Katie, like Johnny did. Her sister smiled as she approached.

"You've been out here for a while," Katie said. "I was wondering if you needed help."

Bekah smirked, although she'd noticed how tired Katie had looked when Bekah had arrived earlier. She didn't look as fatigued now, but she also wasn't her normal self. Keeping the mood light, Bekah set down her basket and said, "I'm capable of hanging up the laundry, thank you very much." She looked back at the dress hanging a little crookedly on the line. "Although it's not *mei* favorite chore."

"You actually have a favorite?"

"I'm getting better at cooking. Does that count?"

Katie laughed. "I think so. What does *Mamm* say?"

"Oh, she's given up on me."

Katie shook her head. "I think she's just trying

43

a different approach than constant nagging."

"Let me guess. She asked you to talk to me."

"*Nee*." But Katie averted her gaze.

Bekah chuckled. "Don't worry. I understand." She folded her arms across her chest. "Say what you need to say."

"I don't think now is a *gut* time—"

"Say it. I want to get this over with so I can move on with *mei* day. And you can say you did your duty."

Her sister sighed. "All right. Bekah, we need to have a talk."

From the other side of the clothesline Bekah nodded. "All right, *Mamm*, er, Katie."

Katie smiled. "Since you already know what I'm going to say, this is pretty pointless, isn't it?"

"Exactly what I've been trying to tell *Mamm*. But will she listen to me?" Bekah shook her head, a wayward light-brown strand of hair escaping from her kerchief. "Of course not. Then she complains that I don't listen to her."

"I'm not sure I want to get in the middle of this."

"You're not, trust me. And I'll tell her what I told you. If—and I mean *if*—I get married, that man is going to have to accept me as I am. Flaws and all, bad cooking and all. He's going to have to be okay with the fact that I like to ride horses, I love to read books, I go fishing at least once a week, and I have a curious nature."

"And *Mamm* wonders why you're not married."

"Also, I speak *mei* mind."

Katie shook her head. "*Nee* argument there."

Bekah folded her hands together and lifted her chin. "Bekah," she said, doing a perfect imitation of her mother. "I know we've discussed this before, but for some reason you don't seem to understand. You are a twenty-five-year-old woman. Yet you don't take your household jobs—or your life—seriously."

"Wow," Katie said, grinning. "You sound just like her."

Bekah continued, pacing the length of the laundry line. "You left a perfectly *gut* job because it 'bored' you. You don't hang the laundry straight. When you wash the floors you don't move the furniture. You seem to think Saturdays are better spent baiting a hook than making sure all the work around the house is done. And shall I mention the time you were kidnapped?"

Katie's mouth formed an O shape. "She brought that up again?"

"More than once." Bekah briefly thought about that time when she was thirteen. Her nosiness regarding their next-door neighbor, Mr. Harvey, had gotten her tied to a chair and a broken arm, thanks to his convict son, who was still serving time. That happened more than a dozen years ago. When she and Caleb had been friends.

A lot had changed since then. Mostly him. Now he was a puffed-up, stuffed shirt who didn't

45

know how to have fun. Work, work, work . . . that was all he was interested in. Granted, she understood work was important. But how boring was life when all one did was work? Even on Sundays, he didn't hang around for fellowship after church, instead choosing to go home, where she was sure he was working on figuring out what he'd work on during the workweek. Or something like that.

She waved away her thoughts. Bekah didn't want to think about Caleb. "Anyway," she said, rubbing her temples in the exasperated way her mother did when she was giving one of her lectures, "out of *mei* three *maed* you've always had the most energy. Been the most curious. Given me the most headaches."

"That's the truth," Katie said with a chuckle.

"You have all that energy. All that quick-mindedness." She looked down her nose. "Why can't you apply yourself and quit being so lazy?"

Katie stopped laughing. "Did she really say that to you?"

Bekah nodded. "*Ya.* She did."

"That's not true. You've helped me out so much around here."

"I guess that doesn't matter. Just like it doesn't matter when I mow the lawn or clean out the barn for *Daed*. She asked me why I can make the barn spotless but my room is a mess." Bekah sniffed. "It's not that bad. I know where everything is." And she did, even though a lot of her possessions were strewn around the room. She liked to see where things were. If they were put away, she often forgot about them.

Katie shook her head. "I didn't realize she was giving you such a hard time. I'm sorry."

"It's not your fault." Bekah eyed her. "Well, maybe a little."

"What did I do?"

"*Nix*, only be perfect." She smiled to show Katie there were no hard feelings. She didn't resent her sister, even though she didn't like being compared to her.

"I'm not perfect," Katie said in all seriousness. "And I think *Mamm* is simply worried about you. She doesn't want you to be lonely." She paused. "Neither do I."

Bekah shook her head. "But that's just it. I'm not lonely. I'm surrounded by family. And now by animals." She grinned. "I also have my books. I may spend a lot of time alone, but I'm never lonely. Even if I was, I wouldn't change myself for someone else."

"*Nee*, you wouldn't. And you shouldn't."

"*Danki* for understanding."

"You're welcome. And I'll ask *Mamm* to leave you alone. Although I can't promise anything." Katie glanced at the clothes basket she had set down next to Bekah's empty basket. It was filled halfway with damp clothes. "Do you mind putting these on the line?"

Bekah eyed the clothing. "I thought all the laundry was done."

"All but Caleb's."

"That figures."

Katie turned toward the house. "I'm going to start on my bread baking. When you're finished, would you mind weeding the garden?"

"I would love to do that."

"I thought you might."

The sisters parted, and Bekah lifted a pair of Caleb's pants out of the basket. As she did so, she did a cursory search through the other clothes, thankful no unmentionables were accidentally mixed in. Not that she would have hung them on the line anyway, but the last thing she wanted to do was deal with anything personal to Caleb.

She quickly put the clothes on the line, then went to the large garden on the other side of the yard. It didn't need much weeding, because as with everything Katie did, she kept up a neat garden. Still, there were a few stray grass blades that needed to come out. She knelt in the soft grass and started to pull.

Despite her half-kidding with her sister about their mother, Bekah couldn't help but replay the "discussion" they had last week. Her mother had accused her of daydreaming, of not taking life seriously. Even worse, she had called her immature.

Bekah curled her fists around a clump of dirt. Her mother would never understand. Books were her escape. What her mother called day-dreaming was Bekah coming up with new ideas. Her mother didn't know it, but Bekah had drawn up the sketch for her father when he expanded the barn last year. At least *Daed* realized she wasn't a complete failure.

She took a deep breath, the scent of the grass and dirt calming her. Couldn't *Mamm* see she was already content? She had joined the church because it felt right. She'd never been drawn to the Yankee world, and she felt part of the community. Her love for the Lord had never been a question. And when she made her vow at seventeen to be *Amisch* for the rest of her life, she'd been completely at peace.

Why did she have to be something she wasn't to please the people around her? Her mother's constant nagging about being a *"gut"* *Amisch* woman wore on her. And as much as she loved her sisters, she would never live up to the ideal their mother saw in them.

Maybe she would never live up to an *Amisch* man's ideal either. Not that there was anyone in mind. Up until recently she had been confident that when the time was right, God would bring the right man into her life.

But if she couldn't be a proper *Amisch* woman, would a man ever be interested in her? Or would he, like her mother, see her as a failure? And then there was Caleb, who had irritated her for so many years when they were kids only to barely speak to her now that they were adults and in-laws. Whatever friendship he'd had for her had dis-appeared. Now he treated her as if she wasn't good enough for him—and never was.

She shook her head. What did she care what Caleb Mullet thought of her anymore? Anytime she went out into the barn to look at the beautiful horses, he would show up and send her away. What? Was he afraid she would prove to be better with the animals than he was? Was he threatened by the fact that she could out fish him, outride him, and make fairly decent banana bread when she set her mind to it?

She stood and walked to the other side of the garden. Forget Caleb. She was ruining her day thinking about him so much.

When she finished weeding the garden fifteen minutes later, she stood and arched her back. She turned and saw Caleb coming out of the house and heading for the barn, as if her thinking about him had willed him to appear.

She groaned, trying not to look at him. Or notice his long-legged stride as he walked. Or how his hat covered what she knew was a thick head of chestnut-colored hair with streaks of gold that glinted in the sunlight. Or how his crooked nose, which he broke three years ago, didn't detract from his handsome face. Or—

Barefoot, she curled her toes in the grass until

they hurt. So much for not thinking about Caleb. Maybe she should just go home. But if she did she might end up having another talk with her mother, and she didn't think she could take that today. She snapped her fingers. She should take a walk in the back pasture. There were woods at the edge of the property that she hadn't totally explored yet. She ran to the house, and in the mudroom she slipped on her shoes before rushing back outside.

As she passed the back side of the barn, she caught Caleb out of the corner of her eye, walking the width of the building toe to toe. She watched him for a moment, then realized what he was doing. Curiosity overrode her decision to explore the woods and ignore Caleb. She walked over to him, putting her hands behind her back, acting as nonchalant as possible. "What are you measuring?"

He didn't look up at her. "We're making a feed storage bin."

"How big are you going to make it?"

"Big enough."

She huffed out a breath. "Brilliant answer."

He glanced at her. "How did you know I was measuring?"

"I saw *mei daed* use the same method when he was deciding on the size of the garden. It's not very accurate, though."

He frowned at her. "I just need a rough estimate."

"But shouldn't you have exact measurements?"

"I know what I'm doing, Bekah."

"Have you ever built a feed bin?"

He glared at her. "Have you?"

She lifted her chin. "*Nee*. But I have drawn up plans for a barn before."

"Sure you have."

"Feel free to ask *mei daed*. He'll tell you all about it."

His eyes narrowed. "Don't you have something else to do besides pestering me?"

She scowled. She remembered she used to call *him* a pest when they were kids. My, how things had changed. "You don't have to be so bad-mannered."

He turned away from her and started walking away. "I've got work to do."

Bekah started after him, furious at his dismissal. Then she stopped. Why waste her time? She had better things to do than argue with such a prideful and rude man.

There were woods to explore. She hadn't been able to thoroughly walk around the farm since she had spent so much time working the past few years. And if she was lucky, maybe there was a secret fishing hole to find—and the last person she'd share that with would be Caleb.

After she finished helping *Mamm* make Rachel's curtains and cleaned up after lunch, Anna Mae quickly left for the Mullets' farm on foot. The moment her feet hit the road, she felt a tiny sense of freedom and relief. She loved her mother, and she didn't like the growing separation between them. But it had gotten to the point where almost everything *Mamm* said irritated her.

She reached the Mullets' almost twenty minutes later. The walk had made her hot and thirsty, but she had enjoyed the rustle of the leaves on the trees, the scent of horses and cows grazing in their pastures, even the intense rays of the sun that had beat down on her back as she had walked along the side of the road.

She went to the front door, knocked twice, and walked inside. It wasn't much cooler in the house than it was outside. David and Amos Mullet lived more simply than many in her district. The off-white curtains on the window were fraying at the hem, showing their age. There were no quilts or candles decorating the wood furniture, only a ratty rug Ella had made years ago from leftover fabric scraps.

Anna Mae went to the windows in the front room and opened them, letting in some fresh air. David spent most of his days outside, either with his cattle or tinkering around in a small work-shop behind the barn. She didn't know what he did back there, and she didn't ask. And Amos . . . well, he wouldn't have remembered to open the windows.

She called out his name but didn't get an answer. Her thirst overwhelmed her, so she went into the kitchen to get a glass of water. Knowing where everything was, she opened a cabinet, took out a small glass, and turned on the tap.

"Hello, Anna Mae."

She glanced over her shoulder and saw Judith Hostetler, Amos and David's next-door neighbor. She shut off the tap and turned around. "Hi, Judith. I didn't realize you were here."

"I just arrived." Judith went to the counter and put a platter of cookies on the table. "I had some leftover cookie dough and thought I'd make some extra for Amos and David."

Anna Mae smiled. Judith had moved into the small house next door almost three months ago, and since then Anna Mae had often run into her here, usually dropping off some kind of bakery treat for the Mullets. Knowing Amos's sweet tooth, Anna Mae was sure that made him happy. She was also glad someone else was nearby. David liked his privacy, but she often felt sorry for Amos, who spent a lot of time alone. Due to his developmental disability, his father kept him fairly sheltered. Anna Mae didn't blame David for his protectiveness, but she had to wonder if it was the best thing for Amos. It wasn't her place, however, to question David about it.

"What brings you by?" Judith said, pulling a dishcloth out of one of the drawers, then wetting it in the sink. Anna Mae noticed how easily Judith moved around the kitchen, as if it were familiar to her. Maybe she had started making meals for Amos and David too.

"I came by to take Amos's measurements," Anna Mae replied before taking a big gulp of water. "I noticed his pants are getting short."

Judith smiled. "I offered to make him some new ones, but he said you always do that for him."

"Since his *grossmutter* died, *ya*, I have."

"He was very insistent that you do it." She wiped down the table, which was covered in crumbs.

"When Amos has something in his head, he doesn't let *geh* of it." She set the glass back in the sink. "Have you seen him this afternoon?"

"He was out in the barn earlier. But I haven't seen him since." She went to the sink and shook out the crumbs, then hung the towel on a hook nearby. "I better get back home. Plenty of laundry waiting for me." She smiled, the soft wrinkles around her eyes crinkling. She seemed to be about David's age, but that was all Anna Mae really knew about her. That, and she seemed very kind.

"If I see Amos, I'll let him know you're here. Bye, Anna Mae." Judith gave her a little wave as she walked out the kitchen door.

"Bye." Anna Mae turned and saw the dishes in the sink. She might as well wash them. If Amos was in the barn, he would be there for a while.

She turned on the hot water and squirted detergent in the sink. As she reached for a dishrag she heard a howl coming from the backyard. She shut off the tap and ran outside.

The deep-throated cries grew louder, and Anna Mae recognized them. "Amos? Where are you?"

As she yelled the words he stumbled from behind the barn, cradling his hand in the other. "Anna Mae! Help!"

She rushed toward him, and they met in the middle of the yard. Blood was smeared on his hands, and he was covering one palm with the other. "Amos, what happened?" she asked, making her voice as calm as possible.

His round eyes widened. He looked scared. "I hurt myself."

"I can see that." She craned her neck to look up at him. He was several inches taller than she, and even at twenty-three he was still growing. "Let me take a look."

He pulled away from her. "*Nee*. It hurts."

"I'm sure it does. How about we *geh* inside the *haus*? You can sit down. That will help you feel better."

He nodded and followed her. A trickle of blood ran down his arm to his elbow, but from a cursory look it didn't seem to Anna Mae like he was seriously hurt. She knew he had a low pain tolerance and a fear of blood, however, and she didn't blame him for being upset.

"Where's *yer daed*?" she asked once he was seated at the table.

"With the cows."

She found a clean cloth and wet it, then sat next to him. "What were you doing when you got hurt?"

"Pounding nails."

Anna Mae winced. Maybe the injury was worse than she thought. "Amos, I need to see your hand."

"I'm scared, Anna Mae."

She smiled. "Don't be. Remember when I got the splinter out of your foot last week? That didn't hurt, did it? You were scared then, but it turned out okay."

"This isn't a splinter."

She laid her hand on his massive forearm. "I know, Amos. But I'll be gentle."

He sniffed. "*Ya.* That's right. You're always gentle." He put his hand on the table and opened it, palm facing up. A small nail was stuck in the center, but it wasn't too deep. "This isn't so bad," she said. "I'm going to pull out the nail, okay?"

His chin trembled. "Okay."

"There's going to be more blood. You may not want to look."

He turned his head and squeezed his eyes shut. "I'm not looking."

"Why don't you count to three for me?" Anna Mae said, lightly grasping the head of the nail.

"One, two—"

"It's out." She pressed the cloth against the wound before he faced her.

"Already?"

"*Ya.*" She let the nail drop, glad that Amos didn't notice the clinking sound it made when it hit the floor. She took his other hand and laid it on top of the damp cloth. "Press on this while I get the first aid supplies."

"Okay." He used two fingers to press on the cloth.

"Does that hurt?" she asked as she rose from the chair.

"Not too bad." His tears had dried up, and the color had returned to his round face.

"*Gut.* I'll be right back, Amos."

She went to the bathroom and crouched in front of the cabinet under the sink, knowing exactly where the first aid kit was. She had doctored more of Amos's wounds over the years than she cared to count, but fortunately none of them had been serious. Just in case, she had read up on first aid and emergency treatment, and had found the information interesting. She admired people in the medical field, those who had chosen to care for the sick and injured. If things were different, she might have done that herself.

Anna Mae grabbed the supplies and went back to the kitchen. David was standing near Amos, his face red from the heat outside. "What were you pounding nails for, Amos?"

"To fix that board at the back of the barn." He glanced up at his father, sheepish, then stared down at his hand.

"*Sohn*, did you forget the rule about tools? That you have to let me know before you use them?"

"I guess I did."

Of course he would have forgotten. Amos's mind didn't work like everyone else's. When they were kids, he'd been called *dummkopf*. Even as an adult he was sometimes teased, more behind his back than to his face, by young *kinner* who needed to learn better.

David shook his head and looked at Anna Mae. "Can you fix him up?"

"It's not bad. Some antiseptic and a bandage and he'll be all right. He had a tetanus shot last year when he cut his foot on the hoe, so we don't have to worry about that." Getting Amos to hold still for the doctor to give him the tetanus shot had been traumatic for all of them.

David nodded, then left the kitchen and went back outside. In the past he would have yelled at Amos, and from the way Amos had cowered, it seemed like he had expected him to. But this time David was restrained. Maybe he was finally learning a bit of patience where his special son was concerned.

Anna Mae bandaged Amos's hand. To his credit, he only winced when she poured the peroxide over the small hole instead of yelping like he'd done in the past. Anna Mae said a silent prayer of gratitude that Amos didn't use the right nail for fixing the barn. If he had, the injury would have been severe. "Now, you have to keep that hand clean for a couple of days. If it gets dirty or wet, you'll have to tell *yer daed* so he can change the bandage."

"Can I tell Miss Judith?"

"*Ya*. I'm sure she wouldn't mind helping."

"She's very nice. Like you." He eyed the platter of cookies. "Did she bring those over?"

Anna Mae pulled off the cellophane wrap. "She did."

"Can I have one? I was *gut* this time, wasn't I?"

She pushed the plate toward him. "You were a *gut* patient."

As Amos chomped on what looked like oatmeal raisin cookies, Anna Mae took the bloody cloth and rinsed it on the other side of the sink, away from the dishes. She breathed out a sigh of satisfaction, glad that Amos was okay, and even happier that she'd been here to help. But the feeling disappeared as she realized how much Amos needed her. Even though she wasn't there every day, he depended on her.

If she ever left, who would be there for him? Maybe Judith, but she couldn't count on that. Judith had known the Mullets for only a few months. Anna Mae had known them her whole life.

She turned off the faucet and wrung out the cloth, twisting it so hard her fingers hurt. She couldn't leave Amos. Her mother was right. He'd been abandoned enough, first by his mother, then his brother. There were so many people she would disappoint if she didn't join the church. Unlike Marie and Jeremiah, she couldn't up and leave, not giving a thought to anyone but herself. She couldn't hurt the people she loved.

CHAPTER 4

"I think that's enough for one day." Doc Miller turned the Open sign over in the front window of the clinic.

Jeremiah glanced at his watch. It was only three thirty. "You sure?"

He nodded. "Don't want to wear you out on your first day."

But as Jeremiah saw Doc lean on his crutches, he could see fatigue dragging at him. Jeremiah could still put in a few more hours of work, yet he kept his mouth shut. He'd spent the morning with Bud's alpacas in Orwell—which were all in great health—and then grabbed some lunch at a diner in town and ran a few errands for Doc until coming back to the clinic several minutes ago. He'd expected to work all day. Now what was he supposed to do?

"You staying at your house?" Doc asked, standing a little taller now.

Jeremiah shook his head. "I thought I'd get a room at one of the bed-and-breakfasts around here. I don't want to put Dad out."

"I'm sure your father wouldn't mind having you around again. I know Amos wouldn't."

Guilt wrapped around his conscience. Of course Amos would want, and expect, Jeremiah to stay at the house while he was here in Middlefield. But Jeremiah had his reasons for not staying, reasons Amos wouldn't understand.

Doc shrugged. "Sorry. This is none of my business." He held out his hand to Jeremiah. "Again, thanks for your help."

He shook it, being careful not to grip too hard. "No problem. I kinda liked being back."

"Feels like home?"

I wouldn't go that far. "I better get going. Need to find a place to rest my head tonight."

"You know, you could stay here too."

Jeremiah gave the idea a split second of thought. He pictured his father's face when he found out Jeremiah had chosen to stay at Doc's instead of his house. Jeremiah wasn't going to borrow that kind of trouble. "Thanks, but I'll be okay."

Doc grinned. "I know you will. See you bright and early tomorrow."

"You bet."

Jeremiah left the clinic and got into his car. He

turned the ignition, letting the blast of cold, air-conditioned air cool down the interior while he pulled out his smartphone. He started to do a search for bed-and-breakfasts but then stopped. He couldn't spend his first day in Middlefield without seeing his brother. Out of everyone, Amos was the only person Jeremiah had written to, and even then it had been sporadic. Amos always wrote back in his scrawling, large handwriting, telling Jeremiah that everything was "okay." With each letter the guilt and pain over leaving his brother had increased to the point that he had hardly been able to bear opening the last couple of letters from Amos.

Now he was less than a fifteen-minute drive from Amos, and he was considering not seeing him. Jeremiah shook his head, disgusted with himself. Whatever problems he had with Dad, Amos needed to come first. Jeremiah threw the car in reverse and backed out of the Millers' driveway, then headed to the place he could never call home again.

"Amos, be still." Anna Mae looked up at him as he tilted on the chair he was standing on.

"I'm trying, Anna Mae."

She put her hands on her waist, the tape measure dangling from one hand. "I know you've had a hard day," she said evenly, "but I'll never get your measurements done if you don't keep still."

"But I don't see anything wrong with the clothes I have on now."

"They're too small. You want to split them when you sit down?"

"Oh. *Nee*. That wouldn't be okay."

"*Nee*, it wouldn't." She approached him again, putting the measuring tape around his thick waist. Maybe she should ask Judith to lay off the extra baking for a little while. She glanced down and noticed the hole in the toe of his left sock. She'd have to darn that for him later.

Anna Mae wrote down his measurements. "All done."

"*Gut*, because this was boring."

She smiled and took his injured hand, checking the bandage. No blood had leaked through, and he didn't seem to be in any more pain. He jumped down from the chair, the kitchen floor shaking when he hit it with a thud. She shook her head and chuckled. Now he was back to normal. Big, lumbering Amos, with his perpetual silly grin, red cheeks, and a sweet innocence that seemed to emanate from his soul.

Anna Mae put the paper with the measurements written on it, along with the tape measure, in her purse. "I'll make several pairs," she said.

"Okay."

"Now take off your socks."

"Why?"

She pointed to the hole.

"Oh." He stripped off his socks and handed them to her, then went back outside, barefoot.

She turned to the basket of dried laundry she'd found outside the bathroom and started folding his and his father's shirts. She picked up a yellow one belonging to Amos, noticed the frayed edge at the shoulder, and set it aside. She'd take it home with the socks.

When she finished folding the clothes, she left them in a neat stack on the table. She looked at Amos's pile. While she would never presume to put David's clothes away, she usually put away Amos's. Scooping them up, she headed upstairs. She might find some other items of his that needed mending.

Once in Amos's room, she saw clothes on the floor. Shaking her head, she put away his clean clothes and then gathered the discarded pants and socks. She found another pair of socks that needed darning, and she rolled them up in a tight ball. She looked around his sparse room, seeing the unmade bed, the stack of drawing pads littered on the floor nearby. She picked up the pads, put them in a neat stack, too, and straightened his bed.

She heard the front door open and close, then the sound of footsteps. More than just Amos's. She walked into the hallway.

"Amos?"

"Down here," he said.

She heard the excitement in his voice, and it

made her smile as she descended the stairs. "What have you gotten into this time?" But once she reached the bottom, she froze.

"Look who came home!" Amos grinned and put his thick arm around his younger brother, Jeremiah.

Anna Mae felt as though her heart leapt to her throat, choking off anything she might have said. She would have expected a parade of horses to rush through the Mullets' living room before the thought of Jeremiah coming home would have entered her mind.

"You've been gone a long time!" Amos said, turning to his brother. He pulled him into a big hug. "I've missed you."

Jeremiah hugged him back. "I missed you, too, Amos."

Her heart pinched as she looked at the two brothers. Although Jeremiah was younger by one year and smaller by a couple of inches and more than a few pounds, he had been Amos's protector before he left Middlefield.

Jeremiah stepped out of Amos's hug. His gaze finally drifted to Anna Mae. "I didn't expect to see you here."

"*Ya*," was all she could squeak out. How much he'd changed since she'd last seen him. He wore Yankee clothes now, slim denim jeans that hung low on his hips and a tucked-in, blue-and-white plaid shirt. His wavy brown hair was cut short, and he had a small mustache and beard just around his chin. A goatee, she thought it was called. He didn't look anything like the gangly sixteen-year-old *Amisch* boy she remembered. He didn't look *Amisch* at all. Then again, why would he? He'd left this life, and everyone else, behind long ago.

Amos moved to stand between her and Jeremiah, his eyes sparking with excitement. "You can stay for supper, right, Anna Mae? Then we'll play checkers, like we used to. I'm on Anna Mae's team. She's a better checker player than you, Jeremiah."

His innocent grin nearly brought tears to her eyes. He wasn't angry that Jeremiah had left, or even curious why he had returned. Amos lived in the present; the past and future didn't cross his mind.

She wished she could look at things with such simple purity. That she could look at Jeremiah and not feel the hurt she'd thought she'd come to terms with until this moment. But now that he was here, saying almost nothing and barely looking at her, the angry feelings came bubbling to the surface again. Had he forgotten how close they used to be? How they had spent so much time together growing up? The adventures they'd had in the tree house? If he did remember, it didn't seem important to him.

She gripped Amos's socks. "I can't stay, Amos.

I promised *Mamm* I'd be home in time to help her with supper." Which was the truth. But she would have come up with any lie to get away from Jeremiah.

He didn't seem to care anyway. He shoved his hands in his pockets and didn't say a word. *Message received.*

"Anna Mae's making me some new pants," Amos said, oblivious to the tension Anna Mae felt tugging at her spine. "And she's fixing *mei* socks. They've got holes in them."

"That's nice of her," Jeremiah said with little emotion.

"Anna Mae is really nice." Amos bit the fingernail on his bandaged hand.

"What happened to your hand?" Jeremiah asked, scrutinizing the bandage.

"I forgot the rule about the tools," Amos said. "But Anna Mae said the hole wasn't big and the nail didn't hurt me that much and there wasn't a lot of blood. I had to look away, though. I don't like blood."

"I know you don't," Jeremiah said softly.

"Anna Mae is really *gut* at making me feel better." He grinned again. "She's real pretty too."

Her cheeks flamed. Amos had always said she was pretty. But he said that about every woman he knew. They were all pretty in his eyes.

When she looked up, she saw Jeremiah's gaze on her. He didn't look away, staring at her with surprise and intensity. His piercing gaze cut through her resentment for a moment, confusing her.

"Amos!" His father's voice sounded from the kitchen. "You here?"

Jeremiah took a step back, flinching at his father's booming voice.

"*Ya*," Amos said. "I'm in the living room, *Daed*."

"I told you to let me know when the horses were out of feed—" David walked into the living room, stopping cold in much the same way Anna Mae had when she first saw Jeremiah.

"I'm sorry, *Daed*," Amos said. "I keep forgetting." He pointed at Jeremiah. "But look who came back home!"

His father's eyes narrowed. "What are you doing here?"

Jeremiah took his hands out of his pockets and squared his shoulders. "Dr. Miller called. He needs some help for a while. I figured after everything he's done for me, I had to come back."

David's eyes, the same color as Jeremiah's brown eyes, sparked with anger. "He calls you, and you come running. Yet we haven't heard from you for six years."

His gaze flicked away, finally showing some emotion. "I know, but I can explain—"

"I don't want to hear it." David stormed past them and went out the front door.

"Jeremiah?" Amos's lower lip trembled.

Jeremiah put his hand on his brother's massive shoulder. "I'll talk to him. We'll have that checker game tonight. I promise." Jeremiah hurried outside, the screen door slamming behind him.

Amos looked at Anna Mae with wide, bewildered eyes. "I wish they wouldn't fight," he whispered. "Why do they always fight?"

She went to Amos and hugged him. Unlike many *Amisch*, he wasn't subdued about physical affection, and he seemed to thrive on simple hugs and touches. Growing up without a mother had something to do with it, she surmised. "I'm sure they'll work it out," Anna Mae said, keeping her voice steady and positive for his sake.

"I hope so." He pulled away and looked at her. "I don't want Jeremiah to leave again."

Anna Mae didn't reply. Jeremiah hadn't come back for her, or even for Amos. He'd come back because of Dr. Miller. A Yankee vet had more sway over him than his family and friends.

Jeremiah leaned back against the hood of his car, crossing his arms over his chest as he stared at his father. It had been a mistake to come here. He should have found a time when he could have seen Amos by himself and avoided his father altogether. After less than five minutes with him, Jeremiah could see nothing had changed between them.

His father kept his distance, standing a few feet away from Jeremiah's car. His lips pressed into a straight line, his bottom lip nearly hidden by the bushy beard he still kept almost fifteen years after his wife left him.

Jeremiah uncrossed his arms. "I came by to see Amos. I won't be staying here."

"We're not *gut* enough for you?"

"That's not what I mean—"

"Doesn't seem that way. You didn't bother to write."

"I wrote to Amos."

"Four or five letters," his father muttered. "Hardly worth it."

Jeremiah flinched. There was no reason to try to explain himself, but could he really give a reasonable explanation? He could have done more; he knew that deep down. Columbus wasn't that far away. He could have visited. But he'd been so focused on finishing college early, then working doubly hard in veterinarian school, that contacting his family and friends had been on the bottom of the list.

For the first time the shame over that bubbled up to the surface. And anger that his father, who had said he would be supportive when Jeremiah started apprenticing under Doc Miller, didn't even try to understand. "I was busy. School, work, internship. It's not like I could snap my fingers and become a vet."

"You make time for what's important to you." ﹒

Jeremiah threw up his hands. He didn't want to argue with his father. "Never mind. I'll see Amos later." He turned to leave.

"Wait."

He looked over his shoulder. His father took a step forward. One small step.

"I don't want Amos to be disappointed. Again."

Jeremiah nodded. "I won't disappoint him. You know how much I love my *bruder*."

"You have a peculiar way of showing it." His father shot a scathing look at Jeremiah's car. The ten-year-old vehicle, covered with small patches of rust, flaking silver paint, and a couple of small dents, was a bit of an eyesore. But he knew that wasn't why his father objected to it. He regarded the vehicle with the same scorn he held for Jeremiah's Yankee clothes and haircut. To him, it all represented betrayal. Even though Jeremiah had never joined the church, even though his father had let him intern with Doc when he was thirteen and knew that being a vet was the one thing he wanted more than anything, his choice had driven a wedge between them. He couldn't see that wound ever healing.

"Where are you staying?" his father said gruffly.

"At a B&B in town. I thought it would be best."

His father paused. "You could stay in your old room."

Jeremiah lifted his brow in surprise. Was his

father extending a tiny bit of kindness? Had something changed during this conversation that Jeremiah wasn't aware of?

"As long as you don't leave that thing here." He gestured toward the car. "Make sure it's out of my way, or I'll have it hauled off."

Guess not. His house, his rules. It had always been that way. "I've already made reservations at the B&B." Not true, but he would as soon as he left here.

"I see." His father started to turn away, only to stop and pause. "How long you staying in town?"

"Not sure. I told Doc Miller I would help him out until his leg healed."

Daed didn't say anything else, just turned and headed for the house.

So much for welcoming the prodigal home.

CHAPTER 5

Jeremiah spun around and kicked one of the tires on his car. The tread had nearly worn off and probably wouldn't last through the winter. He had no idea where he would come up with the money to buy a set of new tires. The only reason he had the car was because a friend from vet school had given him a good deal on the piece of junk.

His shoulders slumped as he wondered yet again

if he'd made a mistake, despite his loyalty to Doc Miller. He could still go back to Columbus and find a job. He had debts to pay—lots of them. His school loans were outrageous.

But he had debts to pay here too—ones that didn't hit him in the wallet.

"Jeremiah!" He looked over the hood of the compact car to see Amos hurrying toward him. His heart swelled with love for his older brother. Man, he had missed him. The innocence that had been there since he was a child still remained trapped inside his large, twenty-three-year-old body.

Amos's face held a worried expression. "*Daed* seemed mad when he came inside."

"He's all right. I surprised him, that's all."

"You surprised me too." Amos grinned. "I like surprises. So you're staying, *ya*?"

"*Ya*."

"Forever, right?"

Jeremiah drew in a breath. "Let's just focus on right now, okay?"

"Okay."

He saw Anna Mae leaving the house. Amos turned and followed Jeremiah's line of sight. "Anna Mae," Amos called out. "Are you sure you can't stay for supper?"

Supper. Although he wasn't prepared to deal with his father's stony silence through a meal, he would stay for Amos's sake.

In response to Amos's question, Anna Mae shook her head, still standing slightly behind Amos. As if she was hiding behind him, eager to get away from Jeremiah. And how could he blame her? They had been close friends once. Now she could barely look at him. When she did, he could see the resentment in her eyes.

"I'm sorry, Amos. I'll see you in a few days, when I've finished your pants and fixed your socks." She moved away from him and started walking down the driveway.

"I can give you a ride home," Jeremiah blurted out. It was the least he could do, considering she'd been taking care of his brother—something he used to do.

"I can walk." Much like his father had earlier, she turned her back on him and left.

"Is Anna Mae mad?" Amos asked.

"She might be."

"Why? She should be happy you're home. So should *Daed*." He frowned. "I'm the only one who seems happy."

His brother's words pierced him. But as usual, Amos spoke the truth. He put his arm around Amos's shoulder. He had to tiptoe a bit—his brother had grown into a huge man since Jeremiah had left Middlefield. He squeezed Amos's shoulder. The muscle underneath was rock hard. Amos always worked hard and tried his best, despite being developmentally delayed. Although his father had never gotten a formal diagnosis for Amos's problems, Jeremiah suspected he had severe learning and processing problems. But that didn't stop him from working the farm, something he'd said he'd wanted to do since he was a teenager. From the neat appearance of the property, it seemed like he was doing a good job helping his father keep up with everything. "Don't worry, Amos," he said. "Everything is fine."

"Okay." Amos brightened as he looked at Jeremiah's clothes. "Maybe Anna Mae can make you some new clothes, like she's making for me."

"My clothes are fine."

"But you're dressed funny. Like a Yankee. Maybe that's why *Daed* is mad. You know he doesn't like Yankees."

"I know. But I have to dress like this."

"Why?"

Jeremiah dropped his arm. "Because." He tapped the hood of his dusty car to change the subject. Now wasn't the time to explain everything to Amos. "How about you go for a little ride with me?"

Amos looked at the car and shook his head. "I don't want to get into the car."

"We're just going to drive to the barn." He tapped the hood again. "I know she's not much to look at, but she's safe." Safe enough. "Nothing's going to happen."

"Don't matter. I don't wanna get into the car."

Jeremiah wondered how sheltered his father still kept Amos from the rest of the world. It wouldn't surprise him if nothing had changed. Dad had never really understood Amos. How special he was. Instead, he'd always seemed disappointed that his oldest son wasn't "normal." Except for church, he probably never let Amos leave the confines of their farm. Maybe Jeremiah could change some of that, at least as long as he was here.

But he wouldn't start with the car. He got in and turned on the engine. Amos jumped back a little. Jeremiah waved at him and grinned, then slowly drove the car toward the barn, parking it in the grass on the side. When he got out of the car, Amos had disappeared.

The soft lowing of the cows in the pasture tugged at Jeremiah. He'd specialized as a large-animal vet in school but had only spent time in the country when he was working. He disliked city living—the traffic, the crowds, the way everyone was too busy to take time for other people. Yet it hadn't taken him long to fall into the pattern he detested.

He didn't know how long he had been standing there, leaning against the slat wood fence he'd helped his father build when he was eleven, mesmerized by the small herd of cattle as they chomped on the sweet grass. From this distance they all looked healthy and well cared for. He'd seen some horrific animal cruelty during his training. Whatever personal issues he had with his father, he had to admire the way the man had always taken care of his own.

Jeremiah made his way toward the barn. When he left Middlefield, his father had owned two horses and a few pigs in addition to the cattle. By the lack of pungent smell in the air, he could tell there were no pigs here. He walked in the barn, wondering what other changes had happened while he was gone.

When he stepped through the doorway, he froze.

The oak slats of the barn were completely covered in drawings. Every spare inch of the walls from floor to ceiling was filled with artistic renderings—accurate chalk drawings of the neighbors' homes, milk paint sunrises and sunsets, and nearly photo-perfect portraits. So many portraits. His father. Their late grandmother, Ella. Himself. Even Anna Mae.

He walked toward Anna Mae's image. Amos had captured her perfectly. Jeremiah studied the drawing, comparing it to the woman he'd just seen. Amos was right. She was pretty. Jeremiah had never thought of her that way before, just as one of his friends he'd hung out with when he was a kid. Their relationship had diminished as he focused on his schooling and she had . . .

What had she done? Only taken care of his brother. Something he should have been doing.

He took in her upturned nose, large blue eyes, and full lips. Amos had somehow matched the exact blond shade of her hair peeking out from beneath her white *kapp*. Unable to help himself, he touched her cheek. He drew away, the pad of his finger covered in rose-colored chalk.

"Do you like it?" Amos came up behind him.

Jeremiah turned to him. "You did all this." It wasn't a question.

"*Ya. Daed* let me. He said I could draw anything I wanted to here. As long as it stayed inside the barn." Amos grinned.

Jeremiah looked at the astounding artwork surrounding them. Maybe his father understood Amos after all.

He continued to look at the drawings, and then he noticed more light coming in at the back of the barn. He walked across the dirt floor and saw that the boards were loose. One was hanging by a single nail.

"That's what I was trying to fix when I hurt myself," Amos said.

"I can help you, if you want."

"Okay."

A short time later, Jeremiah stepped back and regarded their work. "*Gut* job, Amos. Even one-handed."

Amos grinned at Jeremiah. "*Daed*'s going to be happy we fixed this."

"Good."

"He said he hasn't had time."

"Taking care of a farm takes a lot of time."

"I know." Amos wiped the sweat off his wide forehead. "I run out of time all the time."

Jeremiah smiled. "I'm sure you do."

"I'm glad you're back, Jeremiah." Amos pulled him into another huge bear hug.

"Oof," Jeremiah said.

Amos dropped his arms quickly. "Did I hurt you?"

"*Nee*. But you did surprise me."

"I'm sorry." He looked down at his huge boots. "*Daed* said I shouldn't do that. He says I'm too strong. That I might hurt someone."

An ache appeared in Jeremiah's chest. His father was right about Amos's strength. And he knew many people in the district wouldn't understand Amos's hugs. But that didn't matter to Jeremiah right now. He wrapped his arms around his older brother. "You can hug me anytime."

Anna Mae practically ran home from the Mullets' farm. Sweating and breathing heavily, she rushed upstairs to her room and shut the door, leaning against it. She gasped for breath. Jeremiah was back.

The rush of emotions hadn't abated as she'd hurried home. She tried to make sense of the effect seeing him again had on her. Glancing at her hands, she was dismayed to see them trembling. Over Jeremiah. Or maybe heatstroke. She liked that reason better.

She dropped her purse and Amos's socks on her bed, then left her room and went downstairs to the bathroom. She grabbed a washcloth from the drawer, soaked it in cold water, and put it on the back of her neck. Her body welcomed the coolness, but it did little to straighten her thoughts.

Anna Mae patted the washcloth on her heated face. What was she going to do? She didn't want to risk running into him again. Yet she couldn't— and wouldn't—avoid Amos for the sake of his thoughtless brother. He probably wouldn't be there much anyway. *Remember, he only came back for Doc Miller. Not for Amos. Not for his father. And definitely not for you.*

That last thought stopped her cold. She stared at her reflection in the mirror, her cheeks not red from the heat but from her own wandering notions.

It was close to supper time, and she knew her mother would be looking for her. She hung the washcloth over the side of the bathtub and opened the door, only to run into someone standing in the hallway.

"Sorry, Anna Mae."

She looked up at the man in front of her. "Daniel?"

"*Yer mamm* said there was something wrong with the drain in the tub. She asked me if I'd take a look at it."

Anna Mae backed away from him. Despite Daniel Beiler having grown up into a decent man, she couldn't forget how he had mercilessly teased Amos as a kid. Or how he had stolen money that had belonged to her grandmother and Amos and Jeremiah's. Or how he had tried to get away with it by tying her and Amos up and stuffing rags in their mouths, then removing the rungs from the tree house so they couldn't get down. Both she and Amos had been terrified. In the end Daniel had gotten in serious trouble, and from that point on he had changed, leaving Amos alone and being a devoted member of the church.

But he had never said he was sorry. And she would never be able to trust him.

"Oh, Anna Mae, there you are." Her mother appeared in the hallway, her head barely visible over Daniel's shoulder. "Daniel's here to fix the tub."

"I didn't know there was a problem with the tub," Anna Mae said.

Her mother stepped to the side. "There is. Daniel's an excellent plumber. Did you know that?"

"So's *Daed*."

Her mother's face tightened. "Why don't you let Daniel into the bathroom, Anna Mae? I need your help with supper."

Daniel nodded as Anna Mae stepped out of

the bathroom and allowed him in. She followed her mother to the kitchen, barely controlling her anger.

"Why is he here?" Anna Mae whispered.

"I told you, to fix the tub. Could you grate some of that Swiss cheese? That will be lovely on the salad tonight."

Anna Mae looked around the kitchen. Bowls and pots and pans were everywhere, and from the smell in the room it seemed her mother was fixing her best meal—pot roast with potatoes, carrots, and parsnips. Steam rose from the fresh loaf of bread still sitting in the pan on top of the stove. A colorful salad filled *Mamm*'s best ceramic bowl, which she only used for special occasions. From what she could tell, supper preparations were all but complete.

"This is why you didn't want me to be late?" Anna Mae asked. "To grate cheese?"

Her mother didn't look at her as she placed the juicy pot roast on a platter. She picked up a knife. "Never underestimate the importance of cheese, dear."

Anna Mae picked up the block of cheese and started sliding it against the grater, pushing hard. "Why Daniel, of all people?"

"I don't know what you mean, Anna Mae."

She tossed the cheese in the bowl and went to her mother. "You don't think I know what you're doing? There's *nix* wrong with the tub. You've made a feast. And Daniel happens to be a deacon's son—and single."

Her mother finally looked at her. "He likes pot roast too." She picked up the platter and put it on the table. "I expect you to be polite, Anna Mae."

"Don't you remember what he did to me and Amos?"

"*Ya.* And I think he's paid plenty of penance for that. He had to confess in front of the church, rebuild the steps, return the money . . . and he's been a model *Amisch mann* since."

"And that's all that matters, right?"

"People change, Anna Mae." Her mother stopped in front of her. "You certainly have."

"*Frau* Shetler, your tub's working fine now." Daniel walked into the kitchen carrying a toolbox Anna Mae hadn't noticed before. "Just a small clog."

"I'm glad to hear that." She walked over to him, wiping her hands on her apron. "I was worried it was something more serious."

"I think *Herr* Shetler could have taken care of it." Daniel tugged on his straw hat. "But if you have any more problems, I don't mind coming out again." He glanced at Anna Mae, quickly averting his gaze. "I'll be going now."

Mamm shook her head. "I insist you stay for supper. To pay you for your trouble."

"I don't need payment—"

"It's pot roast."

He paused. "It does smell *gut.*" He shifted from one foot to the other.

"Anna Mae's *daed* will be here any minute." *Mamm* smiled. "Please, Daniel. Join us."

Daniel looked at Anna Mae. "As long as it's all right with you."

It was anything but all right. She didn't want him here. Yet what could she do? Her mother looked at her expectantly. To refuse would be rude, would embarrass Daniel, and would make her mother look bad. "*Ya,*" she finally said, praying that God would help her get through the meal.

CHAPTER 6

Jeremiah helped Amos prepare supper. He hadn't seen his *daed* for the rest of the afternoon, which was fine by him. He wasn't looking forward to having supper with him, but Amos was happy, and that was all that mattered right now. "How is it going with those potatoes?" Jeremiah asked his brother.

"I'm mashing them real *gut.* Just like *Gross-mammi* taught me."

Jeremiah winced but didn't say anything as he added a few pats of butter to the canned green beans warming on the stove. His grandmother was another subject he didn't want to talk about.

He turned down the heat on the gas stove and opened up the oven, pulling out several thick slices of ham. His stomach started to growl as he breathed in the aromas of the simple supper. He set the pan of ham on a nearly threadbare towel on the countertop.

"Amos!" *Daed*'s voice sounded from the other side of the house.

"In the kitchen!" Amos left the potato masher standing straight up in the bowl and went to the doorway. "Supper's ready."

"*Gut*, because I'm starv—" His father stopped on the kitchen threshold. "You're still here," he said, looking at Jeremiah.

"I promised Amos I would stay for supper." He faced his father, not flinching.

Daed didn't say anything. He sat down in his usual seat at the head of the table. Amos put the bowl of mashed potatoes in front of him. Jeremiah quietly moved it farther away and took out the masher.

Jeremiah and Amos finished setting the table. As Jeremiah sat down, it seemed like time had stood still for him. His brother was a man now, taller and huskier than when Jeremiah had left. His dad was grayer and even sterner, if that was possible. Yet when the three of them bowed their heads for silent prayer, for a few short moments it was as if nothing had changed at all.

But when Jeremiah opened his eyes, the past

zoomed away. He eyed the chair where Grandmother Ella used to sit, then averted his gaze, guilt taking away nearly all his appetite.

No words were spoken as they all filled their plates with salty ham, lumpy potatoes, and greasy green beans. Jeremiah frowned. He'd added too much butter, which wasn't a surprise. He'd always been terrible in the kitchen.

Yet his father didn't complain, and Amos ate with his usual gusto, like he was consuming a gourmet meal. Jeremiah envied Amos that way, how his brother could sometimes be unaware of the silent tension in the room. But Amos was hyper-tuned in to harsh words and fighting, so it was a good thing that his father hadn't said anything. *Yet.*

"I peeled the potatoes," Amos blurted, grinning, his lips shining from the buttered green beans.

David picked up a forkful, which was dotted with dark spots of potato peel mixed in. "I can tell."

"I like peeling potatoes," he continued. "It's fun. Jeremiah made sure I was careful with the knife."

"Drink your milk, Amos," *Daed* said.

"Okay." Amos picked up a tall glass of milk and drank it all in only a few gulps. He burped. "Excuse me."

Jeremiah smiled. Grandmother had taught them manners when they were growing up. Amos forgot some of them, like not talking with his mouth full of food. But he never forgot to say "excuse me."

A knock sounded at the back door. Amos jumped up from his seat. "I'll get it."

"Are you expecting someone?" Jeremiah asked his father.

His father shrugged, but still didn't look at him. Jeremiah was glad he'd made the decision to stay at a bed-and-breakfast. While he wouldn't see Amos as much as he liked, he couldn't take another one of these family dinners.

"It's Miss Judith," Amos said, walking into the kitchen, "and she brought pie."

Jeremiah looked up to see the woman walking behind Amos. He had never seen her before. She was short, plump, and wore glasses. Her dark-brown hair was streaked with gray underneath her white *kapp*. He guessed her to be about his father's age, mid-fifties or so.

Her hands were protected by potholders, and she held a large pie. Steam rose from the golden crust, and the scent of cinnamon apples filled the kitchen. Jeremiah couldn't remember the last time he'd smelled something so delicious.

"Hello, David," she said, smiling.

"Judith." *Daed* went back to eating.

Her smile dimmed, but only for a moment. She looked at Jeremiah. "I'm sorry. I didn't realize you and Amos had company."

"Oh, he's not company," Amos said. "This is

mei bruder, Jeremiah." He clapped Jeremiah on the shoulder, a little too hard, making Jeremiah jump a little. "He came home," Amos continued. "From his big fancy school."

"I see." Her smile widened, the kindness reaching her eyes. "It's nice to meet you. I live next door. I hope you like apple pie."

Jeremiah stood. "We all do, thank you." He took the pie from Judith and placed it on the counter, nearly burning his fingers on the hot pie plate. Fresh apple pie . . . he hadn't had that in ages. "It looks and smells delicious."

"It is." Amos walked over to the pie and took a big sniff. "Miss Judith makes the best desserts."

"Amos is exaggerating." Judith folded the potholders. "But that's very kind of you to say."

"You're welcome. Can I have a slice?"

"Of course." She turned. "David, may I cut you a piece?"

His father grunted. "Sure."

"I'll get the plates." Jeremiah cast a harsh look at his father. He could be a little more polite and receptive to her neighborly gesture. But Judith didn't seem to mind. She walked to the kitchen drawer and pulled out a pie server, clearly seeming to know her way around their kitchen, which piqued Jeremiah's curiosity. He placed the plates next to the pie.

Judith touched Amos on the arm. "*Geh* ahead and sit down. I'll bring your piece to you." When

Amos walked away she moved to stand next to Jeremiah. "So you're a veterinarian?"

He nodded, handing her a dessert plate. "How did you know?"

"Amos talks about you. A lot." She grinned.

"Just Amos?" The words slipped out of Jeremiah's mouth.

"*Ya.*"

He wished he could take back the words. She didn't need to know about the problems he had with his father. "So you live next door," he said, eager to talk about something else. "In the old Zook house?"

"*Ya.* I've been here for about three months. That was *mei grossmammi*'s house."

"I remember the Zooks." Jeremiah handed her another plate. "We used to go over to their house when we were little. Mrs. Zook always had fresh-baked cookies."

Judith nodded. "She taught me how to cook and bake."

"Her cookies were amazing. She passed away right before my mom—" He paused, the mental stop sign he threw up every time his mother's memory surfaced appearing in his mind. He quickly picked up the two plates. "I better give Amos his pie. I bet his mouth is already watering."

"I'm sure it is." She sliced a third piece as Jeremiah walked to the table. She put the slice in front of David. "This is for replacing the window in the bedroom the other day. I appreciated that very much."

He nodded and picked up his fork. She waited as he chewed the first bite, but he didn't say anything.

Jeremiah gripped his fork. Why did his father have to be so rude? He took a big bite of the pie. The crust melted in his mouth, and the apples exploded with sweetness over his tongue. "Judith, this is wonderful. Best pie I've ever had."

"Told you," Amos said through a bite of the dessert. "She's a *gut* cook."

Judith glanced at her feet, her face turning slightly pink. "I'm glad you like it."

Daed scraped his plate, having wolfed down the pie in three huge bites. If he'd even tasted it, Jeremiah would have been surprised. *Daed* stood and took his hat off the peg near the back door. "Chores," he said. He glanced at Judith, nodded again, then walked out.

Jeremiah shook his head, exasperated. "I'm sorry about that."

"About what?" Judith asked, picking up his father's empty plate.

"*Daed*. I wish I could say he's usually not like that . . . but he's usually like that."

"Pshh. *Yer vatter* is a man of few words. That doesn't bother me." She put the plate in the sink. "How long do you plan on staying?"

"Forever." Amos licked his sticky fingers. "Right, Jeremiah? You're not going to leave ever again."

Jeremiah froze, unable to respond. How could he make Amos understand his stay was only temporary? Any way he explained it, his brother would be hurt. Again.

"Amos, I'm sure your *daed* needs some help with the chores." Judith walked to the other end of the table and put her hand on Amos's shoulder.

"Okay." Amos pushed back from the table. "I'll *geh* help him." He left the kitchen.

"Thanks." Jeremiah put his fork down.

"I shouldn't have asked that question in front of Amos." Judith moved to stand by the opposite side of the table. "It's not *mei* business."

Jeremiah waved her off. "It's fine. The answer is I honestly don't know. I'm here helping out Doc Miller, so it's up in the air."

"I'd heard he broke his leg. He's a wonderful vet. He came out and checked on my Sally about a month ago."

"What was wrong with her?"

"A little colic. *Nix* to be worried about. She's a healthy horse and has been fine ever since."

"If anything else comes up with her, let me know. I'll be happy to take care of it."

"*Danki*, Jeremiah. I will." She glanced at his half-eaten piece of pie. "You don't have to finish it," Judith said.

She reached for the plate, but Jeremiah put up his hand. "Oh, I'm finishing this." He smiled. He liked this woman, and not just because of the pie. There was something calming about her presence. He also liked the idea of someone else looking out for Amos, and he could tell she cared about him. And anyone who could overlook his father's rudeness had to be someone special.

Like Anna Mae. But like the relationship with his father, he wondered if their friendship would ever be repaired.

He polished off the pie and stood, starting to clear the table. But Judith quickly took over.

"I'll take care of it."

"You don't have to. I've washed plenty of dishes in my lifetime."

"It gives me something to do." She put the dishes in the sink.

"I won't argue with you, then." He handed her his glass. "I should get going. I still have to check into a bed-and-breakfast in town."

"So you're not staying here?"

He shook his head. "It's better that I don't."

"I see." She looked up at him. "I do hope you'll be coming around here often. It will be *gut* for Amos." She paused. "And your *daed*."

"I don't know about him." Jeremiah fished his car keys out of his pocket. No reason to pretend around Judith that everything was okay between them. She would realize that soon enough. "But

I'll definitely be visiting Amos. Good night, Judith."

"*Gut nacht*, Jeremiah. It was nice to meet you."

Jeremiah left the house and went to the barn just as Amos was walking out of it. The keys jingled in Jeremiah's hand as he approached his brother.

"Where are you going?" Amos asked.

Jeremiah paused. This was going to be hard. "To town."

Amos's brow furrowed. "But you'll be back, right?"

He shoved his hands in his pockets and took a breath. "Amos, I'll be staying at a bed-and-breakfast in Middlefield." As Amos started to open his mouth, Jeremiah held up his hand. "But I promise I'll come see you."

Amos's frown grew. "I don't understand. Why can't you stay here? You have a bedroom already."

"It's complicated." He kicked at a pebble on the gravel drive, trying to figure out how to make his brother comprehend the situation without upset-ting him. He looked up at Amos. "You know how *Daed* and I argue?"

He nodded. "I don't like it when you're mad at each other."

"I don't like it either. That's why I'm staying somewhere else. *Daed* and I get along better when we aren't together too much. It has nothing to do with you."

"But don't you think if you were here you and *Daed* could try to get along? How can you fix what's wrong if you're not here?"

"It doesn't work that way with me and *Daed*."

"Is that why you stayed away for so long?"

"That's part of it." His brother deserved the truth, at least a version that he could understand. "But mostly I stayed away because I had to work very hard to get through school."

Amos scratched his head. "School is very hard. I didn't like school. But *Frau* Beiler was nice. I remember she helped me learn to read."

"*Ya*, she did. She was a good teacher."

"She doesn't teach anymore," Amos said. "She had *bopplis*, so she's a *mutter* now."

"Amos." Jeremiah put his hand on his brother's arm, guiding him back to the topic at hand. "Do you understand why I can't stay here?"

"You don't want to fight with *Daed*." Amos nodded. "Will you come over for lunch? And supper?"

"That depends on what I have to do for Doc Miller." He rubbed Amos's strong shoulder. "But I'll be here as often as I can."

Amos tucked in his upper lip. Jeremiah could tell he was thinking. Finally his brother smiled. "That's okay with me."

"Good." He hugged Amos. "I have to get going. I'll see you soon, okay?"

"Okay!" Amos started to wave as soon as

Jeremiah got into the car. Jeremiah paused, thinking he should find his father and say good-bye. But that would probably lead to another argument, and he was too tired to deal with that right now. As he drove down the driveway, he looked in his rearview mirror and saw Amos following him, waving and grinning all the way in the dimming daylight. At least someone was happy he'd returned.

Anna Mae picked at the wicker on the old chair, wondering how she ended up out on her back patio sitting next to Daniel. Supper had gone better than she'd expected, since she didn't have to say a word. Daniel was also quiet, but their mother had spoken enough for everyone. Her father ate his meal as usual, making small conversation with Daniel in between her mother's desperate attempts to point out how much he and Anna Mae had in common. Which was almost nothing. Then before Anna Mae had a chance to protest, her mother thrust a glass of iced tea in both her and Daniel's hands and shooed them out the back door. They hadn't said anything to each other since.

The sound of crickets chirping broke the silence of the warm night air. Anna Mae continued to pick at the wicker, trying to pretend Daniel wasn't there.

He cleared his throat. "Supper was *gut*."

"*Ya*."

"Very tender pot roast."

Anna Mae shrugged, still picking at the chair. Why wouldn't he leave? Her fingers froze around a slender wicker strand. Surely he wasn't interested in her?

"Anna Mae?"

Slowly she turned toward him, steeling herself for what he had to say. Never had she thought Daniel Beiler would have notions about her. Maybe he and her mother had plotted this evening together. She wouldn't put it past him to be that devious.

He swirled the ice around in his tea glass as he stared into it. "Um . . . this is awkward. But I've been meaning to talk to you about something for a while."

Don't say it . . . don't say it . . .

He looked at her, his clear blue eyes resembling glass marbles. When he was young they were filled with mischief and meanness. Not anymore. It took everything she had not to bolt from the chair.

He shoved his hand through his brown curly hair. "I never told you I was sorry for what I did when we were kids." He looked down at his glass again. "Every time I think about that I get sick to *mei* stomach. I was stupid." His gaze lifted. "I was mean. I don't know why I acted the way I did back then. But I've been trying to make up for it since."

Anna Mae gaped at him. Was she hearing him right? He was truly sorry? Was her mother right when she said he really had changed?

"I'm sorry, Anna Mae. For all of it. Stealing, lying, tying . . . tying you and Amos up." He shook his head. "Picking on him all those years." He coughed. "I'm ashamed and I'm sorry. Can you forgive me?"

She didn't say anything for a long moment. Her faith required her to forgive him. But she wasn't a member of the church, and being raised *Amisch* wasn't what drove her to say her next words. It was knowing that it was what God wanted her to say. "I do forgive you, Daniel."

His face sagged with relief. "*Danki.*"

But she wasn't ready to completely let him off the hook. "What about Amos? Have you talked to him?"

Daniel smiled, revealing slightly crooked teeth. "*Ya*, awhile back. He forgave me right away, like you did. And if I ever see Jeremiah again, I'll apologize to him."

She glanced away, unsure if she should tell him Jeremiah was in town. He probably wouldn't be in Middlefield long enough to talk to Daniel anyway.

Daniel's smile waned. "I don't know if Jeremiah would be as quick to forgive, now that he's a Yankee."

For some reason his remark hit her wrong. "So

only the *Amisch* forgive? Is that what you're saying?"

"*Nee*. But it can be harder for them, I think."

"It's hard for everyone."

"I suppose you're right." He took a drink of his tea, then stood. "I should get going. Thanks again for supper."

"That was *Mamm*'s doing," she said.

His lips curled in a smirk. "I know. See you later, Anna Mae."

She didn't get up as he set the glass on the patio table and walked around to the front of the house. Before long she heard the crunch of his buggy wheels on the gravel driveway. She slumped in the chair, relieved that was over.

"Why is Daniel leaving?" her mother asked as she flew out the back door.

"Because he had to *geh*."

"When are you seeing him again?"

She stood up. "I'm not."

"But he's perfect for you." *Mamm* stood in front of her. "He's nice, has a *gut* job, is rather *schee* if I do say so myself, he's—"

"*Amisch*."

Her mother straightened. "*Ya*. He's *Amisch*."

"And you thought if we started courting then I would join the church."

Mamm lifted her chin. "The thought had crossed *mei* mind."

"You can uncross it because I'm not interested."

"In him . . . or the church?"

Anna Mae tried to walk past her mother. "I don't want to discuss this right now."

"Then when, Anna Mae? When are you going to talk about it?"

Anna Mae didn't answer. She couldn't talk about this with her mother. Or anyone. No one understood. All her friends and peers her age had their lives planned out. One of her closest friends from school, Lydia, was engaged to another of their schoolmates. The traditional celery for her wedding was already growing in her mother's garden.

A few people had not joined the church, but they had left the district and had moved on and started new lives.

Like Jeremiah had.

Mamm brushed away a fly hovering nearby. "If you have questions about the church, I can answer them. Or the bishop can."

"I don't have any questions."

"Great!" her mother said, a spark of hope entering her eyes. "Then you'll talk to the bishop?"

"*Nee.*"

Mamm spoke, her voice quavering. "I'm worried about you. You've isolated yourself, Anna Mae. You don't spend time with your friends anymore. You don't stay after church service. You *geh* to the Mullets' farm, but I think that's more out of a sense of duty." Anna Mae started to speak, but her mother lifted her hand. "You can't keep living this way. Not forever. You have to make a decision. You have to do what God wants you to do."

Anna Mae bit her lip. How would her mother know what God really wanted for her? She was only concerned with her daughter joining the church—and, of course, getting married to an upstanding *Amisch* man. Following the prescribed course her sister and brother had was the acceptable choice.

"Your father and I have been patient—"

"*Daed* said something to you?" Anna Mae asked, surprised. So far her father had remained silent on the matter.

Her mother glanced away. "He's of the same mind as me."

"You don't sound very sure." Did she have an ally in her father and hadn't realized it?

"Because you're just like him. You keep everything inside. Besides, he doesn't feel comfortable talking to you about it. But trust me, he wants you to join the church as much as I do."

"So this isn't about me making a decision," Anna Mae said. "It's about making the *right* decision. The one you agree with."

Her mother paused. "I would be lying if I said that wasn't true. But can you blame me? I love you. I want you to be happy. You haven't been happy for so long." She stepped away. "I'll leave you alone now." She paused. "I'm sorry about Daniel."

"It's okay." Anna Mae gave her mother a half smile, glad she was finally realizing that she shouldn't have meddled.

"I'd really hoped you two would work out."

Anna Mae heard the screen door bounce against the door frame as her mother went inside.

She closed her eyes, trying to calm the rising tide of resentment. Her mother wasn't sorry about setting her up with Daniel. She was sorry it didn't work.

Lord, what do I do? How can I explain to her what I'm feeling when she'll never understand?

But all she heard were the sounds of the crickets and cicadas as they started their night music. The low croak of the bullfrogs living in the pond a field away. The soft whinny of her father's horse from inside the barn. Noise surrounded her, filling her ears as she listened for the one thing she wanted to hear—an answer.

After waiting a few moments, she shook her head, picked up the tea glasses, and went inside.

Judith finished washing the last dish as David walked into the kitchen. Butterflies flitted in her tummy, as they usually did when she was around him. She hadn't felt this way since she met her late husband, Samuel, and after he died she'd never thought she'd experience that rush of attraction again.

But she had to keep it at bay. She had no choice. Because although David's wife had left nearly fifteen years ago, he wasn't free. He never would be.

"The dishes are done." She turned to him, trying to see him as just another man with a gruff demeanor and very little to say. Yet she saw so much more in David Mullet. Behind his brown eyes was a sadness and vulnerability that pulled at her heart. There was also kindness, buried deep. And love. She'd seen it in his interactions with Amos. How protective he was of him.

And tonight she saw a new side of him. Hurt. She wondered if Jeremiah was aware of how deep his father's pain truly was. She doubted it, because if he were, he wouldn't have left tonight.

She didn't dare bring that up, though. "Would you like me to put on a pot of *kaffee*? Decaf, of course."

He shook his head as he placed his hat on the peg. His hair showed his age. He had as much silver gray threaded through the brown locks as she did in her own. But his hair was still thick, just like Jeremiah's. "I'm going to bed."

"Oh. All right." She wiped her hands on a dish towel and hung it over the counter. "I'll see you later, then. Tell Amos I said *gut nacht*." She headed for the back door, wishing she could stay, knowing she couldn't.

"Judith?"

103

She turned, surprised. Had he changed his mind? Maybe he wanted to talk about Jeremiah. Maybe he would finally open up to her, as she'd been praying almost from the moment she'd met him.

"Don't forget your pie plate."

Or maybe not. "You keep it. There's still a slice left. I'm sure Amos would like to have it in the morning. I'll come back and get it tomorrow."

"Suit yourself." He left the room, leaving her to see herself out.

She left the Mullets' house and walked to her empty one. Samuel had been gone for five years, and she was lonely. God hadn't blessed them with children, and for the most part she had accepted that. But it didn't help during the nights she felt alone. Like tonight.

At first she'd thought her attraction to David was born out of that loneliness. But that wasn't true. There was something deeper there, and she knew there was a reason she was in David Mullet's life. Why else would God have brought her here, telling her she had to leave the comfort of her life in her quaint district in New York and move into her grandmother's old house? At first she'd thought the same thing everyone else had—she was making a mistake. But now she knew she had a purpose here. The specifics of that purpose were unclear, but she trusted that God would reveal them to her when the time was right.

And as for her feelings for David, she would have to deal with those. She hoped and prayed they would fade over time. If they didn't . . . then she would have to deal with that too.

CHAPTER 7

The next morning Caleb waited outside for the taxi that would take him to a livestock auction in Bloomfield. He paced the length of the front porch. He'd been to auctions before, and although he knew what he was doing, he could never calm the jangling nerves he felt before each one. As always, he had to make the right decision or they would lose a lot of money. Money they couldn't afford to lose.

He heard the clop of horse hooves on the road in front of the house and looked up. He frowned at the sight of Bekah turning into the driveway. He'd known she was coming, as Katie had mentioned this morning that the two of them were going to prepare the house for church service this Sunday. He wished she had something else to do, like another job. Or a boyfriend to keep her company.

Why had that popped into his head? Even more confusing, he ignored the pang of jealousy that cropped up at the thought. He shook his head. His nerves were definitely getting the best of him.

Still, that didn't stop his mind from drifting to

the past. At one time they had been close, and had even gone through a pretty harrowing experience when they were thirteen. But as they grew up they drifted apart. He dated Miriam, and when that relationship ended he focused on the farm. Bekah wasn't focused on anything. Except maybe books. And fishing. She did like to do that. He did, too, although he hadn't much time for that. He had work to do. Lots of it. There was no time for lazing around.

Caleb shook his head to get her out of his thoughts, turning away from her buggy as she went past him. Although he couldn't resist a quick look at her. She kept her gaze straight ahead, as if she hadn't seen him standing on the porch, which of course she had. Figures she would be immature enough to ignore him.

Johnny came out of the house, drinking a cup of coffee. "Sleep well last night?"

"Slept fine." Caleb started to pace again.

"You sure you don't want me to *geh* with you?"

He stopped in his tracks. "You don't trust me?"

"What?" Johnny's brow lifted. "Where did that come from?"

"*Nix*. Sorry." He gave him a half grin.

"No problem." Johnny regarded him for a moment. "You look a little . . ."

"A little what?"

"Nervous."

Caleb adjusted his straw hat. "I'm not nervous.

Just wondering when that taxi is going to get here. It's late."

"*Nee*, you're early. By fifteen minutes."

"Oh."

Johnny chuckled and clapped his brother on the back. "Don't worry, Caleb. You'll make the right decision about the horses. You always do. See you this afternoon." He went back into the house.

Caleb forced himself not to pace again. His brother had confidence in him, which meant a lot. Caleb had to believe in his own abilities, his experience with horses, and his keen eye, which his father had pointed out when he was a young *kinn*. And of course there were the prayers he'd said, that God would lead him to the right horses. With all this on his side, he couldn't fail. By the time the taxi showed up, he felt a lot better.

He got in the front seat of the blue compact car and shut the door. "Thanks for picking me up, Roger."

"No problem. You ready for this auction?"

He grinned. "I sure am."

Bekah hid behind her buggy and smiled as she saw Caleb get into the car. One Mullet brother gone. Now she only had to wait for the other brother to leave.

Yesterday when Katie had mentioned that both Caleb and Johnny would be gone today, she couldn't contain her excitement. Even though she was here to help Katie, she would have some time to herself during part of the day. Finally she'd get a chance to ride one of the fine horses Caleb had been training over the past few months. They would be selling them soon, and she had been dying to ride one. Of course, Caleb had said no. His exact word had been *never,* which was ridiculous. He'd been riding these horses, so why couldn't she? She was just as good a rider as he was, even if he didn't think so.

But she couldn't ride until Johnny left. She didn't know if he would care if she rode one of the horses, but she didn't want to get into an argument with him either. Besides, she would only ride for a little bit. It wasn't a big deal.

Bekah went into the house, expecting to find Katie in the kitchen. When she didn't, she called out her sister's name. "Katie?" she said, going into the living room.

"I'll be right out," she called from her bedroom.

Bekah picked up an afghan pattern from the coffee table, looked at it for a moment, then put it back down, not understanding any of the symbols. Katie loved crocheting and knitting, two tasks that bored Bekah out of her mind. She had just sat down on the couch when Katie came into the room.

"I'm sorry, Bekah." She tucked a bobby pin into her red hair and pushed it against her *kapp.*

"Johnny asked if I'd *geh* with him to the lumber-yard today and I told him I would."

"I thought we were going to get the house ready for Sunday."

"We were, but . . ." She blushed. "I thought I'd take the chance to spend some time with Johnny. He's been so busy lately, and it's a beautiful day outside. Are you upset?"

Bekah grinned. This was working out better than she'd expected. With everyone gone she'd have the farm to herself. "You two have a *gut* time."

"Make yourself at home if you want to stay. Johnny's got some fishing poles in the shed if you want to use one and try that fishing hole you found yesterday."

Her sister had just given her the perfect excuse to stay. "Sure. I'll see if the fish are biting." *After I ride one of those beautiful horses.*

Johnny appeared at Katie's side. "Hey, Bekah," he said, nodding at her. Then he looked at his wife. "Ready to *geh*, Katie?"

Soon after her sister and brother-in-law were gone, Bekah walked past the shed and headed straight for the barn. She had the perfect horse in mind—a beautiful gray mare that was so sweet and gentle. She'd had the opportunity to brush her coat and feed her oats once, but that was because Caleb wasn't there and Johnny hadn't minded. He'd actually appreciated her help, something

Caleb never had. Ever since, she'd been eager to ride her.

She opened the stall and walked in. "Sweet thing. I'll miss you when you're gone." She touched the mare's nose and gave it pieces of apple she'd cut up before leaving Katie's house. "You and me, we're going to have fun this morning," she said, stroking the mare's mane. "And best of all? Caleb will never know about it."

Several hours later, Caleb returned from the auction, his experience a resounding success. He'd been able to purchase ten fine young horses and make arrangements for them to be delivered to the farm the next day. He wanted to buy two more, but they didn't have the room, and they wouldn't until they sold the five horses they already had. Next year they hoped to expand the farm further by breeding their own stock.

When Roger pulled up to the house, Caleb paid him. "Thanks again."

"No problem. Let me know the next time you want to go. I always enjoy a good auction."

"But you didn't buy anything."

"I know, but it's fun watching the sales."

Caleb nodded. "I'll call you for the next one."

He got out of the car and headed for the house, planning to change into some old clothes before he cleaned out the extra barn and prepared for the horses' delivery. He glanced up at the sky, which had been clear this morning and had now clouded into solid gray. Out of the corner of his eye he saw Bekah's buggy. He frowned. Great, she was still here. He'd avoid her in the house and quickly dress and get back to work. He wasn't going to let her ruin his good mood.

The house was quiet when he walked inside. Too quiet. "Katie?" he called out. No answer. He'd thought maybe Johnny would be back from the lumberyard by now, but his buggy was still gone. He shrugged. Maybe Katie and Bekah . . . well, he didn't know where they'd gone to, but he was sure they were all right.

After changing clothes he went outside to the barn. As he always did, he checked on the horses. He would let them into the pasture while he cleaned. Caleb opened the side door of the barn that led to the pasture, then one by one he opened each of the stalls and led the horses out. When he got to the last stall, he froze.

Where was the gray mare?

Panic ran through him. Had someone taken her? There had been instances of horse thievery in the area, but not lately. And why pass up the other horses and only take the one in the last stall? It didn't make any sense.

He ran out of the barn and back into the house, calling Katie's name again, even Johnny's, then Bekah's. Again, no one answered.

Caleb rushed outside, yelling for everyone in

case any of them were somewhere where they could hear him. He plopped his hands on his head when he got no response. Where was everyone? What if something had happened—something more than horse theft?

Bekah's eyes fluttered open. Above her was a lush canopy of oak branches from the trees surrounding the fishing hole. She stretched, lifting her arms above her head. She hadn't meant to fall asleep on the warm grass bank of the pond, only to rest her eyes for a few minutes. How long had she been out? She had no idea.

She turned her head and saw the gray mare tethered to the tree where Bekah had left her, still munching on the grass. She had taken the horse for a short ride, then decided to walk her through the woods to the clearing here. Above the horse's head she saw a flash of lightning. The mare lifted her head.

"Bekah!"

She sat up at the faint sound of Caleb calling her name. *Oh* nee. She must have slept longer than she thought. How was she going to get the horse back to the barn without him knowing about it?

A sinking sensation filled her belly. What were the chances that he hadn't gone to the barn when he came home? *None.*

She scrambled up from the ground, not bothering to brush the grass off her dress. What would she tell him? Definitely not that she took the horse for a ride. He would be mad at her for taking the mare out to the field, but not as much as if he knew she had ridden her.

Another flash streaked the sky, followed by a quick crack of thunder. Bekah grabbed the startled horse's reins. She'd have to ride her back to the barn, not lead her on foot like she planned. Caleb would be furious. But right now she was worried about getting the horse back to the barn before the storm started.

She untied the reins and hurtled up on the back of the horse, the skirt of her dress tucked between her legs. Bekah guided the horse through the woods, cringing every time she heard Caleb calling her name, interspersing it with Katie's and Johnny's.

A huge thunder boom sounded right overhead. The horse reared up, and Bekah flew through the air. She smacked her head on the ground. Black spots swam in front of her eyes.

She tried to sit up, but the slight movement made her dizzy. What about the horse? Hazy panic went through her as she realized it had to have run off.

Cold dread pooled in her belly. She had lost Caleb's horse. How could she have been so stupid? She never should have taken it in the first place. All she had wanted was a quick ride, and now she was lying in the dirt, her head pounding in pain, unable to chase down the poor, terrified horse.

I'm an idiot. She put her hand to her head, feeling for any blood. When she was sure she hadn't cut her head, she tried to sit up again, only to have a wave of nausea overcome her, causing her to lie back down. She closed her eyes as heavy drops of rain started to fall, spattering her face. The rain soon became a steady downpour as she tried to stem the dizziness and sit up again.

"Bekah!"

She heard Caleb's voice nearby. Maybe she shouldn't say anything. She nixed that thought when she realized she'd caused him enough trouble. He didn't need to go looking for her in a thunderstorm. "Over here!" She pushed herself to a seated position. Her vision still blurry, she squinted as she saw him approach, holding the reins of the mare. *Thank God.*

"Are you all right?" He moved toward her and squatted down, still holding the reins. His brown eyes darted over her, filled with panic and . . . worry?

"I think so."

"What happened?"

"I . . ." She glanced down at her soggy dress. "I just wanted to ride her once. That was it, and then I was going to put her back. But then I fell asleep by the pond and—" Her head started to pound. "I'm sorry."

"Where's Katie?"

"She went to town with Johnny."

He pressed his lips together but didn't say anything. Rain dripped from the brim of his hat. "Can you stand up?"

Bekah nodded, pushing herself to a standing position. Her head throbbed even more, and a wave of nausea came over her. She stumbled forward, and Caleb's arm shot around her waist. Without a word he swooped her up in his arms and started carrying her toward the farmhouse. "Put me down," she said. "I can walk."

He continued to carry her, leading the horse at the same time. In pain and not thinking straight, she leaned her head against his shoulder. Glancing up, she saw he continued to look straight ahead, his lips still pressed in a firm line.

But despite her hazy mind and roiling stomach, she was aware of his strong arms around her. The warmth of his shoulder beneath his wet shirt. His anger radiated off him in waves, and she didn't blame him. Yet he could have left her behind, or made her walk. Instead, he carried her. She slipped her left arm around his shoulder and sighed.

CHAPTER 8

Caleb was so angry he could barely see straight. Bekah taking out the horse behind his back shouldn't 'have surprised him, but it did. Of all the foolish, irresponsible things to do. Bekah had always been impulsive and was often unmindful of other people, but this beat everything she'd done in the past. Did she realize what could have happened? He couldn't even look at her.

He felt her put her arm around his shoulder, nestle her head against him, and sigh. *Is she enjoying this?* He had a mind to put her down and let her wobble back to the house by herself.

But he couldn't do it. When he had seen Bekah lying on the ground, all thoughts of concern for his horse had fled his mind, replaced with worry and panic for Bekah. And in spite of his anger, when he saw her struggle to walk, it scared him. Picking her up probably wasn't the best thing to do in hindsight, but he couldn't leave her behind.

And now, to top it all off, feeling her cheek pressed against him and her soft breath on his neck . . . he wasn't sure he wanted to let her go.

Once they cleared the field and he saw the horses outside in the pasture, huddled under a tree as another strike of lightning lit up the sky, his anger returned. He stopped walking. "Can you make it to the house from here?" he said tightly.

"I . . . I think so."

He put her down, made sure she was steady on her feet, and walked away, leading the gray horse back to the barn. He resisted the urge to check to see if she was okay. This was her fault, not his, and he had to take care of the horses before they were spooked any further.

As he struggled to get them back in the barn, his fury mounted. It took him several tries to get the last one inside, a black gelding that had taken extra time to break. The last thing this horse needed was to be scared. Once he got the horses in their stalls, he yanked the back door shut and pounded his fist against it.

"What's going on?"

He turned to see Johnny rushing into the barn. Caleb stalked away from the back door and went to the first stall. "Bekah happened." He grabbed a towel, opened the stall door, and went inside to dry off the horse. They could drip-dry just fine, but he had to do something or he would explode.

"Katie's with her. She said she was thrown from one of the horses."

"Is that all she said?" When the chestnut horse started to nicker, Caleb slowed his wiping motions.

Johnny peered over the stall door. "She also said you were furious with her."

"I am."

"Then I'll ask again—what happened?"

Caleb didn't look up. "I don't want to talk about it."

"Fine," Johnny responded, sounding frustrated. "You can tell me later, though I suspect Bekah didn't ask your permission to ride a horse. Are the horses okay, at least?"

"They're wet, but they're fine."

"I was worried they got spooked by the storm." Johnny grabbed another towel and went into the next stall.

"They did, but they're settling."

They dried off the horses in silence. A short while later, Caleb called to Johnny, unable to stop himself from asking the question. "Is . . . is Bekah okay?"

"She's got a huge goose egg on the back of her head, but she seems to have her wits about her."

Caleb let out a relieved breath but didn't respond. Now that he knew she was okay, his anger returned.

"I think she learned her lesson," Johnny added.

"I doubt it," Caleb said. "She never does."

Anna Mae had waited for the afternoon storm to stop before she headed back to the Mullet farm. Steam wafted from the wet road, and the muggy air felt like a wet wool blanket. As she turned into their driveway, she wiped her damp forehead with the back of her hand.

She had decided to take the buggy today, and she tethered her horse to the hitching post in the Mullets' driveway. As she tied the loop, she yawned. She hadn't been able to sleep last night and had stayed up until almost dawn working on two pairs of Amos's pants. Her mother had offered to help her work on another pair today, but she'd rejected the peace offering, instead going out to the barn to talk to her father.

When she found him, he was tying flies for his upcoming fishing trip to Canada. He and his three friends chartered a boat on Lake Ontario for a week each summer. They chipped in to rent a cabin and the taxi to get them to Canada, plus whatever extra food they needed beyond the fish they caught. Her mother always remarked that Lake Erie was close by and full of fish, but her father said it wasn't the same.

"Hi, *Daed*," she'd said.

He'd looked up at her from his workbench. "Well, what brings you out here?"

"I thought I'd see what you were doing."

"Working on this lure. I think it's going to be a beaut."

From that point on he'd talked about how to tie lures, why it was important to tie the strands a certain way, and other things important to fishing that Anna Mae couldn't care less about. He'd never hinted that her mother had said anything to him about their argument last night. Eventually she'd extricated herself from the fishing lecture and left. She was glad he was excited about his trip, and she didn't want to burden him with her problems.

As she'd walked back to her house, she'd realized that she envied his leaving. Not because she liked to fish. She couldn't stand fishing. But at least he was getting away, even if it was for a short time. She'd never had that opportunity.

Her mind ventured back to the present, and she grabbed the cloth bag with Amos's clothes from the seat of the buggy and walked to the house, sidestepping a few water puddles in the uneven driveway. She heard drops of water intermittently sliding from the tips of the leaves on the surrounding trees. Before she reached the house, she glanced around, relieved that she didn't see Jeremiah's car. Not that she'd expected him to be there, knowing he was probably at work.

Then again, what did she know about his life? He'd cut her off a long time ago, and he didn't seem interested in changing that.

She knocked on the door. When no one answered, she walked inside. The first thing she noticed was the fresh smell of lemon cleaner. Then she realized that the living room was spotless. None of Amos's socks or hats were in sight, which they usually were when she came over. The newspapers David read were stacked neatly on the coffee table instead of being strewn all around his chair. She peered down at the table. Not a speck of dust.

Anna Mae smiled. Judith must have been here.

"Hi, Anna Mae."

She turned as Amos entered the room. He had peanut butter and jelly smeared on his chin. She picked up a tissue from the box next to the newspapers—where did that come from?—and held it out to him. "You're wearing some of your lunch."

"Okay." He took the tissue and wiped his face. "Did I get it?"

"*Ya.* Where's *yer daed*?"

"He went to town to buy groceries. We're out of everything," he said. "I ate the last of the peanut butter and bread."

She should have checked the pantry when she was there yesterday. She probably would have if she hadn't been distracted by Jeremiah—and life in general. She handed Amos the bag.

"What's this for?"

"There are two pairs of pants in there. Plus your socks. Try on the pants so I can see if they fit right."

"Okay."

"Meet me in the kitchen when you're finished." As he bounded upstairs, she headed for the kitchen, which would need cleaning considering Amos had just had lunch.

But when she walked in, the only mess she

saw was a plate with bread crumbs scattered on it and a knife smeared with peanut butter. She picked up the plate and shook the bread crumbs into the trash can under the sink, then turned on the faucet and quickly washed the dish and knife. She had just set them in the dish drainer when she heard Amos's voice.

"I think there's something wrong," Amos said.

Anna Mae turned around. Her mouth dropped open when she saw him. "Oh, Amos. I'm sorry."

He looked down at his pants, which had one leg quite a few inches longer than the other.

She went to him and knelt down. "I wasn't paying attention when I did this." That's what she got for sewing when she should have been sleeping. She looked up at him. "I can fix them, though. I'll do it before I leave."

"Okay." He touched the top of Anna Mae's head. "Don't feel bad. *Daed* tells me I have to pay attention all the time. When I don't, bad things can happen around the farm. But sometimes I forget. Like when I fell off the hayloft."

Anna Mae nodded. That had happened two years ago, and fortunately all he had broken was his arm. She had set it in a sling before he had gone to the hospital to get X-rays.

"And look," he said, raising up his bandaged hand. "I'm all better now."

She chuckled, feeling a little bit better about her mistake. "That's wonderful, Amos. Why don't you *geh* upstairs and change. Bring the other pair down with you. I want to make sure they are all right."

"Okay." He turned to leave, the hem of his left pant leg dragging on the floor while the right one was above his ankle.

When he disappeared, Anna Mae went to the back door of the kitchen and opened it. She stepped into the yard, as the Mullets didn't have a patio or deck on the back of their house. She walked in the damp grass and looked at the house next door. The house had been abandoned ever since Mrs. Zook died, although Jeremiah and Amos took turns mowing the grass so the property didn't look totally unkempt. The house still needed a fresh coat of paint, but she saw the small garden just off the back concrete patio and a shepherd's hook that held a flower basket filled with violet-colored petunias. From the outside, it seemed Judith was turning the house into a home.

"Here are *mei* clothes." Amos appeared beside her and handed her the pants.

She took them. "I like Judith's flowers," she said, knowing Amos often looked at nature through his artist's eye. "What do you think of them?"

"I think she needs more. Maybe Jeremiah and I will take her some soon. She's very nice and very pretty. She's always bringing us desserts. She brought an apple pie over last night. Jeremiah said I was right, that Miss Judith makes the best desserts."

Anna Mae looked at the fabric in her hands, brushing away invisible dust.

"Have you seen Jeremiah today, Anna Mae? I hope he comes over for supper again tonight. I asked him if he could stay here, but he said he and *Daed* fight too much." He looked down at her. "If he stays for supper, can you stay too?"

"I don't think so, Amos." She turned and walked toward the house.

"Why not?"

"I just . . . can't."

He followed her. "I wish the three of us would be together again. Don't you?"

Closing her eyes for a moment, she pressed the pants to her chest. She turned and forced a smile. "Things are different now. We're not *kinner* anymore."

"But we made a promise. Remember? I remember that promise. Don't you?"

"Amos, sometimes things change. People . . . they change too."

He nodded. "Jeremiah is different. He wears Yankee clothes now. His hair is also short. I don't like it."

"Speaking of hair," Anna Mae said, reaching up to touch his shaggy locks, "I think it's time for another haircut."

"*Nee*." He shook his head and stepped away.

"I'll only cut off a little bit. Then I'll make you some chocolate milk. How does that sound?"

He grinned. "Okay."

They walked into the kitchen. Anna Mae set the clothes on the table and went to the junk drawer, where she knew they kept the hair-cutting scissors. As she worked to shape Amos's hair into some semblance of an *Amisch* cut, she smiled, her upset over the pants and Amos mentioning Jeremiah replaced by contentment. Being with Amos always made her forget about her problems for the moment. She loved him as if he were her own brother. Impulsively she put her arms around his thick neck.

"What was that for?" he asked, turning to look up at her.

"Just letting you know how much I love you."

"Okay." He turned and faced forward. She continued to snip at his scraggly ends, only to freeze at his next words.

"Me and Jeremiah love you too."

Bekah sat in Katie's kitchen and held an ice pack to the bump on her head. Katie came up behind her and put a bath towel around her shoulders. She rounded the table and sat across from her sister. "How are you feeling?"

The words *stupid* and *selfish* crossed her mind, but she said, "Okay."

"Does your head still hurt?"

She nodded, then grimaced.

Katie frowned. "Maybe we should call the doctor."

"*Nee.*" She didn't need to add a doctor bill to her growing pile of problems. "I'll be fine."

Katie folded her hands together. "Bekah, what were you thinking? You had to know taking one of the horses for a ride was a bad idea."

"But if I hadn't fallen asleep, then it wouldn't have been a problem."

"Do you really believe that?"

She set the ice pack on the table and pulled the towel closer around her. "I messed up, Katie. And now Caleb is really angry with me."

"He has a right to be. And I'm not exactly happy with you either. You told me you were going fishing."

"I was . . . after I went riding." She looked away, shame filling her. "I'm sorry."

"I'm not the one you need to apologize to." Katie stood. "You need to get out of those wet clothes. You can borrow one of my dresses." She took Bekah's *kapp* off the table. Half of it was streaked with mud. "I'll take care of this. There are some kerchiefs in *mei* top drawer." She left the kitchen.

Bekah stood, her head still throbbing but not as much. She touched the lump on the back of her head. Half of her hair had fallen out of its bun. She dragged her bare feet as she went to Katie's room, selected a dress and a kerchief, and headed to the bathroom to change out of her wet clothes.

When she finished dressing, fixing her hair, and pinning the pink kerchief to her head, she opened the bathroom door. Caleb was standing there. He looked down and took a step back, giving her space to leave.

But she couldn't move. Not until she apologized. "Caleb, I'm so sorry."

He lifted his gaze to hers, his eyes narrowing. "You're not."

She balked. "How can you say that? Of course I am."

"You're sorry you got caught."

Bekah bit her bottom lip. "That's not true."

"Isn't it? You planned this. You waited until everyone was gone and you took the horse. Behind *mei* back . . . behind all our backs."

"Because you wouldn't let me ride her. If you would have, then this wouldn't have happened."

"You're unbelievable, you know that?" He raked his hand through his wet hair, slicking it back from his forehead. She could see a vein pulsing on the side of his neck, and she took a step back. She'd never seen him so angry before. "You're blaming me for your lying."

"What?" Her eyes widened. "I'm not lying."

"So you say." He moved past her and into the bathroom. "I need to get cleaned up."

"This isn't over." Bekah crossed her arms. "You

can't accuse me of being a liar and then walk away."

He whirled around, his brown eyes darkening to nearly black. "It's always about you, isn't it? Don't you see the bigger picture here? I'm responsible for those horses. That gray mare? She's already been sold. Johnny has buyers lined up for the other ones. They're not toys; they're *mei* livelihood."

"I know they're not toys," she said, contrite.

"I have to be responsible." He leaned over her and moved close to her face. "I can't fritter *mei* life away. I can't play around at living while I wait for somebody to come along, feel sorry for me, and take care of me for the rest of my life."

Bekah's blood pressure spiked, making her head throb more than ever. She leaned forward until they were nearly nose to nose. "Are you saying the only way I would get a husband is if he *pitied* me?"

Caleb glared at her, not replying. But his silence spoke volumes.

She backed away from him. "I don't see *maed* lining up to *geh* out with you." It was a terrible comeback, but she couldn't think of anything clever. Or witty. Or even smart sounding. She was hurting too much.

"Grow up, Bekah. And *geh* home. We're trying to run a business here, not a playground." He slammed the door in her face.

She turned and stormed away, only to stop a few feet from the bathroom door when she remembered she'd left her dress hanging over the bathtub. She'd have to get it later. She wasn't sticking around to hear more of Caleb's hurtful words.

Tears stung her eyes as she went to her buggy. She wiped at them violently. Why was she letting him get to her? He could have accepted her apology, but no. He had to dig at her, to make her feel worse than she already did. As she climbed in, she tried to force the pain away. His words couldn't hurt her. He wasn't worth it.

Yet the tears wouldn't stop coming. She dropped her head into her hands. Was that what he really thought of her? A dishonest woman? A childish woman who was in the way? Someone to be pitied? Someone who wasn't worthy of real love?

She sobbed into her palms. Why did Caleb hate her so much? And . . . why did she care?

CHAPTER 9

Anna Mae finished repairing Amos's pants—fortunately the pair he tried on were the only ones that were uneven. He had gone outside shortly after she gave him his haircut—presumably to draw in the barn. She was always amazed at his artistic talent, and a bit surprised that his father let him use the inside of the barn as his canvas. But it made sense. Not many people visited the Mullets, mostly by David's design. He'd never been particularly welcoming to anyone after his wife left, and when Jeremiah was gone he had closed himself off more. The chances of anyone seeing Amos's masterpieces were slim.

She frowned as she folded Amos's pants. Knowing that Amos needed to keep his art hidden saddened her, even though Amos didn't seem to mind that no one but his father, Anna Mae, and his late grandmother had seen the drawings. She wished there was a way for him to share them, but that would cause problems for him and David.

Carrying Amos's pants and socks, she went upstairs to put them in his room. She also quickly made his bed, smoothing the old, faded, blue-and-white quilt he had slept with since he was a small child.

She stepped out into the hallway and turned to go downstairs. But she stopped and glanced down the hall at the door next to Amos's bed-room. Jeremiah's old room. She'd been in there one time, when they were almost twelve and he wanted to show her a surprise.

"Close your eyes."

"Jeremiah, I have to get home. It's getting dark."

"This will only take a minute." He shut the door to his room and pulled the shade, leaving them in almost complete darkness. "Are you gonna close your eyes or not?"

"What's the point? I can't see anyway."

"Just close your eyes already!"

"Fine." She shut her eyes and heard him shuffling around in his room, but all she could think about was how much trouble she would be in for being late when she got home. "This better be worth it, Jeremiah."

"It will be. Trust me." He paused. "Open your eyes."

When she opened them, she saw he was holding a jar full of flickering light. She caught his grin, illuminated by the glowing jar. "What do you think?" he asked.

Mesmerized, she moved closer to him. The jar was filled with fireflies and bits of long-stemmed grass. "They're beautiful."

"I caught them yesterday. Underneath the grass is a damp paper towel. I read that you have to keep the jar humid so the fireflies are comfortable."

She didn't really know what he meant by all that, but Jeremiah was smart and knew a lot about animals, even insects. "Can I hold them?"

"*Ya.*" He kept smiling as he handed her the jar. "They're actually beetles, you know."

Anna Mae held it up to her face, watching the

fireflies as they flitted around the glass, their little lights blinking on and off. "I wonder how they do that?"

"Luciferin."

She looked at him. "What?"

"That's the chemical inside their body that makes the light."

"Only you would know that, Jeremiah." She laughed and stared at the beetles again.

He shrugged. "I like to know things." He took the jar from her and unscrewed the lid. "Watch this."

The fireflies escaped. Anna Mae looked around as they circled above them for a moment, then scattered around, spreading tiny lights throughout the room. "You'll never get them back."

"I don't want to. They need to be free." He pulled up the shade, exposing the open window with the screen removed. A couple of them found their way out, but several of them continued to fly around his room.

"They're lost," Anna Mae said. She went to his dresser, where one of the beetles had landed. She put her finger underneath its delicate legs. The firefly glowed as it climbed on. She guided it into the palm of her hand and went to the window. She held out her hand and the firefly took off.

Jeremiah leaned against the window ledge.

"They'll all find their way out eventually." He looked at Anna Mae with a grin. "Pretty neat, huh?"

"*Ya*. Thanks for showing me your collection."

"They're not mine. I captured them for you."

Anna Mae blinked and stared at the doorway. She'd forgotten all about the fireflies, and Jeremiah's comment that he had caught them for her didn't mean much at the time. They were kids, and he was showing off his smarts. Or so she'd thought at the time.

Now the memory was something different. A sweet moment she and Jeremiah had shared. And now she could see it was a glimpse into his kind heart.

She turned away from the door, shaking her head. How could a man who was so tender toward fireflies as a child and who grew up to care for animals so deeply not realize how much he'd hurt her when he left? Or how his return had reopened a raw wound? How could he continue to live his life as if their friendship had meant so little to him, when it had meant everything to her?

"Anna Mae?"

Amos's voice jerked her out of her thoughts. She went downstairs, leaving Jeremiah's room and the memories behind.

"I'm ready for *mei* chocolate milk."

She looked at Amos and smiled. He stood in

the doorway, a huge grin on his sweet, round face, anticipating the treat as if he were eight years old again. She might not have Jeremiah in her life anymore, but Amos was here. He needed her. And she needed him.

Jeremiah pulled his car into Anna Mae's driveway. It was late, nearly sundown, but he knew this visit was overdue. He'd gone to see Amos after work tonight and noticed he not only had a new haircut but new clothes. When he told Jeremiah that they were all courtesy of Anna Mae, he knew he couldn't delay seeing her anymore. He needed to thank her for taking such good care of his brother.

He shut off the engine, hesitating before he got out. He'd thought about what to say to her on the drive here, but he still didn't know what to tell her. What if she refused to see him? He wouldn't blame her if she did. Still, he had to try to talk to her.

And the truth was he wanted to see her. Even though he'd been busy with work and preoccupied with the problems between him and his father, she hadn't been far from his mind. But the desire to see her was tempered with a good dose of anxiety. At least when he kept his distance he didn't have to face the possibility of her sending him away.

He grimaced. His cowardice was repulsive. He opened the door and got out of the car, smoothed down his hair, and skipped up the steps to her front door. Taking a deep breath, he knocked on the screen door. Soft light glowed from a lamp in the living room. He peered inside, but didn't see anybody.

Anna Mae's face suddenly popped up in front of him. He jumped back a bit.

"Jeremiah?" she said through the screen door.

"Um, hi." He started to put his hands in his pockets, then on his hips, then finally he just let his arms rest to his sides. This was already becoming awkward.

"What are you doing here?"

She didn't open the door. Maybe he'd made a mistake in coming here. "I . . . I wanted to talk to you. For a minute. If you had time." He backed away. "But if you're busy—"

"I'm not busy." She opened the door and stepped out on the front porch.

He looked down at her bare feet, the hem of her skirt skimming her shins.

"What did you want to talk about?"

He forced his gaze up to her face. She crossed her arms over her chest. In the fading daylight he could see her clear blue eyes reflecting like cold pieces of ice. He better make this quick. "I wanted to tell you thank you. And that I'm sorry."

"Okay."

He chuckled. "You sound like Amos."

Her shoulders sagged a tiny bit, giving her a

softer shape. "He does say 'okay' a lot. It's endearing."

He nodded. "I appreciate you taking care of him. You gave him a nice haircut, by the way."

"You saw him tonight?"

"Yes, I had supper over there. He couldn't wait to show me his new clothes and hair." He smiled at her. "You made him very happy."

"I'm glad. I care about Amos very much. He's like a *bruder* to me."

Her words made him want to ask her what place he had in her life. But he didn't have the right to ask . . . and he wasn't sure he wanted to know the answer. Instead he brought out his wallet. "Can I pay you for the clothes?"

Her gaze hardened. "Really, Jeremiah? That's why you came over here? To pay me so you don't feel so guilty?"

"That's not what I meant—"

"Doesn't matter." She turned and opened the screen door before looking back at him. "I won't take your money. What I do for Amos I do out of love. I thought you at least remembered that much." She stepped inside and the screen door shut behind her.

He stood on the porch, his mouth dropped open. What had he been thinking, offering to pay her? But words had seemed so inconsequential compared to what she had done for Amos in his absence. He waited for a moment, hoping she would come back. When he knew she wouldn't, he turned and walked away.

Awesome. He ended up making things worse between them. Now he had to apologize for insulting her, not that she would listen.

He glanced over his shoulder at her house. Something was different about her, and he wasn't sure it all had to do with him. She was harder. Guarded. And brittle, like something beneath her was about to snap. That wasn't the Anna Mae he knew.

Something was wrong. He wanted to go back to her, to tell her that whatever was going on, he was here for her, even though he had let her down in the past.

But he went to his car instead. After today she wouldn't be receptive to anything he had to say, and he had no one to blame but himself.

Johnny took off his hat and threaded his fingers through his sweat-dampened hair. "I appreciate you coming to check on the horses," he said to Jeremiah. "When I heard you were back working with Doc again, I didn't hesitate to call."

Jeremiah felt the front legs of the final horse in its stall in his cousins' barn. A week had passed since he'd arrived in Middlefield, and to his surprise, most of Doc's clients were fairly happy to see him. Only a few had politely refused to have him come out to see their animals when they found out Doc wouldn't be the vet. He stood and looked at Johnny. "They all seem healthy and strong." He put his stethoscope around his neck. "Where did you say you got them?"

"Caleb went to an auction in Bloomfield last week. We've bought from them twice. I'm glad to hear they're stout. We did well with the previous group we had."

"Your brother picked some fine ones." They walked out of the horse's stall to the center of the barn.

"*Danki*," Caleb shouted from inside a stall at the other end of the barn.

"They're a little spunky," Jeremiah added. "You plan on breaking them?"

"That's Caleb's job." Johnny plopped his hat on the top of his head and looked Jeremiah up and down, grinning.

"What?"

"I knew you were smart and all. I also knew you had a notion to become a vet. But I never thought you would do it."

Jeremiah crouched on the dirt floor and put his stethoscope in his black medical bag, not sure if he should be insulted.

"Don't get me wrong. If anyone had the smarts to be a veterinarian in our family, it would be you. I reckon it had to be hard for you."

You have no idea . . .

He leaned forward as Jeremiah stood. "Do I get the family discount?"

"Cheap as always," Caleb said, coming out of one of the stalls, his boots covered in straw and debris. "Make sure you charge him double, Jeremiah."

"I should remind you," Johnny said to his younger brother, "that as a partner in this business, that money is coming out of your pockets."

Jeremiah grinned. "Now I'm thinking about tripling my fee."

"That's a sure way to lose business," Caleb said, making a crack.

Jeremiah patted the horse's flanks and smiled. He hadn't seen his cousins in a long time. They were several years older than he, so they had never been close. But he appreciated how accepting they were of his career path.

"Can you stay for lunch?" Johnny asked. "I'm sure Katie has something *appeditlich* whipped up."

"Sure. I've got some time before my next appointment."

The three men walked out of the barn and headed to the house. "This is a pretty impressive farm," Jeremiah said, looking around.

"You should have seen it six years ago," Caleb said. "This place was so run-down. A stiff breeze could have blown the barn apart."

"Hate to say it, but it's true," Johnny said. "I even lived here for a while by myself, before I wised up and sold it."

"What?" Jeremiah asked. "But you own it."

"I'm the primary owner, true." At Jeremiah's questioning glance he added, "It's a long story. But now this farm is thriving, all because of God's timing."

"With a little help from me," Caleb added.

"And Katie," Johnny said. "Plus Bekah helped out too."

Caleb snorted, his good humor gone. "Whatever." He strode ahead of them.

"What was that about?" Jeremiah said as Caleb entered the house.

"He and Bekah are on the outs."

"So they're together?"

"Just the opposite. Pretty much can't stand each other. Although Katie says it's because they really love each other." He stopped at the back door and looked at Jeremiah. "I appreciate your opinion on the farm. It really means a lot."

Jeremiah was touched, especially since the compliment came from family. The *Amisch* eschewed pride in favor of humility, but there was a difference in being conceited about work and knowing others took value in it.

"I know what it's like to pursue a dream." Johnny gestured to the farm. "I didn't think this one would come true. But God provided."

"He always does."

Johnny looked at Jeremiah. "I'm glad to hear you still believe that."

"Of course I do." He'd never been close to

Johnny, but there was something about the man that made him feel like he could trust him. "It hasn't been easy. Not gonna lie about that. But I don't regret what I've done."

"Leaving the *Amisch*?"

"It's more than that. I didn't just leave a religion. I moved toward something else—veterinarian medicine. I can't imagine doing anything different."

"So you're planning to stay around for a while?"

Jeremiah rubbed his stubbly beard. He hadn't been as conscientious about the appearance of it since he'd arrived in Middlefield. He should shave it tonight. "I'm not sure. Depends on how long Doc needs me."

"How's his leg?"

"He's moving around on the crutches better. It's only been two weeks since he broke it."

"I hope he recovers soon."

"Me too." But then what? He assumed he would go back to Columbus and renew his job search. But could he just leave again after a few weeks? Could he do that to Amos?

Anna Mae's image came to mind. Could he do that to her . . . again? He hadn't tried to see her since she shut the door on him last week. Not that he hadn't driven by her house almost every night, trying to come up with the right thing to say to her but inevitably chickening out. He realized during that time, first driving aimlessly around in his car, that while he was focused on his schooling and himself, he had assumed Anna Mae would always be there for him. He had taken her for granted, and he should have known better.

But how could he make up for that? Was it even possible?

"We better get inside," Johnny said. "Before Caleb eats all the food. Though he would tell you he deserves it."

"How so?"

They resumed walking. "Because he's a better horseman than me. He shoes faster than I do."

"Is that true?"

"It pains me to say so, but *ya*. It is. But I have better business sense. Which requires an extra helping of dessert."

"I'm sure it does," Jeremiah said wryly. "Are you sure Katie won't mind an extra mouth to feed?"

Johnny shook his head as he opened the door. "You know the *Amisch*. When it comes to company, we always have plenty."

Bekah stared out her bedroom window, looking at her backyard. Her gaze landed on the large oak tree near the small pond, her favorite of all the trees in the yard. She leaned her chin against the window ledge as memories flooded over her.

"What do you always got your nose in a *dumm* old book for?"

Bekah rolled her eyes at Caleb. But she refused to look at him. Instead she calmly turned the page. "Maybe if you read a book sometime you'd understand."

He snatched the book from Bekah's hands. "Maybe I should read this one."

"Hey!" Bekah popped up from beneath the tree and rushed toward him. She wished his family had never stayed for lunch after church. Then maybe she would have a moment's peace. "Give it back!"

He held it up over her head, flashing an annoying grin. Although they had both just turned thirteen, he was taller than she was. Chocolate-colored eyes, filled with teasing glee, gazed back at her. "You'll have to catch me first!" He spun off and ran toward the pond. He held the book over the edge. "Say good-bye to Nancy Drew!"

"Don't you dare, Caleb Mullet! That's a library book. If you ruin it, you're going to pay for it!"

He dangled the book above the water. She hurtled herself toward him, ready to grab the book out of his hands. But just as she reached up, he tossed the book over her head and onto the grassy bank behind her. She slipped on the wet bank and tumbled forward, headfirst into the murky water.

Caleb doubled over with laughter as she sputtered and tried to catch her breath.

Bekah smiled. She had been furious with him that day. But now she could look at the situation for what it had been—childhood teasing that had gone too far. Her smile faded. They weren't children now, and his anger with her was anything but funny.

She lifted her head, still replaying every word Caleb had said to her last week in front of Katie's bathroom. While her head had healed with no problem, she couldn't say the same thing for her ego. Or her feelings. It hurt even more that she knew he was right.

A knock sounded on her bedroom door. "Bekah?"

She got up from the window and opened the door. Her mother stood there, holding a glass of lemonade. "I thought you might want something to drink."

Bekah looked at the glass. She wasn't thirsty, or hungry, but she took the glass from her anyway. "*Danki.*" She started to close the door, but her mother slipped inside her room. She sat on Bekah's bed and smiled. "I thought we could talk."

Bekah sighed. "I'm not in the mood for a lecture, *Mamm.*" She walked over to the window and looked outside again. It was a gorgeous day, almost the end of June, and the sun shone brightly in the cloudless sky. A perfect day for fishing. Or reading under a tree. Or riding a horse—

She shook her head. *Childish things.*

"I'm not here to give you a lecture." *Mamm* paused. "I'm worried about you."

"You always say that. Right before you tell me I need to grow up." She looked at her mother, tears blurring her vision. "Well, you're right. I'm immature and childish."

"Bekah, that's not what I was going to say. Come here and sit down."

She paused, then set her lemonade on the nightstand beside her bed and sat next to her mother. "I'm sorry," she said through tears.

Mamm put her arm around Bekah's shoulder. "Oh, *lieb*. What for?"

"Being . . . me."

Her mother pulled her close, and Bekah laid her head on her mother's shoulder. "I love you, Bekah. You have no reason to apologize for being the person God made you."

"I think God messed up."

Mamm pulled away and gave her a sharp look. "God never makes mistakes. You know that."

Bekah looked down at her lap. "He doesn't, but I sure do."

"We all do. I'm starting to think I've been making a mistake with you these past years."

Bekah looked at her. "What do you mean?"

"I've been lecturing you about your life. That's not *mei* place."

"Even if you're right? I *am* lazy. I *don't* take things seriously."

Her mother took her hand. "I was wrong to call you lazy. I know you work hard when it's something you want to do. And when you don't want to do it . . . you at least try. That's important."

Bekah looked at her mother. "Katie told you what happened, didn't she?"

Her mother folded her lips inward before admitting Katie had. "She was concerned about you when you weren't at church last Sunday. I told her you were still nursing a headache, but we both know that wasn't true."

It wasn't, but it was the excuse she'd given her mother when it was time to get ready for the service. She could add being a liar to the list of her sins. Caleb had been right about that too. And she couldn't face him after what she'd done.

"It was a stupid thing to do," Bekah said. "I know that now." She cast her mother a side glance. "Are you going to ground me?" she asked, only half-joking.

"I think you're punishing yourself quite well, staying holed up here in your room." Her mother released Bekah's hand. "I know you'd rather be outside." She rose from the bed and looked down at her. "Katie misses you. I do too. It's not like you to mope, Bekah. I think there's something else going on here."

"Maybe I've just decided it's time for me to finally change. To be more serious." She got up.

"Do the floors need mopping? Or the dishes washing? I can clean out the kitchen cabinets or scrub out the oven. Whatever you need me to do."

"Bekah, stop it." Her mother's brows flattened above her eyes, as they usually did when she was annoyed. "You made an error in judgment. Fortunately no one was seriously hurt, and the horse you took out is fine. Have you apologized to Caleb?"

"I tried to."

"Then put this behind you." She touched Bekah's face. "You don't have to change who you are because of one mistake. You only have to make sure you don't repeat it." She patted Bekah's cheek. "Katie would like for you to go over tomorrow. She's thinking about putting up a *grienhaus* next to the garden."

"Why?"

"She'd like to have fresh fruit and vegetables year-round, if possible. Also, she was thinking about growing flowers in part of it, and maybe selling them in early spring at the market."

"That's a *gut* idea."

"Johnny and Caleb are too busy with the horses and the farm to help her, and we all know how *gut* you are at designing and building things."

So her mother *did* know she helped her father design his barn expansion. Bekah lifted her chin a bit. "I do enjoy doing that."

147

Her mother smiled. "That sounds like *mei* Bekah." She headed for the door, then turned and faced Bekah again. "But until tomorrow, I do have plenty of laundry for you to do."

Laughing, Bekah said, "I'll be glad to."

Her mother shook her head. "I never thought I'd see the day you'd be happy to do laundry." She looked up at the ceiling. "Thank God for small miracles."

Her mother left, and Bekah sat back on her bed. She wasn't thrilled about the laundry, but she also realized she needed to do her fair share when it came to chores, even the ones she didn't like. She took a sip of the sweet lemonade. Once she finished her work around here, she would sketch out some drawings to take to Katie tomorrow.

She frowned. Going to her sister's would mean facing Caleb. She could ignore him, like she had done in the past. Like driving up the driveway and pretending she didn't see him, even though it was hard for her not to watch his every move. He had a commanding presence about him, as if he had a secure sense of himself. She still remembered the way his arms felt around her, the way he'd scooped her up without hesitation. He was such an appealing man—

Her eyes widened. Where had that come from? She opened her palm, which had grown damp. She gave her head a good shake. Caleb would probably never speak to her again. Whatever she felt for him was moot.

What did she feel for him, exactly?

"Bekah!" her mother called from downstairs.

"Coming!" She shoved Caleb to the back of her mind and left her room, ready to tackle the laundry.

CHAPTER 10

Judith ran the push mower across the width of her backyard, pausing to wipe the sweat from her forehead. This was a lot easier to do when she was younger. But the grass was in need of a trim, and it wasn't going to cut itself. She continued to push the mower until she got to the edge of her yard and David's.

She saw booted feet approaching. She recognized them. Lifting her gaze, she smiled. "Hello, David."

He nodded, his usual curt greeting. Perhaps one day he would actually tell her hello. He stopped in front of her. "I'll do that," he said, reaching for the mower.

"It's okay. I don't mind the work." Although the sweat dripping down her back told another story.

He ignored her and took the mower from her hands. Gently, she noticed. Judith stepped back, and David started to mow. She watched him for a moment, trying to puzzle him out, to see the man underneath the brusque demeanor. She knew he had experienced great pain in his life. They both had. But God had never promised anyone a life free from trials. It was how a person handled those trials that mattered.

She strained to pull her gaze from him. She shouldn't stare. But she couldn't help it. David had the broad build of his son Amos but moved with quick sureness like Jeremiah. She could imagine how handsome he had been in his younger years.

He's plenty handsome right now.

The thought propelled her back into the house. She had to stop looking at David Mullet through rosy emotions. She was too old for that. He was only showing her kindness because it was part of his beliefs. She was a widow, and she needed looking after. And despite her independence, there were things she appreciated having a man do. Like mow the lawn on a hot summer day.

She went to the kitchen and pulled a few lemons from her fruit basket. Twenty minutes later she had finished making fresh-squeezed lemonade just as David was putting the mower into her small barn.

Judith met him in the middle of her yard. The scent of fresh-mown grass tickled her nose, making her sneeze.

"*Gesundheit,*" he said.

She nodded and handed him the lemonade. With extra ice. He took a long swig.

"Would you like to sit on the back porch with me for a little while?" she asked, telling herself she was being neighborly.

"I have to get back to work." He finished off the lemonade and handed it to her. "That was *gut*." He turned and started to walk away.

"David," she said, catching up to him.

He stopped and turned, looking at her expectantly.

"I wanted you to know . . . if you need anything . . ." She looked down at the two glasses in her hands. Beads of condensation dripped off the glasses and rolled over her skin. "I mean, if you ever want to talk about . . . anything." Oh, this was awkward. Painfully so. She should have kept her mouth shut.

David looked at her for a long moment. "Next time you need the yard mowed, let me or Amos know and we'll do it." He turned and walked away.

She pressed her lips together. Clearly he wanted to keep his distance. She should do the same. But she couldn't release the nagging feeling that despite her budding attraction for him and his efforts to keep her and everyone else at arm's length, she still needed to try to reach him. *Lord, tell me what you want me to do. How do I handle David Mullet?*

Carefully.

The word came to her mind as clearly as if she'd heard it spoken aloud.

Bekah sat in Katie's kitchen, a drawing pad in front of her and a pencil in her hand. She looked at the rough sketch of the greenhouse and frowned. This wouldn't do at all. She tore the paper out of the pad, balled it up in a wad, and aimed for the open trash can near the pantry. It bounced off the edge of the can and missed, joining five other balls of paper littering the floor.

The back screen door opened with a squeak and closed with a bang. Johnny really needed to oil that hinge. She turned her pad so it faced horizontally. Maybe a change of perspective would help. Inspired, she started to sketch.

Caleb walked into the kitchen. She glanced up, then quickly looked down. She'd hadn't seen him since she'd arrived this morning, when he was coming out of the barn. He didn't say anything to her, and she kept her mouth shut. She could tell he was still mad at her. Would he ever forgive her? He had to, eventually. Forgiveness was something they strongly believed in. However, he sure was taking his sweet time about it.

He walked toward the pantry, looked at the floor, and sighed. She looked up and saw him pick up the balls of paper. Great. That wasn't going to help her case.

Caleb opened the pantry door and took out bread and butter. He went to the cooler and grabbed some trail baloney and Swiss cheese. Now she realized her chance. She popped up from her chair just as he was moving to the counter. They slammed into each other, causing him to drop the baloney on the floor.

"Oops," she said, bending down. That was a mistake, because he bent down at the same time. They knocked heads.

"Good grief, Bekah!" He stood up, the heel of one hand pressing against his hairline above his forehead. "Would you just stop?"

"I'm sorry." She set the baloney on the table. "I was going to offer to make your lunch."

"I can do it." He scowled. "Without your help." He snatched the meat off the table and shoved past her.

"Caleb, stop being ridiculous. You're the one who always says I should spend more time in the kitchen." She held out her arms. "Well, here I am."

"Causing a disaster, as usual."

"I gotta be me," she said, taking the food from his arms and putting it on the counter. "And I'm going to make you a sandwich whether you like it or not. So sit down and shut it."

To her surprise, he clammed up and sat in the chair. She turned and smiled. Maybe being in the kitchen wasn't so bad after all.

Caleb drummed his fingers on the table as Bekah made him lunch. He should be angry with her. Furious would be more like it. She left a mess everywhere she went, the balls of paper being yet another example. Not to mention crashing heads together. His noggin still smarted. Yet he'd been rude to her, and she hadn't responded in kind. Instead she made a joke and fixed him lunch.

He wasn't sure what to think about that.

His eye caught the sketchpad in front of him. So this was where the paper wads came from. He leaned forward in his chair and peered at it. Instantly he could tell what it was . . . and it was good. "A *grienhaus?*"

"*Ya.*" Bekah put the sandwich in front of him. "Katie wants Johnny to build one later this summer. She asked me to design it."

"Really?"

She sat down across from him. "Really." She took the sketchpad, eyed her drawing, and started erasing a line.

He looked down at his sandwich. The bread was sliced at an angle. He picked up the top piece and saw that she'd smeared the butter only on the center of the bread instead of taking it to the edges like he always did. The baloney looked like it was slapped on top of the cheese, which hung over one side of the sandwich. One of his horses could have put this together better than Bekah had. Caleb's eyes lifted to see her staring at him.

"What's wrong with the sandwich?" she asked, her eyes narrowing.

"*Nix.*" He let the bread drop. "It's perfect."

"I understand sarcasm, Caleb."

"I know." He looked at her. "You're fluent in it."

She slammed down the pencil. "Why can't you eat the food instead of dissecting it?"

"Just making sure you didn't poison it or anything."

"Don't tempt me." She leaned over the table, her gaze matching his. He expected her to flinch, but she remained still, staring at him, her blue eyes growing rounder, the pupils becoming larger.

His pulse thrummed. He knew what she was doing—having a staring contest. There she was again, playing her childish games.

But this one was different. Her gaze wasn't only focused on his eyes. It dropped down to his mouth, only to fly back up again. He saw a beautiful pink tinge appear on her cheeks. Suddenly he was staring at her mouth and thinking thoughts about Bekah Yoder that were very, very far from being childish.

This was no longer a game.

He rammed his chair back and stood up. He grabbed his sandwich off the plate and hurried out of the kitchen, nearly running into Katie in the hallway.

"Sorry," he said, keeping his head down.

"Caleb?" Katie called after him as he rushed down the hall.

"Gotta *geh!*" he said, ducking into the nearest room and shutting the door. He turned and realized he was in the bathroom.

A knock sounded on the door. "Are you all right?" Katie asked.

"I'm fine." He dropped the sandwich in the trash and stared in the mirror, irritated to see his own face as red as a fresh-picked strawberry.

"Okay. Let me know if you need some peppermint tea."

He groaned, thrusting his hand through his hair. Now his sister-in-law thought he had stomach trouble. He had trouble all right, but it wasn't with his stomach.

Caleb splashed cold water on his face and stared in the mirror. What was he going to do about Bekah? More specifically, his *feelings* about Bekah?

He didn't have time to think about that now. He quickly slipped out of the bathroom and made his way unnoticed out the front door.

Bekah sat back in her chair, willing her heart to slow. What had just happened? One moment she was trying to lighten up Caleb, the next she was gazing into his eyes and thinking about kissing him. Even more bewildering, he looked like he wanted to kiss her too.

Maybe. She wasn't sure. It's not like she had any experience with dating. Yes, she was twenty-five, but she had never been out on a date. And that had never bothered her before, because she had never found anyone she was interested in. Until now. And he could barely stand to be around her.

But if that was true, then why did he look at her like that?

"Is Caleb okay?" Katie came into the kitchen and looked at Bekah. Then she stopped. "Are you okay?"

"What? Why?" She put her hands on the table and started twiddling her thumbs, trying to look casual. "I'm fine. Why would you ask such a dumb question?"

"Because you look like someone set fire to your face."

Bekah touched her cheek. It was warm. And probably glowing, thanks to her fair complexion. "It's summer. What do you expect?"

"It feels cool in here to me."

"*Ya*, well, I'm roasting." She stood up.

"Where are you going?" Katie asked as Bekah left the kitchen.

"To splash some water on *mei* face," she said, hurrying away.

"But there's a sink in here!" Katie called out.

Bekah ignored her and snuck into the bathroom. She leaned against the door, closing her eyes. But all she saw was Caleb's face. Her eyes flew open, and she turned on the water faucet.

Was it possible she wasn't imagining things? Could Caleb be attracted to her? The thought brought a smile to her face. Then she glanced down at the trash can.

Her sandwich was there. Uneaten.

She shut off the water and clenched her teeth. Figured. Her sandwich wasn't good enough for him. She wasn't good enough for him. Whatever she thought she saw in his eyes moments ago, she'd imagined it.

"Stupid," she said to her reflection. But why should she be surprised? He made it clear she didn't measure up to his standards.

Her shoulders dipped. Knowing that didn't ease the hurt and rejection. It only made it worse.

"You're going over to the Mullets' farm again?"

Anna Mae wrapped foil around the plate of gingersnaps she'd made earlier and set it on the counter. They were Amos's favorite cookies, although pretty much any dessert was a favorite. She didn't mind cooking and baking when she knew it was appreciated. She looked at her mother. "I made cookies for Amos."

"I think you're spending too much time over there." *Mamm* was sitting at the kitchen table, rolling out pie dough. She sprinkled a little bit of flour on the ball of pastry dough. "Why don't you help me with these piecrusts?"

"I already promised Amos I'd bring him the cookies." She'd done no such thing, but she had to get out. Her home seemed more and more confining, maybe because the tension between her and her mother was becoming thicker than the cookies she'd just made. And now that her father had left for Canada and it was just the two of them, being at home was like balancing on a razor's edge.

"Take them tomorrow," *Mamm* said. "They won't spoil."

Her mother's tone brooked no argument. Anna Mae left the cookies on the counter and grabbed the extra rolling pin from its drawer. She plopped down in a chair and took one of four balls of dough, placing it on the floured surface of the table.

"Make sure you add extra flour," *Mamm* said.

"I know." She reached for the flour canister and snatched a healthy pinch. "I've made piecrust before."

Her mother gave her a sharp look before pushing her rolling pin back and forth.

Stifling a groan, Anna Mae patted down the dough ball. "What are the pies for?"

"Church next Sunday. I'm making them ahead of time and freezing them."

"Where?"

"The Donaldsons'," she said, referring to their Yankee neighbors down the road. "Vicki said she had extra space." She took the dough and rolled it onto her rolling pin, then laid the pin on the pie dish and unrolled the dough. It lay perfectly on the glass.

"Oh." Anna Mae rolled out her own dough.

"I heard there was a singing that Sunday evening."

"You know I don't *geh* to singings."

"You used to." Her mother took another ball of dough from the bowl. "Maybe you should give it a try. It would be *gut* to reconnect with your friends."

"They don't *geh* to singings either."

"Why not?"

Anna Mae sighed. "Because they're mostly married."

"Ah. So you don't have any friends you can meet up with after church?"

"Not any I'm interested in." She mimicked her mother's movements and laid the piecrust on another dish. She should have gone to Amos's. Then she wouldn't have to deal with her mother's relentless attempts to get her involved with the church. She also didn't want to admit that she really didn't have any friends anymore, and it was her own fault. She had chosen to keep herself separate over the last year or so. Other than seeing the Mullets, she hadn't socialized much at all. She quickly finished rolling out the last piecrust. "Done." She stood up and washed her hands in the sink. When she was finished she picked up the cookies. "I'm going to Amos's now."

"Is Jeremiah going to be there?"

Anna Mae stilled at her mother's accusatory tone. "*Nee.*"

"Are you sure he won't drop by while you're there?"

I hope not. She hadn't seen him since he'd stopped by last week. But there was something strange in her mother's tone. "What are you getting at?"

"It seems like quite a coincidence, you suddenly spending more time at the Mullets' since Jeremiah came home."

"That's exactly what it is, a coincidence. I have hardly seen Jeremiah. He's busy with his job."

"You mean the one that took him away from the *Amisch*?"

"The one he always dreamed of doing?" Anna Mae scowled. "*Ya.* That one."

"He could have taken care of animals without going to school. Without leaving his family behind."

"Not this again," Anna Mae muttered as she grabbed the cookies and headed out of the kitchen.

"Don't take the buggy," her mother called out, stopping Anna Mae. "I might need it later."

Anna Mae mustered a sweet smile. "I was planning on walking anyway." Her temple throbbed as she headed for the Mullets' place.

Twenty minutes later, damp with sweat from the trek, she walked up their tree-lined drive, her skin welcoming the cool shade of the oak trees' overhanging branches. Her face felt warm, like she'd gotten a bit of sunburn. She strode up the steps, feeling more relaxed as she reached for the front door. Here, she wouldn't be judged. She wouldn't be pressured to make a decision she wasn't ready to make. She wouldn't have to listen to snide digs at her friends . . . if Jeremiah was even her friend anymore.

Anna Mae opened the door. "Amos? Are you here? I brought you some gingersnaps." She heard footsteps upstairs and headed for the staircase. She called up the stairs. "Amos?"

Jeremiah appeared instead.

CHAPTER 11

"Hi, Anna Mae," Jeremiah said softly.

She gripped the banister, willing her suddenly bumped-up pulse to slow. "What are you doing here?"

He came downstairs, his short hair damp, his face freshly shaved. Her breath caught unexpectedly. He'd had a short scruffy beard the last time she'd seen him. Now that he'd shaved she could make out the strong line of his jaw. He no longer looked like a boy . . . but like a man.

She glanced away before he caught her staring.

"I had some free time this afternoon, so I stopped by to see Amos," he said casually, as if the tension between them didn't exist. "Took a shower while I was here."

"Oh." She stepped off the bottom step. "I brought some cookies for him. That's why I stopped by."

"Between you and Judith my brother is in heaven with all these treats." He smiled.

So much for slowing her pulse. If anything she thought her heart would jump out of her chest. "I'll put them in the kitchen." She turned to go, desperate to get away, when his words stopped her.

"I fell into a pigsty today."

She looked up to see him grinning. She couldn't help but smile at the idea of him stuck in pig muck. "Seriously?"

"Not my finest moment." He slicked back his hair and leaned against the railing. "I was checking on a sow that had just given birth. I took a step forward in the mud and *whoosh*." He thrust his hand forward in an upward motion. "My legs went one way and my rear went the other."

"Ha," she said, her smile widening. "Wish I could have seen that."

"Mr. Ellis, the pig farmer, even laughed. He said you haven't lived if you haven't fallen in a sty a time or two."

"Sounds gross."

"Trust me, it was." He pulled on his white T-shirt. "I feel and smell much better now." He looked at the foil-covered plate. "I smell cinnamon. Gingersnaps?"

"*Ya*. They're Amos's favorite."

"Mine too."

She already knew that. Forgetting that she was supposed to be ignoring him, she uncovered the plate. "Do you want one?"

"Depends. Did you make them?"

She lifted her chin. "Does it make a difference?"

He leveled his gaze. "Yes."

Anna Mae held out the plate to him. "Made fresh this morning."

"Good." He snatched one off the plate and took a bite. "Just as delicious as they look," he said as he chewed.

His continued gaze caught her off guard. She glanced away again. "Where's Amos?"

"In the barn."

"I'll put these in the kitchen and *geh* out there, then."

Jeremiah jumped over the last step. "Do you mind if I join you?"

She paused. He was right behind her, smelling of soap and his own distinctive scent. Her palms turned damp as she held on to the plate of cookies. Trying to be nonchalant, she shrugged. "It's a free country."

"Thanks for the reminder." He reached over

her shoulder and grabbed another cookie. "Amos will never miss it. I'll go grab my shoes. I think I still have a spare pair of sneakers in the closet too. I'll meet you at the barn." He turned and bounded up the stairs.

Anna Mae went to the kitchen and set the cookies down on the counter. She put her palms on the scratched-up Formica and took a deep breath. What just happened? Things had seemed *normal* between them. Jeremiah was in a good mood, especially for someone who had spent part of the day in a pigsty. She missed his playfulness, the way they used to be at ease with each other. The way they had just been moments ago.

She crumpled the foil in her hand and took a cookie. As she bit into the soft, sweet yet spicy treat, she pondered those few moments when he had seemed like the same Jeremiah she remembered. One of her best friends, and a man she had missed more than she was ever willing to admit.

Jeremiah waited for Anna Mae before going into the barn. The taste of cinnamon and ginger still lingered on his tongue from the cookies. But even stronger was the attraction he'd felt seeing her unexpectedly at the bottom of the stairs. He couldn't help himself from trying to make her smile. It was the least he could do after the last time they'd talked, when she'd rightly sent him on his way for trying to pay her for helping Amos.

He would be willing to fall in a thousand pigsties to see her smile like that again.

As she walked toward him, he took in her clothing. Stiff white *kapp*, a plain, light-green dress that stopped midcalf, short white socks, and tennis shoes. He'd seen plenty of flesh while he was living outside of the community. Plenty of young women who caked on the makeup and wore provocative clothing. But none of them were as beautiful as Anna Mae in her simple, modest dress. He could see the real her, beyond the trappings of fashion and the mask of cosmetics. He hadn't appreciated the plain style of Amish women until he had been away from them.

"I think Amos wants to show you something," he said, smiling again, hoping to elicit a smile from her.

"Another drawing?"

He gestured for her to go inside the barn. "Find out for yourself."

"Hi, Anna Mae!" Amos met them at the entrance. "I drew something today."

She smiled, a relaxed excitement shining in her blue eyes. "I can't wait to see it."

Amos led her to the opposite end of the barn while Jeremiah followed. The new drawing was of one of the cows. It was pretty detailed for being a pastel drawing on rough oak barn slats. Jeremiah put his hands at his waist and stared at the picture, marveling at the realism and what

166

Amos had been able to do with simple pieces of chalk. His brother had so much talent. But as an *Amisch* man, he could never show the world what he was capable of. Not that Amos minded. He'd never been interested in anyone seeing his art, except for those he was closest to. Like Anna Mae.

"Do you like it?" Amos said, chewing on his fingernail.

She moved closer to the drawing, examining it further. "Of course I do."

The grin on his face as Anna Mae complimented him couldn't have been any wider.

She kept staring at the image. "I love all of your artwork, Amos. But this one seems a little more . . . special."

Jeremiah frowned. What did she mean?

"It is." Amos pointed to the top of the cow's head. "See her birthmark? It's shaped like a heart."

She looked at Amos, her eyes widening. "You drew Belle?"

He nodded. "She was *mei* favorite."

"Mine too." She took Amos's hand.

"This is the perfect place for her, *ya*?" Amos asked.

"It is." She turned to the drawing again. "It definitely is."

A strange sensation went through Jeremiah. It wasn't jealousy, although he longed for the time when the three of them were still close. He was intruding on a private moment, two special people bonding over a cow, of all things. Yet he understood why. Animals, whether they were pets or livestock, could find their way into a person's heart.

Still, it was more than that. His gaze dropped to Anna Mae and Amos's hands entwined together. She cared deeply for his brother. No one else had protected him as fiercely from the stares and the whispers, from the teasing, from people assuming Amos was just a *dummkopf*. No one, except Jeremiah—and she had taken over for him when he left. When he had put his dreams ahead of his family.

Guilt and shame made him turn away.

"I'm hungry," Amos said suddenly.

Anna Mae chuckled. "I brought gingersnaps. They're in the kitchen."

"Okay. Those are *mei* favorite. Do you want one?"

She shook her head and let go of his hand.

"What about you, Jeremiah?"

Composing himself, he looked at his brother. "None for me." His voice cracked, and he cleared his throat. "Help yourself."

"Okay." He lumbered out of the barn.

Anna Mae remained in front of the drawing, studying it. With a little hesitation, Jeremiah moved to stand next to her. She didn't look at him, keeping her attention focused on Amos's latest masterpiece.

"Who's Belle?" Jeremiah asked. He didn't remember any of his father's herd having such unique markings.

"She was born early a couple of years ago. Amos and I used to take turns bottle-feeding her. She grew up, but she was never completely healthy. Doc Miller said he was surprised she'd managed to live longer than nine months."

Jeremiah took in a deep breath. "I'm sorry."

"It was hard on Amos." She touched Belle's dusty nose. "On both of us." She withdrew her hand. "But that's life, isn't it?" She looked at Jeremiah. "You lose the ones you love."

He couldn't look away from her. There was something in her eyes, a darkening of the crystal blue he'd never seen before. Then as soon as it was there, it disappeared.

"I mean, you and Amos have lost a lot in your lives." She walked to the other side of the barn, picked up the broom leaning against the wall, and started to sweep. "That's all I meant."

"Oh." He went to her. "You don't have to do that."

"It's all right." She kept sweeping. "I don't mind."

But there was a break in her voice as she spoke. The tension between them appeared again. He had to dispel it. He took the broom from her. "Do you want to talk about it?"

"About what?" She looked up at him, her lips

twisting into what he thought she meant as a smile. Instead it looked more like she had just sucked on a lemon.

"About what's bothering you."

She laughed, but instead of it sounding natural and sweet, it sounded forced. "Nothing's bothering me." She moved past him. "Why would anything be bothering me?"

Now he was sure she had something on her mind. "I know you, Anna Mae."

She whirled around, any trace of mirth disappearing. "*Nee*. You don't."

He cringed, knowing he'd stepped in it big-time. "All right. I deserved that. But it's obvious you've changed since I've been gone."

"I have?"

Their gazes locked, and something moved inside him. She had no idea how appealing she was. Fragile, yet strong. Troubled, but brave at the same time. Why hadn't he noticed this before? Because he hadn't paid attention. He'd only been focused on himself, even since he'd been back. But he could see there was something she was fighting with, an inner battle that she tried to hide from everyone. "I'm hoping we can be friends again," he said, knowing he needed to clear up the past before he had a right to pry.

"For how long, Jeremiah? A month? Maybe two? Until you decide to leave again without saying good-bye?"

He flinched. "I was wrong not to see you before I left. I . . . I don't have a good excuse, and I'm not sure you'd understand. I had to leave as soon as I had the chance. And I had to go right away because leaving . . ." He blew out a breath. "Saying good-bye—"

"Was too hard."

Jeremiah cocked his head. Her words weren't harsh or accusatory. Simply matter-of-fact, as if she were inside him, able to feel the conflict he'd gone through the day he'd taken that bus to Columbus and left the community.

She took a step toward him. "How did you manage it?"

"Manage what?"

Her gaze dropped, then lifted to his again. "Being alone?"

This time he didn't have to ask her what she meant. During college and vet school he'd been surrounded by people. Had made friends, even a couple of good ones. But there were many, many times he'd felt completely alone, lost without his brother, and even his father. Lost without Anna Mae, he realized now. "I prayed," he said softly. "I prayed a lot."

"Were you scared?"

He frowned. Where were these questions coming from? "Yes." He swallowed, finding it difficult to admit his weakness out loud, even to her. "I was terrified."

"And now?" She took another step closer until less than a foot separated them. "Are you still afraid?"

Jeremiah tried to speak, but the words didn't come. Yes, he was afraid, but of something different from loneliness. He feared the feelings that had rushed over him as she searched his face, gazing into his eyes as if he held the answers to her questions . . . and more. When he finally found his voice, he could only speak her name, his tone sounding like he'd swallowed a handful of gravel. "Anna Mae—"

The chime of his cell phone startled him. She backed away as he dug the phone out of the pocket of his jeans. Technically he was still on the job, even though he didn't have anything on his schedule for the afternoon. "I have to take this."

She quickly nodded and turned away.

He pressed the answer button. "Dr. Mullet speaking."

"Jeremiah. It's Johnny."

He heard the panic in his cousin's voice. "What's wrong?"

"The horses . . . five of them have taken sick."

"All at once?" Jeremiah frowned.

"*Ya.* It's the strangest thing I've ever seen. I don't know what's wrong with them."

"What are the symptoms?"

"They haven't been eating much the past couple of days. Their breathing is shallow too.

We've got one . . . we're having a hard time keeping her on her feet, Jeremiah."

Those symptoms could mean a number of things, but he didn't want to upset Johnny further. "I'll be right over." He hung up the phone and went to Anna Mae.

"Something's going on with Johnny Mullet's horses. I'm sorry. I've got to go."

"Take me with you."

Surprised, he said, "I don't know how long I'll be over there."

"I don't care. I want to help."

He paused. "I don't know what we'll find. It could be bad."

She lifted her chin. "I understand."

They hurried to his car. Amos came out of the house, gingersnap crumbs on his face. "Why are you leaving, Jeremiah?"

"I have to check on some horses. I'll be back later." Jeremiah opened the car door.

"Anna Mae is going with you?" Amos wiped his mouth with the back of his hand.

He nodded, tensing. What if Amos wanted to go too? He couldn't waste time arguing with him.

"Okay." Amos shrugged. "Can we play checkers when you get back?"

"Yes, we'll play checkers." Jeremiah scrambled into the car, grateful for Amos's lack of curiosity. Anna Mae joined him, buckling the seat belt across her chest.

"I'm still not sure this is a good idea," he said.

"I can handle it." She turned and faced straight ahead, a determined tilt to her chin that he'd seen before over the years. He had no doubt she could handle anything.

With a nod, he threw the car into drive and hurried to Johnny's farm.

CHAPTER 12

Anna Mae opened the door when they arrived at the Mullets' place. Despite the urgent circumstances, she noticed how beautiful it was. Although they had become family when her brother married Johnny's sister, Anna Mae hadn't visited the horse farm in years.

Jeremiah rushed out of the car. Johnny met him at the barn. She waited slightly behind Jeremiah while Johnny explained in more detail what was wrong with the horses. From Jeremiah's frown, she could tell it didn't sound good to him.

"Hi, Anna Mae."

She turned around and saw Bekah standing behind her. Her expression was streaked with the same worry as the men's. "Jeremiah will make sure they're all right," Anna Mae reassured her.

"I hope so." Bekah looked past Anna Mae's shoulder as the men went inside the barn. "If something happens to those horses, I don't know what Caleb will do."

Anna Mae glanced around. Caleb was nowhere in sight. "Where is he?"

"In one of the stalls. He's making sure the one horse is staying upright." She wrung her hands together. "He's so worried. And he blames himself."

"What do you mean?"

"He's the one who bought them at an auction." She shook her head.

"Surely they weren't sick when he purchased them."

"That's the strange part. Jeremiah was here the other day looking them over. He said they were fine." She let her hands drop to her sides, her brows furrowing. "Wait, what are you doing here with Jeremiah?"

"I wanted to help," she said simply. Bekah didn't need to know any other details.

"So do I, but Caleb says there's nothing I can do." She looked away. "He doesn't think *mei* help is *gut* enough, apparently."

"I'm sure that's not it."

Bekah rubbed her finger. "You don't know Caleb, then." She pulled up her chin. "But that doesn't matter. The horses are what are important."

"I'm sure there's something we can both do." Anna Mae led Bekah to the barn door. Right before they went inside, Bekah put her hand on Anna Mae's arm.

"I'm glad you're here."

As they walked in they heard Johnny say, "So what's going on with them, Jeremiah?"

Their voices came from the back stall. She and Bekah moved closer but didn't go in. Anna Mae peered inside. The horse was standing on shaky legs, its chest heaving with labored movement. Caleb stood close beside the animal, scrubbing his hand over his pale face, his eyes wide with panic. Now Anna Mae knew why Bekah was worried about him.

"I'm not sure." Jeremiah listened to the horse's chest with his stethoscope. Anna Mae realized she'd never seen him in his professional capacity. While he had a serious expression on his face, he also looked in control. "Her breathing is very shallow." He looked at Johnny. "Whatever it is, it's strange that these five horses have come down with the same symptoms while the rest of your horses are fine. I'm going to need to run some blood tests. I'll have to go back to Doc's and get more needles. I don't have enough with me."

"What should we do in the meantime?" Johnny asked.

"Make sure they're as comfortable as they can be." He looked at Caleb. "I'll need to see what you're feeding them. Also, I want to take a look at your pasture."

Caleb nodded. "I'll take you out there, but all our horses eat the same feed and graze the same pastures."

"I'll still need to take a look."

Anna Mae grasped Jeremiah's arm. "How can Bekah and I help?"

"Stay with the horses until I get back. Keep track if anything changes, especially with this one." He gestured with his thumb to the sick horse behind him. "Make sure she stays on her feet. If she can't stand up . . ." He glanced at Caleb before giving a slight shake of his head.

Anna Mae didn't question him. She knew what happened to horses that stayed down. Blood would pool in their intestines, and fluid would build up in their chests. If they couldn't be upright within a day, they would die.

"I'll stay with her," Bekah volunteered. "Anna Mae, keep an eye on the other ones, please." She walked into the stall, not looking at Caleb.

He opened his mouth as if to say something. Instead he left the stall and stood by Jeremiah.

Jeremiah nodded, then looked at Johnny and Caleb. He had Johnny's attention, but Caleb was staring at the stall. He had been since Bekah had walked in. "Caleb?" Jeremiah said.

He turned and faced him. "Right. The pastures."

"Show me your feed stores first."

The men left, with Caleb glancing worriedly

over his shoulder before they walked out the barn door.

Anna Mae set to work. She checked the other stalls. While none of the other young horses were as sick as the first one, she could tell something was wrong. She entered the last stall in time to see the horse collapse to the floor. "Bekah!" she called out.

Bekah quickly appeared. "Oh *nee*." She crouched down next to the animal. "That's exactly what happened to the other one."

"I'll run and tell Jeremiah," Anna Mae said. "Can you keep an eye on all of them?"

Bekah nodded, touching the flank of the poor horse. "I can't imagine what's happening to them," she said, her voice thick.

"Whatever it is, I'm sure Jeremiah will figure it out."

Bekah looked up at her, tears welling in her eyes. "I hope so. We couldn't bear it if the horses didn't make it."

As Anna Mae left the barn, she realized Bekah had used the word *we*. She didn't know what Bekah's exact interest was in the farm, other than it belonged to family, but it was clear she cared about the animals . . . and about Caleb.

Jeremiah checked the horses' feed and pastures, finding nothing unusual in his observations. The feed was fresh, and the pasture grass seemed fine.

Yet the horses still exhibited signs of some type of poisoning—information he didn't share with the Mullets or Anna Mae and Bekah. He would need to run tests on the feed, grass, and soil, but his priority was getting the horses stabilized.

"Jeremiah!"

He turned to see Anna Mae running toward him as he stood next to the car. "What is it?"

"Another one of the horses collapsed."

Panic rose inside him, but he maintained his professionalism. Calmly, he took Anna Mae by the arm, and they hurried to the barn. Caleb and Johnny were already there, slapping the horse on his flanks and yelling at him to get up. Jeremiah was about to jump in and help when the horse rose to his feet.

He let out a heavy, relieved breath. He looked at Johnny.

"*Geh*," Johnny said. "Get what you need. We can take care of them while you're gone."

Jeremiah glanced at Anna Mae. She nodded, her chin lifted in confidence. Her calm certainty reassured him. He rushed out of the barn, jumped in his car, and hurried to the clinic.

When he arrived, Doc Miller was in the back, checking on a cat that had been spayed the day before. Although Doc still used the crutches, his leg was healing enough that he could limp around fairly well. Jeremiah dashed to the storage cabinet and threw open the doors. He grabbed the needles and blood tubes and put them in his bag.

"What's the rush?" Doc asked, hobbling as he turned around. He leaned forward on his crutches.

Jeremiah explained the horses' symptoms. Doc frowned. "And you checked the feed?"

"The pasture too. Nothing seemed out of the ordinary, and the rest of the animals are fine."

"You know what this sounds like?" Doc moved toward Jeremiah. "Years ago I worked with a vet who had several horses die from lead poisoning."

"How did that happen?"

"They never found out. The symptoms were similar, though. Make sure you test for lead."

"I will."

"You should probably take the calcium versenate and IV equipment."

"I'll load it into my car."

Doc followed him out to the front of the clinic. "Do you need any help?"

"Actually, I have plenty." Anna Mae's image flashed through his mind.

"Wish I could go out there with you." He lifted up a crutch. "I'm sick of these things."

"I bet. I'll keep you posted."

After Jeremiah put the medicine and equipment into his car, he hopped inside and turned on the engine. As he drove back to the Mullets' farm he thought about lead poisoning. Had someone poisoned his cousins' feed? He'd test it to make sure, but who would do such a thing? Cruelty to horses in the area was unimaginable, but it happened. Did someone want to see the Mullets fail?

Jeremiah gripped the steering wheel and pressed down on the accelerator. He'd do everything medically possible to make sure those horses didn't die.

Caleb paced back and forth between the stalls in the barn, peeking over each of them to check on the horses. They were all still standing, and Anna Mae and Bekah were with the ones that had collapsed. Johnny had gone inside to check on Katie, who had been feeling ill the past couple of days. So much so that Bekah had practically moved in to help her with the household chores. Seeing Bekah more often had been something he'd wanted to avoid.

But he couldn't think about that now. He put his hands on his head, almost literally sick over the horses. This was his fault. There was something wrong with the animals and he had missed it. But what had happened? They had only been at the farm a little longer than a week, and he and Johnny had done everything to make sure they had the best of care. The only thing he could think of was that they were ill when he bought them at the auction. His stomach lurched. How could he have not realized they were sick? He clenched his hands. He could hardly bear it, knowing they were suffering.

His boots scraped against the dirt floor of the barn as he continued to pace. When he got to the last stall, Bekah's head popped up. "Caleb," she said, motioning to him.

He rushed over, hoping to see the horse feeling better. But she wasn't. He touched his forehead to the top door of the stall. "What do you want, Bekah?"

"You have to stop pacing." She moved closer to the door of the stall. She lightly touched his shoulder, and he looked up. "It's not helping, and you're going to make the horses nervous."

"Sorry." He shouldn't have needed Bekah to point that out. Desperate to do something, he opened the stall door and went inside. He stood by the horse, her head hanging low. When he touched her, she twitched. "I don't understand it," he said in a low voice. "How could they be so sick? They were fine the other day."

Bekah moved beside him. "I know they were."

He glanced at her, anger rising within him. "You've been out here with them?" After what had happened last week, he'd thought she'd honor his wish for her to stay away from the horses. He should have known she wouldn't have listened.

"*Nee*." She shook her head. "I know you don't want me around them. But I watched them in the pasture the other day." She looked into the horse's eyes. "They're beautiful, Caleb."

He watched her gaze, seeing her appreciation as she whispered to the horse, hearing how much she cared in the tone of her voice. He'd never realized until that moment how emotionally invested she was in the animals. He'd thought Bekah had snuck off and ridden the gray mare because she was trying to get his goat, or to be rebellious, as she had often been when they were growing up. Now he could see she had a true connection with them.

"I hate that they're going through this." Bekah's voice was barely above a pained whisper. "But Anna Mae said Jeremiah's a *gut* vet. She has faith he'll figure this out."

"I hope so." He stood and went to the water trough, which was still full from last night. The horse hadn't eaten or drunk anything for nearly twenty-four hours.

"We need to pray that he will," Bekah said.

He felt her fingers touch his lightly, almost like a feather brushing up against his skin. The contact surprised him, as did his reaction. He grabbed her hand and held it tight. They both closed their eyes and prayed silently.

Thud!

Caleb's eyes flew open, and he ran out of the stall and looked inside the next one. Another horse had fallen. He went to him and knelt down.

The horse was still breathing . . . but for how long?

"Johnny, it will be okay." Katie came up behind her husband and put her arms around him. He leaned his forehead against the window of their bedroom. He'd come in there earlier after leaving the barn, his face crestfallen, his shoulders slumped as if the weight of twenty horses rested on them.

"I'm trying to believe that." He turned and faced her. "It just doesn't make sense. Just when I had started to believe everything was falling into place. These animals have been the best herd we've had. Now they're sick and I don't know what's going to happen . . ."

"Shhh." She kissed him gently. "God's will. That's what's going to happen."

"But how can it be God's will to let the animals suffer like this?" He shook his head. "I don't want to sound callous, but I have to be realistic. If they die . . ." He swallowed. "We'll take a huge hit financially. It will set us back years."

Katie brushed his cheek, then let her fingers trail down the length of his short beard. "Whatever happens, we will persevere. I believe that. You're always telling me to trust. Now I'm reminding you." A wave of nausea suddenly struck her. *No, not now. This isn't the time—*

She ran out of the room, barely making it to the bathroom to throw up in the toilet.

"Katie?" Johnny's voice sounded tentative on the other side.

"I'm okay."

He opened the door as she stood up. He put his arm around her shoulders. "Maybe you should see a doctor. You've been feeling off for days. It's not like you to be this sick."

She shook her head. "I'm not exactly sick."

He stared at her for a moment before realization dawned. "*Nee.*"

She managed a smile, despite still feeling queasy. "I was going to tell you, but I wanted to be sure." Another, less violent attack of nausea assaulted her. She put her hand over her stomach. "I'm pretty sure I'm sure."

"Oh, Katie." He hugged her.

"I know the timing isn't right—"

"The timing is perfect." He sounded happy, although his normally lighthearted tone was still tempered. "Have you told anyone else?"

"I don't want to." She looked up at him. "I want to keep it between us for a while."

"You got it."

"Oh *nee*, not again." She shoved away from him. "Johnny, you need to *geh*."

"I don't want to leave you when you're sick."

She pushed him out the door. "Believe me, this isn't an experience we need to share."

∙ ∙ ∙

Jeremiah was more concerned than ever when he returned to the Mullets' farm and found out another horse had collapsed. But thanks to Doc he had a lead to follow. "I'm going to take some blood samples," he told Caleb as he went into the last stall. This horse was the weakest, and he wanted to take care of her first. "Where's Bekah?"

"She went in the house for a few minutes."

Jeremiah gave the horse another close examination. Now that he knew what to look for, the signs were plain—this horse had lost weight since he'd examined her last week. She, along with the other horses, had intermittent coughing. And although he had missed it before, he could now see the slight knuckling of her fetlocks. All symptoms pointed to lead poisoning.

"I'm going to administer IVs to each of the horses." He stood up. "Calcium versenate. That will chelate the lead and dissolve it."

Caleb scratched his head. "I have *nee* idea what you just said, but if it will cure the horses then do it."

"Between the six of us we can get the IVs going as soon as possible."

"I'll get Johnny and Katie and Bekah."

Jeremiah opened another bag he had brought from the clinic. He looked up at the ceiling to see where he could hang the IV bag. The rafters were low enough that he could drive a hook into the beam and hang it there. Not an ideal situation, but it would have to do. "Anna Mae!" he called out. "I need your help."

She walked into the stall, determination set on her face. "What do you need me to do?" she said without hesitation. He looked at her, grateful she was here by his side.

"We have to get an IV going right away."

Anna Mae watched as Jeremiah opened a huge bag. Inside were tubes, needles, and a large, clear bag of liquid. He tilted his head toward the horse. "I have more medicine in the car that I'll get once we take care of her."

She nodded as he pulled out clippers and felt along the horse's neck. He zipped the clippers over a patch of hair, leaving behind smooth skin. "Anna Mae, check for a step stool or short ladder in the barn. We'll need that."

She left the stall and ran into Caleb, Bekah, and Johnny, with Katie right behind them. "Jeremiah needs a step stool."

"There's one in the shed," Bekah said. "I'll get it." She ran out of the barn.

"Caleb! Johnny!"

The men hurried to Jeremiah. Anna Mae turned to Katie, frowning when she noticed how pale she looked. "Are you all right?"

"I think I'm coming down with something." She averted her gaze as she spoke.

"You should *geh* inside," Anna Mae said. "We can take care of this."

"Are you sure?"

She smiled. "Positive."

Relief crossed her features. "*Danki*, Anna Mae. And can you keep an eye on Johnny and Caleb? They're both very worried."

"I will."

Katie left just as Bekah brought in the step stool. Anna Mae took it from her and went back to the stall.

"You'll need to harness the horses that are standing," Jeremiah said to Caleb and Johnny. "Make sure they're stable. This girl is too weak to fight me, but the others won't like me shoving an IV in them, even if it's for their own good."

He stood when he saw Anna Mae. He took the stool from her and placed it on the ground near the horse. He stood on it and reached up, his fingers barely grazing the beam above his head. "We have to put a hook here for the IV bag to hang." He looked down at Caleb. "You're the tallest. Pound a hook in the beam over each stall. Make sure it's a thick hook that's sunk deep in the wood. It has to be strong enough to support the bag."

Jeremiah stepped down and Caleb snatched the stool. Soon the sound of him pounding nails, along with the whinnying of the horses, filled the barn.

With quick movements Jeremiah cleaned the shaved spot using an alcohol wipe. Anna Mae watched, fascinated, as he worked. He searched for what she presumed was a vein. When he found it, he quickly inserted what looked like a thick needle into the horse's flesh.

"All right, the catheter is in," he said, tossing the plunger to the side.

"Catheter?"

"It widens the vein in order to deliver the medication." He put a piece of tape over it, leaving a small dangling portion of tube with a tiny hole in the end. "Good girl," he murmured as he touched the horse's side. He grimaced.

Anna Mae clutched her hands together. "Jeremiah?"

"She's still breathing." But he didn't look at her. He pulled out a spiral tube with the big bag attached to one end. The top of the bag had a flap with a hole attached to the top. He handed the bag to her. "I need you to hold this as high as you can while I insert the needle into the catheter."

She took the bag and did as he asked. He wiped the end of the dangling tube with alcohol and placed a needle inside. "Caleb!" he called. "Bring the stool!"

Caleb appeared and set the stool on the floor. Without waiting for instructions he hammered a hook in the ceiling beam, then took the bag from Anna Mae and hung it. "How long before she'll start feeling better?" he asked, getting off of the stool.

"With lead poisoning, four to five days."

"Lead?" Caleb looked bewildered. "Are you sure?"

"Pretty sure. The next few hours we'll know more."

"But how can they be poisoned?"

"I don't know, but after the horses are stable we'll find out." He looked at Caleb, as serious as Anna Mae had ever seen him. "I'm going to be straight with you. This one is pretty bad off. We'll have to watch her very closely over the next twenty-four to forty-eight hours."

Caleb nodded. "I've got all the hooks hung."

"Good. Anna Mae and I will start an IV on the other horse that collapsed. I'll need your and Johnny's help too."

"What can I do?" Bekah said, standing at the entrance of the stall.

"Stay with her," Jeremiah said. "Watch her breathing."

Bekah walked into the stall and sat down next to the horse. She stroked her chestnut-brown forelock. "Everything will be okay," she said. "I'm here to watch over you."

Jeremiah picked up his equipment and left the stall. Anna Mae followed him, nearly bumping into Caleb, who kept staring at Bekah and the horse, anguish in his eyes.

As she left the stall, her gaze locked with Jeremiah's. He shook his head, then went into the next stall. A lump caught in Anna Mae's throat. *Please, Lord . . . save these horses.*

CHAPTER 13

Several hours later, Jeremiah was finishing up the stitching on the IV catheter of the last horse. Anna Mae hadn't blinked when he said he would have to apply the stitches to the healthier horses to make sure they didn't pull the catheter loose. She calmly assisted, handing him what he needed with each horse.

"Do you mind cutting this?" he said, gesturing to the thread coming out of the horse's skin.

She took a small pair of scissors from the bag of supplies and snipped the thread close to the stitching. "Now what do we do?"

"We wait." He looked down at his hands and saw the blood on his fingertips. This horse had been feistier than the others, and it had taken two tries to get the catheter into his jugular vein. "And wash our hands."

"I was thinking the same thing," Anna Mae said.

They walked out of the stall. Bekah was still in with the first horse, and Caleb was popping in and out of the other stalls. Johnny had alternated between the barn and checking on Katie. At this point, Jeremiah felt like he could leave the horses for a bit and go to the house. "We can put the rest of the supplies in my car," he said.

Anna Mae followed him to the vehicle. "What

do you think will happen to the horses?" she asked as he opened the trunk.

He put the box of extra tubes and needles in the trunk and closed the lid. "If lead poisoning is what's causing their illness, then we should see improvement soon, especially with the healthier ones."

"And if it's something else?"

"That's why I want to stay here and make sure it isn't." He turned to Anna Mae. "I can take you home."

She shook her head. "I'm staying here."

"Your mother will be worried."

"She'll understand. I can't leave, Jeremiah. Not until I know they'll get through this, and I don't just mean the horses."

He nodded. Truth was he was glad she was staying. It was going to be a long night for all of them . . . and he didn't mind spending it with her.

They went inside the house and found Johnny in the kitchen. He was cutting up slices of ham. A bowl of boiled eggs and a stack of sliced cheddar cheese were on the table, along with a pitcher of iced tea and a bottle of mustard. "It's not much of a meal, but with Katie feeling . . . poorly, I wanted to make sure you all had something to eat."

Jeremiah went to the sink and washed his hands. Anna Mae joined him. He handed her the soap and they lathered up. "Thanks, Johnny," he said. "We do need to eat."

He stuck his hands under the running water at the same time Anna Mae did, their fingers touching each other. He glanced at her, and she gave him a shy smile. He dried his hands and then handed her the towel.

He joined Johnny at the table. "I still need to get the blood samples. I'll have to send them away for testing. I also want to test the soil."

"Why?"

"If the lead poisoning isn't in the grain or grass, it might be in the ground. Pesticides can leach into the soil over time, and it can be toxic to animals."

"But we don't use pesticides."

Anna Mae came to the table. She put two plates of food down, one in front of Jeremiah and one in front of Johnny. But Johnny pushed his away. "I'm not hungry."

Jeremiah pushed it back in front of him. "We still have to eat, though. All of us will have to keep a close eye on the horses throughout the night. I thought we could do it in shifts. Anna Mae and I can take the first one." He looked over his shoulder at her, at the counter fixing another plate of food. "If you're okay with that."

"*Ya*," she said as she turned to sit down at the table next to him. He turned his attention back to Johnny. "You and Caleb can take over around midnight."

Johnny looked torn. "I think maybe Bekah should do it," he said. "I want to stay with Katie."

"She's that sick?" Anna Mae asked.

Johnny looked down at the table. "You could say that."

"Stay with Katie," Jeremiah said, peeling an egg. "I'm sure Bekah can help Caleb just fine."

Johnny pushed away from the table. "I'm going to take Katie some crackers and water. Maybe that will settle things."

Jeremiah paused for a second, looking at Johnny again. Katie wasn't sick—she was expecting. No wonder Johnny seemed at his wits' end.

After Johnny left, Anna Mae placed a slice of cheese on a piece of bread. "I know why you wanted to take the first shift."

"You do?" He bit into the egg.

"You're worried about Caleb."

She really did know him well. "The next few hours are going to be crucial. I don't want Caleb to be there if something . . ." He couldn't even bring himself to say the words.

She rested her hand on his arm for a moment. "It won't. You're doing everything you can." Then she folded the bread and cheese in half. "What did you mean about pesticides possibly causing the poisoning?"

"Lead poisoning is pretty rare. Usually it happens if a horse eats some feed that's been contaminated. But sometimes if the pasture they graze on has been sprayed numerous times over a long period of time, the poison can get into the soil, which in turn affects the grass. I'm not convinced that's the case, though."

"Because Johnny said they don't use pesticides?"

He grabbed another egg. "That, and because the lead poisoning symptoms the horses have are severe. That can only be for two reasons—they were poisoned with large amounts at one time, or they were grazing on toxic grass and had accumulated enough lead in their bodies that kicked in the symptoms. But they haven't been at this farm long enough for chronic lead poisoning to occur. And if it's acute—"

"Which means they were poisoned quickly, right?"

"Right. If it's acute, then how come no other animals have been affected? I know Johnny and Caleb have never had problems before."

"That is strange." She took a bite of her sandwich and chewed thoughtfully before swallowing. "The blood samples will tell us if they were poisoned quickly or over a period of time, won't they?"

"They should give us some insight, yes. Also, the soil sample testing will determine what's going on with the land, if anything." He wiped his fingers on a napkin. "I'm going to get the blood samples from a couple of the more stable horses. Then I'll get the soil samples and take it all back to Doc Miller's to get sent off to the lab. I have to pick up some more supplies while I'm there too."

"I can get the soil samples," she said. "Just tell me what you need me to do."

"You want to do that?"

"I'm here to help, remember?" She polished off her last bite of the sandwich.

"You've been a big help already," he said. He'd still be trying to establish those IVs if it weren't for everyone pitching in. Caleb and Johnny and even Bekah all had a stake in the farm, so it made sense that they would do everything they could to save their horses. But Anna Mae didn't have to. He knew that. "I'll give you the supplies and instructions when you're finished eating," he told her.

She took a fast drink of iced tea. "I'm done."

Despite the gravity of the situation, this was the most lively he'd seen her since he came back to Middlefield. She was not only interested in the science behind the problem, she was also adept at handling a stressful situation. As they left the kitchen, she asked, "Is your job always this exciting?"

"Fortunately, no. But it is always rewarding."

She nodded, as if mulling over his words. "I'm starting to understand why."

Bekah walked outside into the warm night air. She looked up at the stars as she headed for the barn, carrying two mugs of coffee in her hands. The clear sky revealed what looked like hundreds of stars twinkling against a deep black backdrop. Everything seemed so peaceful tonight, in contrast to the turmoil of the day.

She walked into the barn and saw Caleb sitting on a short stack of hay bales, three wide and two deep. He was leaned over, his hands dangling between his legs. She was tired, and she knew he had to be exhausted. He'd fought Jeremiah about leaving the barn to sleep for a little bit while he and Anna Mae watched over the horses. "I'm not leaving them," he'd said. But Jeremiah had insisted—and if there was anything she'd learned about him today, it was that when Jeremiah was in charge, his word was practically law. She and Caleb had retreated to the house and taken showers, but Bekah hadn't slept much.

She doubted Caleb had slept at all.

She walked over to the hay bales and sat down next to him. The hay scratched the back of her legs. It wasn't the most comfortable place to sit, but it was better than the floors in the stalls, which was where she'd spent most of the afternoon.

"Here," she said, handing him one of the mugs. "Extra strong."

He accepted the drink and took a sip. He choked. "What is this, liquid tar?"

Bekah wanted to snap back at him, but she couldn't muster the energy. She reached for the mug. "You don't have to drink it."

He shook his head. "It's fine. I'm sorry." He glanced at her, exhaustion evident on his face. "It's been a long *daag*."

She nodded and took a sip of the coffee. Ugh. She probably should have tasted it first before she brought it out. "You're right. This is terrible." She put her coffee mug on the dirt floor, fatigue and defeat engulfing her. "I can't do anything right."

"Bekah." Caleb angled his body toward her. "That's not true. You proved that today."

"And what exactly did I prove? That I can babysit a horse?"

"You know you did more than that." He took another sip of the coffee and swallowed. Hard. "See?" he said through gritted teeth. "It's not that bad."

She chuckled and took the mug from him. "Nice try." She set the mug down and stood. "I need to *geh* check on Promise."

"Who?"

"The chestnut. I made her promise me she would fight to live."

Caleb tugged on her hand. "I was just with her. She's asleep. Her breathing is a little better."

She sagged with relief. "Thank God." She sat back down. "I'm not going to stop praying for her. Or the others."

He paused. "Me either." He rubbed his hands over his thighs. "Jeremiah's a *gut* vet."

"He's a great vet. I never realized how smart he was."

"Me either. He also made me realize something."

"What's that?"

"That I need to learn more about the medical side of taking care of horses."

"But that's what vets are for."

"Still, to run this farm properly, I've got to educate myself. Maybe after all this is over Jeremiah will teach me a few things."

"I don't think he'd mind that." She smiled at him, then glanced away and brushed the toe of her shoe in an arc on the barn floor. "Look at us."

Caleb arched his brow. "What do you mean?"

"We're actually talking without fighting." She looked back at him and grinned. "I didn't think it was possible, considering how you feel about me."

"How I feel about you?" The words came out scratchy, like he was forcing them through a wire sieve.

"You know." Why was she bringing this up? Maybe the exhaustion was getting the better of her. But that still didn't stop her from continuing to talk. "You think I'm . . . beneath you."

"What?" He faced her. "When have I ever said that?"

"You don't have to." She shrank back from him a little. Over the years Caleb had grown into a large, muscular man. Sometimes his size could be intimidating. "I can tell."

"How? Because you can read my mind?" He turned away from her. "Bekah, you've never understood anything about what I feel for you."

She froze. Was she hearing him right? He had *feelings* for her?

A shuffling sound came from one of the stalls. Bekah and Caleb jumped up from the hay bales. Although she didn't hear a thudding sound, she steeled herself for the worst. But the horse was drinking out of the trough. They watched him for a few moments.

"I think the medicine is working," Bekah whispered, not wanting to startle the horses.

"I think you're right." He moved away from the stall, and Bekah followed. When they were in the middle of the barn, he turned and looked at her, his grin melting her heart.

Without thinking, Bekah threw her arms around him. She'd intended to hug him just for a second, but when she felt his arms circle around her, she moved closer. He smelled like horse and sweat and barn debris—and she didn't care. All she cared about was that the horse was improving.

Bekah had no idea how long they stayed in each other's embrace. Finally she started to move away from him—only to feel his lips brush her ear. "Bekah," he whispered in a husky, spine-tingling voice.

Suddenly he jumped back from her. Caleb turned his back, running his hand through his hair.

While she was still getting her bearings, he spun around. "I need to tell Johnny and Jeremiah," he said, darting for the stall door. Then he disappeared out of the barn.

Frowning, Bekah touched her ear. Had she imagined the tiny kiss? Maybe he'd accidently made contact when she had pulled away. And of course he hadn't whispered her name. *Had he?*

Except he would have had to bend to reach her ear. He was nearly half a foot taller than she was.

She went back to the stall and looked at the horse, who moved his head to the side and looked at her. "Am I going *ab im kopp*?" she asked the animal. She lifted up her hands and turned around. "Of course I am. I'm talking to a horse!"

She left and went to Promise's stall. Her ear still tingled. She touched it again, her fingers brushing just underneath the pale-blue kerchief she'd exchanged for her *kapp* earlier in the evening. The whole thing seemed like a blur to her now. Was she so tired that her mind was playing tricks? That had to be it. No other explanation made sense.

After checking on Promise, she peeked in on the other horses, happy to see another one drinking from the water trough. She went back to the hay bales and sat down, waiting for Caleb to return. Unable to help herself, she smiled.

A few moments later, Johnny and Jeremiah entered the barn. Caleb was nowhere in sight. She glanced away as they went to the horse's stall, murmuring about the progress the horse had made in such a short time.

"Where's Caleb?" she asked, forcing a steady tone.

"Still in the house," Johnny said. "I told him I'd take over for him for the next hour or so."

"And he agreed?"

Johnny tilted his head. "Why wouldn't he?"

She backed away, feeling stupid for asking the question. She turned and blew out a breath, disappointed that he hadn't come back—and a little hurt that he'd been in such a hurry to get away from her. Again.

Bekah walked to the entrance of the barn and looked up at the stars. For a few sweet moments she and Caleb had had a regular conversation. No insults. No sarcasm. For once things between them had been *normal*.

But she didn't want normal—she had never wanted normal.

She looked down and hugged herself, remembering the feel of Caleb's arms around her, his warm whisper in her ear. That was as far from normal as life could get.

It was also what she wanted.

She put her hand up to her cheek, stunned. She was attracted to Caleb. How was that even possible? She lifted her gaze to the sky once again. More importantly, what was she going to do about it?

CHAPTER 14

As Jeremiah pulled into her driveway, Anna Mae looked at the outline of her parents' house, shaded in the low light of dawn. Now that the horses were healing, she didn't have a reason to stay at the Mullet farm. Jeremiah was going to go back, but Anna Mae's time with him had come to an end, which disappointed her. Though it would be good for both of them to finally get a shower and some rest.

He put the car in park and looked at her. "I hope your mother won't be too mad at me."

"Why?"

"For keeping you out so late. An entire day late."

"I didn't mind."

He angled his body toward her. "I could tell. I've never explained so much about veterinary medicine to anyone before."

She smiled. "It was interesting. Fascinating, actually."

"All that talking helped me stay awake. I appreciated you being there." His words warmed her. It was nice to feel needed, and not just by Amos and his father. Tonight she'd felt like she had a purpose, and it wasn't to be someone's wife or daughter or a proper *Amisch* woman. A new world had opened up to her, thanks to Jeremiah including her in his work. "Don't worry. If she's mad, she'll get over it."

"I hope so. I wouldn't want to get you in trouble."

"If I'm in trouble, then it was worth it. I know now why you love your job."

He nodded. "It's not just the animals, though. I'm helping people too. You saw how important those horses are to Johnny and Caleb. Every time I'm able to save someone's livestock or pet, I'm making a difference in the owner's life too."

Anna Mae nodded. They both had that in common, the desire to be needed, to know that they made someone's life a little better. "It is something special."

He continued to look at her, his eyes gazing at her intensely. He glanced down at his lap for a moment before looking at her again. "We make a pretty *gut* team, *ya*?"

She curled a corner of her upper lip in a small smile. This was the first time he'd spoken *Deitsch* to her since returning to Middlefield. She nodded, not needing to say anything. When they were teenagers, they could communicate with a look. At that moment in the car, it was as if they had traveled back in time, to when their relationship had been unshakeable.

They locked gazes for another long moment before she glanced at the house. "I better *geh* inside." She opened the door, not eager to leave, wishing she could stay with him a little longer. *Or a lot longer . . .*

"I'll see you later?" Jeremiah asked.

The tentative way he asked the question, as if he was afraid she would reject him, touched her. "*Ya*," she said.

He grinned as she got out of the car. She shut the door and hurried up the steps, unable to stop herself from smiling.

Before she reached the door, her mother was out on the front porch. "Where have you been?" she asked, her voice shaking. Then she brought Anna Mae into a hug. "I was worried sick about you."

Anna Mae pulled away, looking over her shoulder to see if Jeremiah had seen the exchange. But she saw him backing out of the drive. Her mother saw him too.

"Who dropped you off?"

"Jeremiah."

Her mother crossed her arms. "You couldn't find another ride home?"

"*Mamm*, can we talk about this inside?" They didn't have any close neighbors, but she didn't want to have an argument with her mother on the front porch.

Mamm nodded and they went inside. Exhaustion finally hit Anna Mae. All she wanted to do was fall into bed.

"I want an explanation," *Mamm* said. "I went to David Mullet's looking for you last night when you didn't come home." Her face looked pinched. "Amos said you left with Jeremiah. He said you were going to Johnny's but that you were coming back later." She shook her head. "You were gone all night, Anna Mae!"

"I'm sorry." She went to her mother, feeling the first twinge of guilt. "Jeremiah needed *mei* help—"

"So this is his fault, keeping you out all night, letting me get sick with worry—"

"Don't blame him." She explained what had happened at the farm, expecting her mother to be more understanding once she knew the reason Anna Mae hadn't come home.

Instead, her mother's face flamed with anger. "How could you be so inconsiderate?"

"*Mamm*, can't you see how important this was? Johnny and Caleb needed us."

"They needed Jeremiah. Sounds like they had plenty of help without you being there. Unless you were using that as an excuse to be with him."

Her eyes widened. "With Jeremiah? You think I would really do that?"

Turning away, *Mamm* said, "I don't know, Anna

206

Mae. I don't understand anything you do anymore."

Anna Mae sighed. "We're both tired. Why don't we get some sleep? We can talk about this later."

Mamm spun around. "You always want to talk later. Or not at all." She stormed to Anna Mae and grabbed her arm. "Let's *geh*."

Shocked, Anna Mae tried to pull from her grasp. "Where?"

"To see Bishop Esh."

Anna Mae yanked her arm away. "I'm not going to the bishop!"

"You are. You owe me that after what you put me through last night. You're going to talk to him, and he's going to set you right."

"Set me right?" Anna Mae clenched her hands together. "There's nothing wrong with me."

"If you think I'm going to allow you to live in this house while you stay out all night with a . . . *Yankee* . . ."

"*Mamm*, please." She'd never seen her mother so upset. "You're talking nonsense."

"Am I? Then tell me, Anna Mae. Tell me what you're going to do with your life. Tell me your plan, because it seems like the only reason you're here is to have a place to lay your head at night."

"That's not true."

Her mother put her fists on her waist. "Then tell me the truth."

"I want to be a nurse," Anna Mae blurted. Her eyes widened. She'd surprised herself with the admission. But as soon as she said the words out loud, her tilted world seemed to right itself. Working with Jeremiah had revealed what had been buried deep inside her for so long. "I want to help people. I want to heal them. I want to make a difference in their lives."

"But you can do that and still be *Amisch*."

"How is that possible?"

"There are needs here. People get sick all the time. You can learn about healing here, among us." Her mother put her hands on Anna Mae's shoulders. "You can join the church," she said, laughing with relief.

Anna Mae touched her mother's hand. "*Nee*," she said softly, "I can't."

Hope fled from her mother's eyes. "I don't understand."

"It's more than me wanting to be a nurse. I've been questioning things for a long time. Since I was sixteen."

"Around the time Jeremiah left." *Mamm* shook her head violently. "I knew he had something to do with this."

"He doesn't. I promise." Although that wasn't completely true. She didn't know what would happen between her and Jeremiah, but the decision not to join the church was her own. "I've prayed about this. I've agonized over it." Tears came to her eyes. "I believe God wants me to follow a different path."

"Away from the church? From *yer* family?" *Mamm* began to cry. "You're confused. I understand now. I've been putting too much pressure on you—"

"I'm not confused. For the first time, I'm seeing things clearly."

Her mother stepped away, her expression hardening. She didn't say anything for a long time. Then she finally spoke, her tone sharper than a razor's edge. "Then leave."

"What?"

"I don't want to hold you back from your *path*."

"*Mamm*, please . . ."

But her mother turned around. "I said *geh*, Anna Mae."

The words slammed into her like a raw punch to her stomach. She moved toward her mother, who spun around, her eyes red-rimmed but dry.

"*Geh*!" *Mamm* shoved past her and walked out of the house. The screen door bounced against the frame as Anna Mae tried to come to terms with what had just happened. She ran after her and stood on the front porch, holding the door open. The sun was now well above the horizon. "Where are you going?"

Her mother was headed for the back of the house. Without looking at Anna Mae, she said, "To pray."

Anna Mae leaned against the doorjamb. She knew where her mother was going—to her prayer garden, a patch of gorgeous wildflowers with a small wooden swing in the center. When Anna Mae was younger she used to join her mother there, and they would pray together.

Not anymore.

She started to shake. Her mother was throwing her out. Without discussion or much more than a minute's thought. Anna Mae didn't know what to do. She couldn't talk to her father because he was still on his fishing trip. But her mother had said they were both of the same mind when it came to Anna Mae joining the church. Would he have told her to leave too?

She fought the burning in her eyes, the lump lodged in her throat. Should she wait until her mother had calmed down so they could talk? Yet talking wouldn't change anything. Regardless of whether she became a nurse—which seemed like an impossible dream—she wouldn't join the church. And if she didn't join the church, she wasn't welcome here. Now she knew where she stood with her family—apart, in all the ways that mattered.

She ran inside and up to her room, threw a couple of dresses and some undergarments in a travel bag. She glanced at her Bible on the night-stand and picked it up. Who had remained the one constant in her life? The Lord. *I will never forsake you* . . . But where was he now? She'd never felt so alone.

Anna Mae sat on the bed clutching her Bible to her chest, tears slipping down her cheeks. She knew God had never promised that life would be easy and free from pain. But he had promised he would be there during the low times as a comforter, a counselor, a spiritual Father, and so many other things she desperately needed.

But she didn't need promises right now. She needed answers. She had no idea what she was supposed to do.

After a few moments she stood. Wiped her tears and put her Bible in her bag. Her mother had made her wishes clear, and Anna Mae was tired of the fight. She took a deep breath and walked out of the room. Down the stairs and out of the home where she'd spent her entire life. Glancing over her shoulder, she wondered if she would ever see her family again.

Jeremiah yawned as he maneuvered his vehicle down Anna Mae's road. After he'd dropped her off, he'd gone back to the Mullets' farm, just to make sure the horses were still responding to the medication. Satisfied they were doing well, he headed toward the B&B for a shower and some rest.

He could have taken another route to the B&B, but he found himself driving past Anna Mae's house one more time, in case he could catch a glimpse of her. It was silly and immature, something a young kid would do. But he couldn't help it. Something had changed between them. Their friendship seemed to be rekindled, which he was grateful for. But that wasn't it.

He felt different when he was with her. Like having her back in his life filled in a piece he didn't know was missing.

But he didn't see anyone, and he yawned again. Anna Mae was probably asleep by now. He should be too. He craved a hot shower and a soft bed. He'd go back to the farm after he had a good nap, but he was sure he'd left the horses in good hands for a few hours.

After a few minutes, Jeremiah saw an Amish woman walking on the side of the road, her back to him. But as he neared, he leaned forward, recognizing her.

He slowed and pulled up beside her. When she didn't turn to look at him, he rolled down his window. "Anna Mae?"

She glanced at him but kept on walking. He called to her again, but she ignored him. Finally he pulled over on the side of the road in front of her, left the engine running, and got out of the car. As he walked back toward her, he saw her face was blotchy. There was only one thing that would cover Anna Mae's perfect skin with large red spots. She'd been crying.

When he reached her, she didn't stop. "Leave me be, Jeremiah," she said, quickening her pace.

But he stepped in line right beside her, matching her stride. "Not until you tell me what's wrong." She didn't say anything. Realizing he wasn't getting anywhere, he jogged ahead and blocked her way. She finally stopped.

"You've been crying."

She glanced away. "So?"

His heart constricted. "What happened?"

Anna Mae opened her mouth, but no sound came out. Then she started to sob.

Without hesitation he put his arm around her and led her to his car. He opened the passenger door, and she got in without protest. He scooted around and slid into the driver's seat, shifted the car into drive, and turned into the closest driveway to turn around.

"What are you doing?" she said, her voice heavy and thick.

"Taking you home."

She gripped his arm. "You can't."

He looked at her, bewildered. "Why not?"

"I can't *geh* back home." She released his arm and looked out the passenger window. "Ever."

He started to ask her why, but he knew she wouldn't give him an answer. When he saw her reach for the lever to open her door, he put the car in reverse. "All right. I'll take you to my place." Jeremiah expected her to object, but she said nothing. Only took her hand off the door handle and stared out the window.

Although the drive to Priscilla's Bed-and-Breakfast wasn't a long one, it seemed interminable in the heavy silence hanging between him and Anna Mae. What a difference from their last conversation. He couldn't imagine what had happened for her to say she couldn't go home. She clung to the lumpy duffel bag in her lap like it was a life preserver.

Finally he turned into the driveway of the B&B and drove around the back, where his room was situated on the second floor. A stairway led from the parking lot to the balcony outside the two top-level rooms. He turned off the motor. "Can I take your bag?"

She shook her head and got out of the car. She waited for him, not moving until he reached her. "My room is up there," he said, pointing to the door right next to the stairwell.

Anna Mae nodded and started toward the stairs.

Jeremiah paused. What was he doing, bringing her here? Yet where else could they go? She couldn't go home, and he didn't have one. He had to find out what was wrong, and if he hadn't seen her, who knew where she would have ended up? He silently thanked God for the good timing. Anna Mae was ascending the stairs by the time he propelled himself forward. Strangely enough, if she had a problem going to his room, she didn't express it.

He joined her in front of his door, then fished for his room key in the pocket of his jeans. He opened the door, breathing in the cloying smell of lavender and vanilla from the potpourri Mrs. Henson insisted on leaving in his room every time she cleaned it. He scooped up the small glass container of twigs and dried flowers and moved it to the bathroom. "Sorry about the smell," he said.

Anna Mae didn't answer. When he returned from the bathroom, she hadn't moved. Now he could see her face clearly, her swollen, yet still beautiful eyes filled with pain. She clutched the bag to her chest. He gently took it from her and laid it on the floor near the small wood table in front of the window. He closed the curtains, feeling the need to ensure privacy. "Do you want something to drink?"

She shook her head.

"Are you hungry?"

"*Nee.*" She sounded hoarse, and he saw the patches and streaks of dirt on her dress from working with the horses. She seemed to be in a state of shock. He picked up a light quilt that was lying on the end of his bed and put it around her shoulders.

"I'm not cold."

"Humor me." He led her to the one chair in his room and helped her sit down. He perched on the edge of the bed in front of her. "Tell me what happened."

Tears pooled in her eyes, slipping from their blue depths and trickling down her cheeks. "I made *mei* decision," she whispered.

"Decision?" He frowned.

"About the church."

"Wait." He sat up, surprised. "I thought you had joined the church."

She gave him a hard look.

"I just assumed—"

She wiped her eyes. "Of course you did." She shrugged the quilt off her shoulders and glared at him. At least she wasn't as pale as she had been a moment before. "You always assume things."

"Hold on. This isn't about me."

"Isn't everything about you?"

He withered under her pointed stare. He rubbed the back of his neck. "Let's start over. You were telling me what was wrong."

"I wasn't telling you anything." She stood up and grabbed her bag.

"Where are you going?" He was back on his feet too.

"Anywhere but here." She put her hand on the doorknob.

He covered her hand with his. "You're staying here until you tell me what's going on."

She didn't move, and Jeremiah thought she'd challenge him again. Finally she let go of the knob. "Doesn't matter. It's not like I have any-where else to *geh*." She went back to the chair and sat down, her shoulders slumped.

He went to the closet where he kept not only his clothes but a few dry goods and several cans of pop. He pulled the tabs off two of them and handed her the diet version. "Just in case you change your mind."

She put it on the table and stared. He waited for her to speak. When she didn't, he tried to think of a way to get her to talk. When he realized he wasn't going to get anything out of her, he said, "Maybe I should go get your *mamm*."

She grabbed his arm, making him spill a little of his drink. "Don't!"

"Why not?" He set the can on the table and took her hands in his, not caring that she resisted him. "Just forget about the past for a minute, okay? I'm here now, and I'm ready to listen."

"How did you do it?" she asked.

"Do what?"

She licked her lips. "When you left . . . how did you forget about your family . . . about me?"

He looked down at their hands clasped together. "I never forgot about them." He looked up at her. "Or you."

"I told *Mamm* I wasn't going to join the church," she whispered. "Then she told me to leave."

His brow shot up. "What about your dad?"

"He went fishing in Canada on a charter for the week." Her eyes grew moist. "I may never see him again."

She was gripping his hands, and he wasn't about to let her go. "I'm sure that won't be the case."

"She doesn't want me there if I don't join the church."

"And you're sure you're not going to?"

She nodded. "More sure than ever."

He sat back on the bed. He felt like he should say something, try to convince her that she needed to think about this some more. Dozens of thoughts flew through his mind, mostly arguments his father had made right before Jeremiah left for college, trying to get him to change his mind and remain *Amisch*. But he knew none of them would sway her, just as they didn't sway him. He recognized the determined set of her eyes, the permanent way she'd stated her intention. She wasn't changing her mind. "I have to say I'm surprised. I had no idea you were struggling with this." Guilt crawled inside him like a worm through dirt. "When did you start having doubts?"

"Before you left."

"And you never said anything?"

"I didn't know what to say. I wasn't doubting because I was pursuing a dream, like you were. And it was more of a feeling than anything else. Every time I thought about getting baptized, I would freeze up inside." She looked away. "It's hard to explain."

"I get it. Even though I knew I would never be *Amisch*, the decision wasn't easy. But it was the right one, for me." He peered at her. "You have to make sure it's the right one for you. Have you thought about what you're going to do?"

She shrugged. "I don't know. I hadn't expected this. Any of it. It's not like I take my faith lightly." She stood up and started to pace. "I'm not turning my back on God."

He nodded. He hadn't either. But it was difficult for his father—and Anna Mae's mother, apparently—to understand. Still, he was surprised her mother was being so harsh. "I'm sure she didn't mean what she said. She was upset. You know how my father gets when he's angry."

"She meant it." Anna Mae looked at him again, this time her expression haunted. She halted in front of him. "*Mein Gott,*" she said, her voice trembling. "What am I going to do?"

Jeremiah stood, inches away from her. He could still smell the horses and barn scents on both of them. He said the first thing that came to his mind. "Take a shower."

Her blond brows shot up. "What?"

"There's plenty of shampoo and soap in the bathroom. Some sweet, girly-smelling stuff. I'm sure you'll like it."

"So you're saying I stink."

"We both do." He stepped farther away from her. "A shower will make you feel better." *And give me some time to think.* "I'll be out on the balcony," he said, opening the door. "Let me know when you're finished."

He stepped onto the wooden balcony, breathing in the hot summer air. How could he help Anna Mae? Growing up, she'd never said anything about wanting to leave the *Amisch*. Now he understood a little more about why she was so angry with him about leaving. If he had stayed, or at least had said good-bye, she might have revealed her doubts about joining the church. They could have talked about it, and maybe she could have avoided this. He had a plan when he left. She didn't, and she needed one.

He closed his eyes and listened, something he usually did when he was troubled. Being outside, hearing the sounds of nature, whether it was the twittering of birds during the day or the chirp of crickets at night, the sounds always calmed his emotions. But not this time.

He opened his eyes and started to pace the length of the balcony, thinking, praying . . . and coming up with nothing.

The door to his room opened. Anna Mae tentatively came outside wearing a fresh dress, her blond hair combed smooth and fashioned into a long braid coiled at the crown of her head. This was the first time he had seen her without her head covered. All he could do was stare. Her hair was beautiful . . . she was beautiful.

She touched her braid and averted her eyes. "You were right. The shower felt *gut.*" She scrunched her nose. "Your turn."

"Are you saying I stink?" He winked at her, glad for the break in the tension.

She pushed him toward the room. "You know you do."

He went inside, noticing she closed the door behind him and stayed outside. *Good idea.* He quickly showered, put on fresh jeans and a white T-shirt, and finger combed his damp hair. He hurried, not wanting her to be alone for too long, not when she was this vulnerable.

But when he came out of the bathroom, she was in the room. She had unbound her hair, and it flowed over her shoulders like a shimmering blond curtain. He clenched his fists, fighting against the attraction that hit him hard. *Lord, help me!* When she walked toward him, he took a step back.

She stopped a few inches in front of him. She looked down at her feet, which were bare. Then she looked up at him, those beautiful blue eyes filled with pain and longing.

"I'm sorry you're going through this." He put his arms around her and brought her close to his chest, wanting to absorb at least some of her pain. He expected her to pull away, but instead she snuggled against him.

He rested his chin against the top of her head, inhaling the scent of the shampoo. The next moments were a blur. She pulled away from him, only to reach up and place her hand on the back of his head. He couldn't resist when she pulled his mouth to hers for a kiss.

For a split second, he allowed himself to enjoy it.

She drew away from him and touched his face. "Let me stay here tonight," she whispered in his ear.

He closed his eyes and groaned. The temptation was almost overwhelming. The word *yes* danced on his tongue. It would be so easy to let her stay here. So easy to keep kissing her. So easy to forget everything they both believed and had followed for their entire lives. So easy . . . and so wrong.

He removed her arms from around his neck and backed against the wall. "We both know you can't."

"Why?" Her voice grew husky, but with a heated edge. "Because our parents said so?" She put her hands on his shoulders. "Because it wouldn't be the *Amisch* thing to do?"

He removed her hands from him. "Because it wouldn't be the right thing to do."

Her brows flattened, her cheeks glowing bright red as her eyes ignited with anger. She turned from him and picked up her travel bag.

He came up behind her. "Anna Mae—"

"Of course you're right." She kept her back to

him, the bitterness in her voice clawing at him. "It would be wrong for me to stay."

Jeremiah jumped in front of the door, preventing her from bolting as he was sure she was going to do. "What about Judith?" he said as the thought formed in his mind.

"What?"

"Judith," he said again. "You can stay with her. I'm sure she wouldn't mind."

Anna Mae looked up at him. "I barely know her. You don't either."

"I know she's been kind to my family. That's enough for me." He looked at her, willing her to agree to the idea. "I'll drive you over there."

She shrugged as if she didn't care anymore. "Fine." She went into the bathroom, taking her bag with her, and shut the door.

As they left his room, her braid, head covering, and shoes restored, Jeremiah hoped he was right about Judith. If he wasn't, he didn't know what they would do.

CHAPTER 15

Anna Mae wanted to crawl into a hole and die.

What had she been thinking, kissing Jeremiah, asking him if she could stay the night? He was right to reject her, and she knew better. *Foolish, foolish, foolish.*

She squeezed against the car door, trying to put as much space between them as possible. Rejection seeped through every ounce of her body. She needed someone to accept her, to stand by her side. Why didn't she just tell him that instead of letting her feelings for him get in the way?

She rested her forehead against the palm of her hand. She'd messed up, again. What if Judith didn't want to have anything to do with her? She had no obligation to Anna Mae or Jeremiah. But what other choice did she have? And if Judith refused to let her stay, where else could she go?

Jeremiah didn't speak during the short drive to Judith's house. It took everything she had to keep from crying. Had she ruined their friendship? When they were talking, he had understood. Not just her decision, but everything. Her pain. Her loneliness. Her confusion. And one impulsive move might have driven him away.

He eased the car into Judith's driveway and turned off the engine. His hands remained on the steering wheel. "Everything will be all right, Anna Mae."

He sounded more like he was trying to convince himself than her. Suddenly she went numb. None of it mattered anymore. Her family had cast her out, Jeremiah had rejected her, and now she was dependent on the kindness of a woman she barely knew. Maybe she would just spend the night in Amos's barn.

"Do you want to wait in the car?" Jeremiah asked. "I can talk to her first."

Anna Mae opened the car door and got out. Without a word she went to the front door and knocked on it, aware of Jeremiah behind her but not caring anymore. He could go back to his room, back to his job being a vet, and then back to his life away from Middlefield. From now on she had only herself.

Faint footsteps sounded in the house. Judith opened the door. "Anna Mae," she said, smiling, her kind eyes peering from behind the rims of her silver-framed glasses. "This is a nice surprise."

Anna Mae took a shuddering breath. "I'm . . . I'm sorry to bother you, but . . ." Unbidden tears threatened her resolve. She held them back. "I need a place to stay."

"Of course." Judith opened the screen door wide. "Come in, please."

Anna Mae didn't move. "Don't you want to know why?"

Judith shook her head and placed her arm around Anna Mae's shoulders.

Something broke inside Anna Mae as the screen door shut behind them. She turned and buried her face in Judith's shoulder and started to sob.

Jeremiah watched Anna Mae go inside Judith's. He had gotten out of his car, but hung back when he realized Anna Mae didn't need him. He shoved his hands into the pockets of his jeans and waited, just in case she couldn't—or wouldn't—stay. After a few minutes, he let out a sigh of relief. He'd finally done something right where Anna Mae was concerned.

He had started to get into his car when he glanced at his father's house. Memories came flooding back, as they always did when he was here. Some were good. Many were not.

Yet he realized that most of the happy memories of his childhood involved Anna Mae. When he and Amos were with her when they were kids, he could forget about his problems. She was there during the bad times—his mother leaving, his arguments with his father about becoming a vet, his trying to protect Amos from people who didn't understand him. He could turn to her when he needed to. With Anna Mae he could let down his guard. He could be a *kid*.

They weren't kids anymore, but they still had a bond. He thought about the kiss, and realized he wanted something more than friendship. But that wasn't what she needed right now. She needed him—the same way he needed her when they were growing up.

And right now, she needed some sleep. He did, too, but falling asleep wasn't going to happen anytime soon. He shut his car door, assuming Judith wouldn't mind him leaving it in her driveway for a little while, and walked over to his father's house.

He checked the barn to see if Amos was there, but he wasn't. He walked out back and to the fence surrounding the pasture and gazed at the grazing herd. His dad wasn't anywhere in sight either. He thought about checking inside the house, but he changed his mind and leaned on the sturdy oak fence. As he watched the cows, their tails flicking away the flies as they chomped on the grass, he wished things could be different. Not his vocation or his place in the *Yankee* world. He was sure he was exactly where God wanted him to be.

He wanted things to be different with his family. With Anna Mae. They were all so broken. How could he put the pieces back together? He couldn't make Anna Mae's mother accept her daughter's choices. He couldn't snap his fingers and make his father happier. He couldn't give Amos a book and make him smarter.

He couldn't make his mother come back. He couldn't make her love him. He had tried . . . and failed.

"Amos is inside." His father came up beside him. Jeremiah hadn't even heard him approach. He stood by the fence, keeping a good distance between him and Jeremiah. "You said you were coming by last night."

"I was at Johnny and Caleb's farm." He told

his father what had happened to the horses.

Daed nodded. "So what's your excuse today? *Yer bruder*'s in the house, wondering where you are."

"I didn't realize that." Jeremiah moved to leave. "I'll *geh* see him now."

"Why bother?"

Jeremiah froze. He looked at his father's stony profile, his gaze dropping to *Daed*'s hands, his knuckles white from gripping the edge of the fence. "Because he's my brother. I care about him."

"You have a funny way—"

"*Daed*!" Jeremiah said in a storm of anger and frustration. "How many times are we going to have the same argument?" He lowered his voice. "Why can't we just talk to each other?"

His father slowly turned toward him. "I'm listening."

But Jeremiah suddenly couldn't speak. What could he say to his father that he hadn't already said? And he wasn't going to apologize for who he was. "Why are you so angry?" He asked the question as soon as it hit his mind.

"I'm not." His father faced the pasture again.

"You have a right to be. *Mamm* left us. Amos is . . . Amos. And I—"

"You could have stayed," *Daed* said evenly. "You could have stayed."

"No, *Daed*. I couldn't." He wiped his hands over his face, feeling the perspiration on his skin. "I didn't want to."

His father paused. "Then I guess we've got nothing to talk about." He turned and walked back to the house.

Jeremiah hung his head. So much for mending fences. He'd made things worse by telling the truth. He sighed and looked at the cows again. Simple, and sometimes stupid, animals, but they made sense to him. Animals he understood. He knew what to do when an animal was sick or in trouble.

People, on the other hand, were a different story.

Anna Mae crept downstairs, making sure she didn't wake up Judith. Her head throbbed and her eyes ached. She glanced at the living room window, surprised to see it was dark outside. She remembered Judith showing her to an upstairs bedroom, where she'd fallen on the bed and cried herself to sleep. Had she slept all day?

She heard the clanging of dishes in the kitchen. Anna Mae followed the sound and pushed open the swinging door. She hadn't seen one of these before. The air from the door's movement followed her. She saw Judith standing on a short stepladder, pulling bowls from the top shelf and putting them on the counter. She turned, looked at Anna Mae, and smiled.

"Sleep well?" she asked.

Anna Mae nodded. "What time is it?"

"Ten o'clock or so. I'm a night owl."

She couldn't believe she'd slept that long. "I'm sorry."

"Don't be." Judith stepped down from the ladder and handed a bowl to Anna Mae. "You were exhausted. I've got some sandwich fixings in the pantry and cooler. Do you want something to eat?"

"I'm not really hungry."

Judith nodded. "It's ready when you are." She glanced at the dishes littering the countertops. "I've been meaning to clean out these cabinets since I moved in. I've also been wanting to wash all these extra dishes and bowls so I can give them away."

"They're not yours?"

"They belonged to *mei grossmutter*. She and *mei grossvatter* used to live here. Maybe you remember her and her cookies. Jeremiah and Amos do. She loved to bake cookies for children, especially after *mei mudder* married and moved to New York with *mei* father. She stayed here after *mei grossvatter* died, then she died as well and left this house to me."

"Yes, I do remember her."

Judith turned on the tap and poured dish detergent into the sink. "Would you rather wash or dry?"

"Dry," Anna Mae said.

"*Gut*, because I like to wash."

Anna Mae moved beside Judith as the bubbles

rose in the sink. She braced herself for the inevitable questions. But Judith didn't say anything, only washed each dish and rinsed it before handing it to Anna Mae to dry.

When they were nearly finished, Anna Mae said, "*Danki* for letting me stay here tonight."

Judith plunged her hands into the water, fished around the bottom until she found one of what seemed like dozens of spoons that had been stored in various drawers. "You're welcome to stay as long as you want. It's nice to have the company."

"I don't want to impose."

"It's not an imposition when you're invited." She smiled at Anna Mae again, her round cheeks lifting up the bottom edge of her glasses. She handed Anna Mae the spoon.

Anna Mae took it and wiped it until it shone. "Do you usually invite strangers to stay with you?"

"You're not a stranger." She paused. "You care a lot about Amos. Anyone can see that. That makes you as special as he is, in my book."

"Amos is special," Anna Mae said.

"So is his brother."

"That's a matter of opinion." Anna Mae put the spoon in the pile harder than she intended. "Sorry."

"Struck a nerve, I see." Judith pulled the plug out of the sink, and the water and suds gurgled as they went down the drain. "I won't bring up Jeremiah anymore."

Anna Mae sighed. "That's okay." She put her hands on the edge of the counter. "Jeremiah and I are . . . complicated."

"When are relationships not complicated?"

"But we're not in a relationship—"

"You are." Judith took the dish towel from Anna Mae. "Not a romantic one, perhaps, but you do have a relationship with him."

Anna Mae lowered her head, her cheeks heating as she remembered the kiss. But romance was far from her mind right now. She hung the towel on a tiny peg attached to the side of the window casement. As they stacked up all the extra bowls, dishes, and silverware, Judith said, "I feel like making banana bread. Would you like to help me?"

Baking this late at night? Her mother would be sound asleep by now . . .

Anna Mae tried to ignore the pinch in her heart. "Sure."

As Judith brought out the bananas and all the ingredients to prepare the batter, and Anna Mae mashed the bananas and then greased and floured the bread pans at the kitchen table, Anna Mae waited for Judith to ask her what had happened that morning. Finally, unable to stand it anymore, Anna Mae said, "I told *mei mudder* I'm not joining the church."

Judith paused for a moment before cracking an egg on the counter and letting the insides fall into a bowl. "And she asked you to leave."

Anna Mae nodded. "If you want me to *geh*, I'll understand."

Judith turned to Anna Mae. "Do *yer* parents know you're here?"

"*Nee*." She explained that her father was away. "*Mei daed* doesn't know what happened."

Judith nodded as she cracked another egg. She picked up a fork and scrambled them before adding them to the batter bowl along with the bananas. "What do you think *yer daed* will do when he finds out?"

Anna Mae ran her finger over the rim of one of the bread pans. "I don't know," she said wearily. "But I don't want to cause you any trouble."

Judith stirred the batter, pausing for a moment to rub her chin. "I'm sure *yer mamm* needs a few days to think about things," she finally said.

"That's what Jeremiah said."

"And when *yer mudder* is ready to talk," Judith added while pouring batter into one of the pans, "she'll be welcome here."

"I appreciate your understanding."

"I understand because I've been in your shoes." Judith filled the other bread pan and put them both in the oven. She sat down at the table next to Anna Mae. "You're not the only one who has struggled with joining the church. It's a commitment—the biggest one you'll make in your life. And if you're feeling pulled in another direction, it's only fair you explore it."

"Is that what you did?"

"For a time. I was nearly thirty when I joined. I won't bore you with what happened during the time I was away."

"I'm sure it's not boring."

Judith folded her hands. "It's not exciting either. Or filled with moments I'm proud of. *Mei mudder* felt the same way as yours. Although I didn't give her the chance to tell me to leave. I left on *mei* own. We didn't speak for years." She rubbed her lips together. "I regret missing that time with her. But we were both stubborn."

"Sounds like *mei* and *Mamm*."

"Maybe. Or maybe you need some time apart. To pray and figure things out. As hard as it is for you right now, she's suffering too. Parents have dreams for their children. When God has something different in mind, it can take time to accept it."

The faint scent of banana bread wafted in the air. "What made you decide to become baptized?" Anna Mae asked. "What brought you back?"

"God. Him, and the sense that when I was in the *Englisch* world I was out of place. Like I was constantly on the outer edge of things, not a part of them. Here, for example," she said, holding her arms out, "it's different. Even though I haven't lived here long, I feel part of the community. My purpose is being fulfilled. I felt that way in my community in New York, too, but I never felt that way out in the world." She yawned and patted Anna Mae's hand. "I guess the day has finally caught up to me. Do you mind taking the bread out of the oven when it's done?"

"I will."

Judith stood. *"Gut nacht,* Anna Mae."

Anna Mae stayed at the table, pondering what Judith had said. A woman she barely knew had given her the insight and advice she needed. She prayed while the bread baked and asked God for forgiveness for what she'd done in Jeremiah's room, for direction in her life, and for her relationship with her mother to be healed.

The wind-up timer went off, and she pulled out the bread. Despite Judith's hospitality, she couldn't stay here indefinitely. Her mother was right—she couldn't live in limbo anymore. She needed a plan, and she needed to make some hard decisions. She would have to do them alone.

No . . . not alone.

Anna Mae smiled. For the first time in a very long time, she heard that still, quiet voice in her soul.

CHAPTER 16

Bekah stood by her parents' buggy as she watched Caleb walk out of his barn after church service. Three days had passed since the horses had fallen ill. She'd stayed at Johnny and Katie's until Promise had shown improvement. Katie had started to feel a little better, but Bekah still helped her around the house. And if she was honest with herself, she'd admit she'd wanted to stick around the farm so she and Caleb would have a chance to talk.

But Caleb had something different in mind—ignoring her completely.

That frustrated her, yet it still didn't keep her from thinking about him. All the time, which annoyed her too.

She kept her gaze on him as he stood by Johnny, the two of them talking to a few of the older men she didn't really know very well. Discussing business, no doubt. Before she left, Bekah had overheard Johnny saying he would make sure everyone knew what Jeremiah had done for the horses. From what she gathered, most, but not everyone, had welcomed Jeremiah's return to Middlefield, even though it was temporary. Bekah was grateful he had come back. Promise and the other horses were alive because of him.

Caleb put his hands on his waist as he spoke, his white shirt crisp and bright against his dark vest and trousers. He laughed at something one of the men said. It was good to see him relaxed. Happy. Except when he was around her.

"Bekah. Bekah!"

She jumped, not realizing Katie had walked over to her. "What?"

"I called your name several times. Didn't you hear me?"

Bekah pretended to be interested in the buggy. "I had my mind on something else."

"Caleb, perhaps?"

She gave her sister a sidelong glance. "Definitely not."

Katie laughed. "I'm only teasing."

Bekah relaxed a bit. "I'm glad you're feeling better today."

"Me too—though it, uh, comes and goes. Some kind of . . . something, I guess." Bekah looked at Katie then and saw her smile, almost sheepishly. It seemed like her skin was glowing. What was that about?

"I appreciate you helping me out the past few days. Especially getting ready for the service here today," Katie added.

Bekah's shoulders snapped back. "I haven't minded at all. I can still come over. Maybe I should, for a few more days. Just in case you start feeling poorly again."

"I don't want to take up all of your time," Katie said. "I know you don't like doing the chores. Besides, I thought you'd be looking for another job by now."

Bekah scratched her nose. She probably should be finding work, but she had saved up a lot of her money from her waitressing job, so she wasn't in dire straits. "I'm still pondering possibilities. And I can ponder and help you out at the same time." Her smile grew wide enough that her mouth hurt.

Katie tilted her head. "I know what this is about."

Her eyes widened. She knew Katie had caught her staring at Caleb. She hadn't been careful enough.

"I know you're concerned about Promise. You've been with her every chance you get."

Bekah breathed an inward sigh of relief. "You're right. That's it."

"You're welcome to come over anytime to check on her. I know Johnny won't mind."

"What about Caleb?" She bit her bottom lip.

"He hasn't said anything to me about it." Katie turned and looked at Johnny, who was saying good-bye to the men. Caleb had disappeared. "I better get going. Why don't you come over tomorrow morning? I'd like to see what you came up with for the *grienhaus*."

The greenhouse. Bekah had forgotten about that. Now she had a legitimate excuse to be at the farm. And if she accidentally on purpose ran into

Caleb, she would give him a talking to. There was unfinished business between them, and she was tired of being ignored. "Great! I'll see you tomorrow, then."

Her mother and father appeared. She climbed into the buggy, waiting for her mother and Katie to exchange a few words. Then her father took the reins as her mother got into the buggy.

On their way home, Bekah said, "I didn't see Anna Mae in church today. She's not sick or anything, is she?"

Her mother didn't answer right away. Finally she said, "She's not sick."

Bekah sat back on the bench seat in the double buggy. "I wonder where she was, then."

Her mother sighed, then turned around. "I guess you'll find out soon enough. Anna Mae has decided not to join the church. She's no longer living with her *mutter* and *daed*."

Bekah sat back, shocked. Anna Mae hadn't given a hint that anything like this was going on. "Where is she now?"

"Judith Hostetler took her in." *Mamm* shook her head. "That's all I'm going to say on the subject." She faced forward, ending the conversation.

Bekah understood. Any more of the conversation would be akin to gossiping. Still, she couldn't stem her curiosity. Or the niggling idea that something had gone wrong. Her mother's reticence to talk about Anna Mae was part of it, but it was more about how Anna Mae was the other day. She had seemed content and focused while working with Jeremiah. Bekah never would have suspected something as serious as leaving the church was on the horizon.

When they arrived at home, Bekah asked for the horse's reins. "Where are you going?" her father asked.

"To see Anna Mae." She glanced at her mother. "I think she might need someone to talk to."

Judith walked to her buggy after the church service, keeping her chin lifted. She'd noticed the looks and sidelong glances several of the ladies had given her since she'd arrived for church this morning, and she understood them. Some were curious, and some were clearly stating that they were being loyal to Caroline Shetler. She had expected all of it, knowing the risk she took by letting Anna Mae stay with her.

Still, it stung a bit. And it reminded her of how some of her friends in her youth had reacted when she had waited longer than usual to be baptized. Judith hadn't gone very far from her district in New York during that time, and she had occasionally run into some of her old friends. Some were polite, and some ignored her as if she weren't there. As if she was supposed to be shunned.

She climbed inside her buggy and picked up the

reins. None of this made her question letting Anna Mae stay. The young woman needed guidance, guidance she wished she'd had at her age. Judith hoped that somehow she could keep Anna Mae from wandering in the wilderness for too long, the way she had years ago.

"Judith?"

She turned to see Ada, a woman close to her age whom she'd been friendly with during the past couple of months. "Hi, Ada. Wonderful service this morning, *ya*?"

Ada narrowed her eyes. "You need to send Anna Mae home."

"I'm not keeping her against her will."

Ada glared at her over her eyeglasses. "You have *nee* business letting that *maedel* stay at your house. You're supporting her disobedience, and you're meddling in their affairs."

Judith kept her voice even. "Aren't you also meddling?"

"Caroline is my oldest friend. I am standing up for what's right. You should be doing the same, not encouraging a *yung* one to *geh* against her family."

"I'm doing what I think is best."

"You have *nee* idea what's best." Ada shook her head and walked away.

Judith sighed. For the first time she questioned her decision. *Is giving Anna Mae refuge your will, Lord? Or is it mine?*

Anna Mae sat on Judith's back patio holding a glass of iced tea that she had barely sipped. Today was the first time she'd missed church. Ever. She stared at the cubes floating in the tea, her heart suddenly aching for her mother. She'd had to go to church at Johnny and Katie's alone today, as Anna Mae's father wasn't due back from Canada until tomorrow. Was she peppered with questions about Anna Mae's absence? What did she tell everyone at the service? Did anyone help her carry all those pies she'd made? She squirmed in the chair, her conscience nearly overwhelming her.

She heard the sound of David and Amos's buggy coming home. David pulled the buggy in front of their barn, and Amos hopped out, wearing his Sunday best. She steeled herself, thinking he might come over and ask her why she wasn't at church. But she could hear David's stern voice telling him to go inside and change clothes.

Anna Mae took a small sip of tea. This morning she had prayed and read from a devotional book she found on Judith's coffee table. It wasn't the same as going to church, but it hadn't felt wrong either. She couldn't picture herself not praying and worshipping God, no matter where she ended up. Her faith in the Lord would always be a large part of her life.

She leaned back in the chair and lifted her face to the hot sun. Seeing Amos and David reminded her of Jeremiah. She hadn't seen him since he brought her here. She didn't blame him for staying away. Part of her was glad he had. She was confused enough about her future. She didn't need to deal with her sudden attraction to him too.

But she couldn't lie to herself either. She missed him, and she hoped that kissing him hadn't driven him away forever. She wanted him back in her life, and if that had to be as a friend, even one she rarely saw, that would be better than nothing.

Anna Mae heard the crunch of another buggy's wheels on gravel, this time closer than before. Thinking Judith must be home, she rounded the house and walked to the front, surprised to see Bekah pulling her buggy to a stop. She got out and tethered the horse to the hitching rail near Judith's tiny barn.

Bekah smiled and waved as she walked toward her. But Anna Mae didn't move, unsure why Bekah would be here.

"I hope you don't mind that I dropped by," Bekah said. She smiled, but it looked a little forced and nervous. "I wanted to let you know how the horses are doing. Unless Jeremiah has already told you." Her smile faded. "I didn't think about that," she added, almost to herself. She looked at Anna Mae again. "I didn't see you in church, and, ah . . ." She let out a breath. "Bother."

Anna Mae couldn't help but chuckle at Bekah's flustering. "It's okay, Bekah. You can tell me why you're really here."

"I wanted to see how you're doing." She clasped her hands together. "I . . . I heard you decided not to join the church."

"I did." Anna Mae straightened. Saying it out loud had become easier now and sounded right.

"Do you want to talk about it?"

"Not really."

"Oh. Okay." Bekah's face fell.

"But I'd like to talk about something else." *Anything else.* "We can sit on the back patio and visit if you'd like."

"I'd like that very much."

When they were situated on Judith's white plastic chairs, Bekah with a glass of tea, too, Anna Mae asked, "How *are* the horses doing?" As Bekah filled her in on their progress, especially the one she named Promise, Anna Mae smiled. "I'm so glad they're improving."

"Jeremiah's been out to check on them every day. The results from the tests came back."

"And?" Anna Mae leaned forward.

"Definitely lead poisoning."

"Do they know how?"

Bekah shook her head. "But the horses weren't poisoned by anything at the farm. All the feed and soil samples were fine."

"Strange."

"Very. Johnny's not sure what to do. I do know that he and Caleb put a lock on the feed bins, just in case someone does try to get into them."

"*Gut* idea."

Bekah leaned back in her chair. "Everything is getting back to normal. Katie's feeling better, even Caleb is . . ."

"Caleb is what?"

"He's just being Caleb."

"What does that mean?"

Bekah sighed. "I have *nee* idea."

Anna Mae hid a smile. It had been so long since she'd had this kind of talk with a female friend, and Bekah's cluelessness about Caleb was amusing.

"I mean, I thought when he kissed me—"

"Wait." Things just got more interesting. "He *kissed* you?"

She held up her hands and waved them. "Not that kind of kiss. His mouth brushed *mei* ear, that's all. And it was probably an accident. I wasn't sure what end was up. I was so tired that night."

"When we were all over at the farm?"

"*Ya.* I also thought he whispered *mei* name. A . . . special kind of whisper." She flushed. "But that sounds stupid, and now he's back to acting like I don't exist." She fiddled with the skirt of her Sunday dress. "He threw *mei* sandwich away," she said sadly.

"What?"

"Never mind."

"Hmm." Anna Mae set her glass on the plastic patio table that matched the chairs. "I'm the last person to give insight when it comes to men, but from what I can tell, I think he likes you."

"That's ridiculous."

"Maybe. But the more important question is, how do you feel about him?"

Bekah stilled her hands. "What do you mean?"

"Do you like Caleb?"

"Wow," Bekah said. "Talk about getting to the point."

"I'm learning that it's better to be more direct sometimes."

Bekah fidgeted in the chair. "How I feel doesn't matter. Nothing will ever happen."

"How can you be so sure?"

"Because." She looked down at her dress again. "I'm not the kind of woman he wants."

"How do you know what he wants?"

Bekah glanced away. "I guess I really don't. I just know it's not me."

Amos came out of his house at that moment wearing old clothes and bounding to his barn. She couldn't see his face, but she could imagine his smile. Life delighted him in so many ways, most of them the simple ones. "I wish we could all be like Amos."

"Amos?" Bekah asked. "Jeremiah's brother?"

Anna Mae nodded. "He sees everyone, including himself, as the same. We're all equal in his eyes.

We're all *gut* enough, no matter what we think of ourselves." She smiled at Bekah. "And if we're female, we're all very pretty."

Bekah smiled back. "He really is sweet."

The back door opened and Judith appeared, holding a plate of sliced watermelon. "I thought you *maed* might like a snack."

"I didn't realize you were back," Anna Mae said. She gestured to Bekah. "You know Bekah Yoder, *ya*?" At Judith's nod, she asked, "Why don't you join us?"

"I don't want to intrude."

"You're not intruding." She rose and pulled out another chair. They spent the next hour visiting, avoiding any touchy subjects and just having a good time.

When it was time for Bekah to leave, Anna Mae walked her to the buggy. "I'm glad you came by," she said, giving her a hug. "I really needed this."

Bekah hugged her back. "Me too. You've given me a lot to think about."

"Does it have to do with Caleb?"

"Maybe," she said coyly. "I'll see you later." She waved as she got into the buggy.

Before Anna Mae turned to go inside, she looked at the Mullets' house at the same moment Amos came out of the barn. He'd been in there for over an hour, and Anna Mae was sure he'd added something new to the amazing mural of his life. As if he'd sensed she was watching, he looked over and waved.

Sweet, sweet Amos. He didn't worry if people accepted him, and not everyone did. He didn't fret over the future; he lived in the moment. The things that did bother him—his father and Jeremiah fighting, for one—sprang from him loving others, not a focus on himself.

She'd do well to follow his example. Everyone would.

"I win!" Amos's booming voice sounded from the living room downstairs.

David sat on the edge of his bed, his hands pressing on the mattress, the one he had bought almost twenty-five years ago when he and Marie had gotten married. Jeremiah had surprised him tonight by coming over to see Amos. Of course, Amos had invited him to play checkers with them, but David had refused. Amos didn't understand. Neither did Jeremiah.

Maybe they didn't remember, or in Jeremiah's case, refused to. How their mother used to play games with them when they were little. How she took so much care cutting their hair, making their clothes, preparing their favorite foods. Just seeing a checkerboard brought back memories he kept running away from. Memories that wouldn't stop chasing him down.

He opened the drawer in the nightstand next to

his bed. It was nearly empty. He didn't have many things, and what little he did have served him fine. Marie had been the collector. Candles she never lit, fabric for quilts she never made, cookbooks filled with recipes she never prepared. When he'd realized she was never coming back, he'd boxed up all those things and thrown them in the trash. A waste, he realized now. But back then he'd wanted it all out of his sight.

David looked at the three letters in the drawer. They had come the day before, postmarked from some city in California he'd never heard of. But he recognized the handwriting. His knees had buckled when he pulled them out of the mailbox.

One addressed to him. One to Amos. And one to Jeremiah.

He pulled them out and held them in his hand. Now would be the time to give them to the boys. He stopped himself. *Men.* His sons had grown into fine men, despite neither of them turning out the way he had imagined when he held them in his arms after they were born. He'd had hopes for them both, for their family. For the grandchildren he'd thought he'd have someday.

But God had a way of changing plans. Of taking a straight road and twisting it into a pretzel, a maze, and finally a crooked slope that crashed into a dead end. This was his life. Caring for his disabled son. Remaining distant from his other one.

Never being with a woman again. Never finding that kind of comfort, touch, and love.

He ran his hand over the letter with his name on it. He hadn't opened it. What could be in here that would change anything? Didn't want to hear her apologies. Didn't want to know if she was asking for forgiveness.

Because he didn't want to give it to her.

Tossing the letters back where they'd been hidden away, he slammed the drawer shut and went to the bedroom window. He put his arm above his head and leaned on the frame. The window looked out the front of the house, and he saw Jeremiah leaving. He skipped down the steps wearing his Yankee clothes and driving that wreck he called a car. David had driven a few cars in his younger days, not that he would tell Jeremiah that.

Jeremiah opened the car door, paused, and looked over at Judith's house. But not because he was interested in whatever Judith was doing. He was hesitating because of Anna Mae.

David jerked away from the window. Was Jeremiah the reason Anna Mae wasn't joining the church? He'd heard about that at the service this morning. Had he convinced her to leave the *Amisch*? He wasn't content enough to break up his own family? He had to fracture another one?

He balled his hands into clenched fists, feeling like his blood was boiling inside. He wouldn't let this happen. He wouldn't let her destroy any-one else. Marie wouldn't get away with it—

He froze. Looked down at his clenched fists, then out the window to see Jeremiah get into his car and drive away. Turning away from the window, he sat down on the bed again, his entire body shaking.

CHAPTER 17

Anna Mae stirred her tea, the spoon clinking against the cup. Not a night owl this time, Judith had gone to bed several hours ago. But Anna Mae couldn't sleep.

A knock sounded on the kitchen door. She rose, frowning. Who would be here at this time of night? When she looked through the window in the door, she saw Jeremiah standing there, holding two Styrofoam cups. She couldn't help but smile as she swung open the door. "How did you know I'd be up?"

"I took a guess." He held out one cup. "Don't worry. It's decaf. Two sugars and a cream, just like you like it, right? I noticed the other night at the farm."

Anna Mae took the cup from him and let him inside. She briefly thought about what her mother would say. She and Jeremiah together, alone even though Judith was just upstairs, late at night. But she wasn't beholden to her mother or the church rules anymore. She could do whatever she wanted, and her mother would never know.

Yet Anna Mae would know. *God* would know.

She kept her distance from Jeremiah, moving to the other side of the small kitchen table. "I haven't seen you for days. Why are you here now?"

"I'm worried about you." He looked down at his coffee. "Okay, that's not completely true." He gazed at her. "I wanted to see you." He set the cup on the table. "Anna Mae, I think it's time we're honest with each other."

She gripped the back of the chair. "About what?"

"Us."

She froze. "I . . . I don't know what you're talking about."

He rounded the table, his eyes never leaving hers. "Are you sure?"

Backing away, she said, "Jeremiah, what are you doing?"

"Nothing you don't want me to." He took her head in his hands and leaned forward, his mouth hovering over hers.

"Jeremiah," she whispered.

"Anna Mae . . . Anna Mae . . ."

"Anna Mae!"

Her eyes flew open to see Judith standing next to her. Anna Mae lifted her head off her arms, which had been resting on the kitchen table.

Judith put her hand on Anna Mae's shoulder. "Are you awake now?"

She'd been dreaming? She stared at the cup of tea, trying to get her bearings—and hide her embarrassment. "What time is it?"

"Four in the morning. I went to bed so early last night that I'm wide-awake now."

Anna Mae rubbed the back of her aching neck. "I couldn't sleep. The last thing I remember is making that cup of tea."

Judith picked it up. "It's cold now." She walked to the sink. "That must have been some dream. I had to say your name a few times before you'd wake up."

Her face heated, and she looked away from Judith. Faded images of the dream lingered in her mind. What had triggered it? She'd thought about Jeremiah over the past few days, but not in the romantic sense. Apparently her heart had other ideas.

"I'm making pancakes this morning," Judith said. "I thought I'd take some over to Amos and David in a little while."

Anna Mae rubbed her eyes, hoping to erase the dream from her memory even as unfamiliar—and pleasant—emotions remained. "I can help."

"All right. But first, *kaffee*." Judith filled the percolator coffeepot with water and set it on the stove. She turned on the gas burner underneath, then sat down across from Anna Mae.

Anna Mae took a napkin out of the holder on the table and began to fold it. "Judith, do you mind if I ask your opinion about something?"

"Of course not." She smiled.

"What do you think about me getting a GED?"

"You want to *geh* to college?"

She creased the napkin. "*Ya*. I think I do. But I'd have to study and take the GED test before I can focus on college."

"Sounds like you've been thinking about this for a while."

"Thinking . . . praying . . ." She matched the corners of the napkin until they formed a triangle. "You've been kind to let me stay, but I have to start acting on *mei* future."

"Have you talked to Jeremiah about this?"

Her head snapped up. "Why would I talk to him?"

"He's been through the process. He'd be able to help you. Give you advice."

Rubbing her palm on the napkin, Anna Mae said, "I don't know if that's a *gut* idea."

"Why not? I thought you were friends."

"We are." She paused. "I think."

"I see." Judith got up and moved behind Anna Mae.

What did she mean by that? Anna Mae whirled around in her chair. "Jeremiah and I have had our problems recently. But we're okay now." So okay that he hadn't stopped by to see her. Not that she wanted him to. But her dream said otherwise.

She was *so* confused.

"Sugar and cream in your *kaffee*?" Judith asked as she took two mugs from a cabinet.

"Please." Anna Mae rose from her chair. "I think we're at a *gut* place, Jeremiah and I," she said, as if stating the words out loud would make them true.

"Is that so?" Judith turned and leaned against the counter, waiting for the coffee to be ready.

"*Ya*. We won't ever be as close as we were when we were younger—"

"Because people change," Judith added.

"Right. They grow up. They have different priorities."

"And different feelings."

Anna Mae paused, the napkin still in her hands now crumpled. "You could say that."

Judith's lips curled into a slight smile. "Have your feelings changed for him?"

"That's a pretty personal question."

"Sorry. I don't mean to pry." Judith turned to check the coffeepot. "But I sense you have something on your mind, and it's more than taking a test."

Anna Mae stilled.

Judith turned toward Anna Mae and put a hand on her shoulder. "I'm glad you're making some decisions about going forward with your life.

From what I can tell, you've been at a standstill for a while."

"But?"

"But . . . before you can move forward, you have to make peace with your past. You need to settle things with Jeremiah. You need to talk to *yer* parents. You weren't thinking of leaving Middlefield without seeing them again, were you?" She dropped her hand and waited.

Until Judith mentioned it, Anna Mae hadn't realized that the thought had crossed her mind. It would be easier if she didn't have to face her mother and father. If she could forget about kissing Jeremiah and ruining their friendship. She could leave, put the past behind her, and start her new life . . . the same way Jeremiah did.

Yet she knew firsthand how much pain that caused. And she and David and Amos weren't the only ones who had suffered. Jeremiah had too. Could she really do that to her family and friends?

Judith poured coffee into both mugs, handed one to Anna Mae, and said, "I better get started on those pancakes."

Anna Mae nodded. She sat back down at the table and swiped one hand across it. She knew Judith was right. "I'm afraid," she whispered thickly.

Judith came up behind her and gently put her hands on Anna Mae's shoulders. "I know," she said quietly. "We're always afraid of the unknown. That's why you need to prepare yourself. Spend more time in prayer. Be open with God. Tell him your fears and worries. Most important, be open to listening to him." She put her arm around Anna Mae's shoulder, leaned down, and gave her a squeeze. "I'll be praying for you too."

Anna Mae turned and hugged Judith back. "*Danki*," she said into her soft shoulder. "For everything."

Judith patted her on the back. "You don't have to thank me." She pulled back from Anna Mae and touched her cheek. "It's why I'm here."

Bekah stood at the edge of the corral and watched as Caleb brought Promise out from the barn. She smiled. It was good to see the horse healthy again. And she was such a beautiful animal. She wished she could ride her someday, but knew she couldn't. And she was content with that.

The past couple of days she'd spent time reflecting and praying, thinking about her life in ways she hadn't before. She couldn't remember the last time she had been still and just listened to what God had to say. At first she had trouble calming her mind, but now she was spending regular prayer time in the morning and really focusing on God.

She had to accept herself; that was true. But there were also things she needed to change. Her attitude toward Caleb was a good place to start. He had his opinion of her, and she couldn't change that. But she could change her own behavior. She could stop being so self-centered. So selfish. She could live the way her faith directed her, the way she'd promised to live when she joined the church.

Caleb let go of Promise's bridle, and she joined the other horses under the shade of a huge maple tree at the other side of the corral.

Bekah turned at the sound of a car pulling into the driveway. At first she thought it might be Jeremiah, but she didn't recognize the car. A man stepped out of the vehicle and headed for the front door of the house.

Knowing Katie and Johnny had gone out for the day—they didn't say where and Bekah didn't ask—she hurried to intercept the stranger. "Can I help you?"

He glanced around the farm and nodded, an old baseball cap shading his eyes from the bright sun. "I'm looking for Caleb Mullet."

"That's me." Caleb appeared beside them, brushing his hands together. Then he paused. "You're from the auction."

"Yeah. Jerry Freemont." He extended his hand to Caleb, who shook it. Jerry frowned, creases of weariness evident around his eyes. "I've got some bad news about those horses I sold you."

"They were poisoned," Bekah blurted. Caleb

258

shot her a look. She shut her mouth and took a step back.

Jerry rubbed his eyes. "So they got sick too."

"Very sick," Caleb said. "But they're healthy now."

Relief crossed Jerry's face. "Thank God. Not all the horses were as lucky."

Bekah reeled at the news that some poisoned horses didn't make it. She looked over at the herd under the tree, thanking God for sparing them.

"I've been tracking down everyone who bought from me at the auction. I promise I didn't know they were poisoned when I sold them."

Caleb remained stone-faced. "What happened?"

"Little over a year ago I bought some new property. Wanted to expand my business a bit. It's a beautiful place, on the surface. What the guy who sold it to me didn't say was that it had been a dumping ground for chemical waste in the sixties. Apparently that stuff doesn't go away. It ended up making the pasture toxic, which gave the horses lead poisoning." He sighed. "It happened so slowly I didn't notice it until my own herd started getting sick. That's when I found out. I'm really sorry."

His expression softening, Caleb said, "It's all right. I appreciate you telling us. We were wondering how they'd gotten sick because our feed and pastures are okay."

Jerry shoved his hand in the back pocket of his

jeans and pulled out a thick billfold. "I'm paying everyone back. Full price. This never should have happened, and I take full responsibility."

Caleb held out his hand. "You can keep your money."

Jerry's bushy eyebrows rose. "At least let me pay the vet bill."

"We've got it covered."

"Are you sure?" When Caleb nodded again, Jerry blew out a breath. "You're the second person who's said that to me today. This whole thing has put me out of business, at least for a while."

"Even more reason to keep your money." Caleb walked with Jerry to his car while Bekah held back. They said good-bye, and Jerry drove off.

Caleb walked toward her. She turned away, her eyes burning as she fought tears.

"Bekah?"

The soft tone of his voice both surprised and comforted her. She sniffed and turned around. "I'm sorry. But those poor horses . . ." She blinked.

He nodded. "I know. The *gut* thing about this is Jerry's making it right. Also, the horses weren't poisoned on purpose."

"I can't imagine someone would do anything so horrible." She glanced down at her feet.

"You really care," he said, sounding surprised.

"I do. I care about all animals." She managed a smile. "But horses are special."

"That they are." His gaze darted around before briefly landing on her. "I better get back to work." Caleb walked past her.

She hurried to catch up to him. "It's almost lunchtime. Do you want something to eat?"

He turned to her. "You're offering to make me lunch?"

She nodded. "I know that sandwich I made last week didn't turn out very *gut*. And I do have a little problem with making *kaffee* too strong. But I promise this time I'll make you something better."

He eyed her for a moment. "Don't worry about it. I'll get something later." He walked toward the toolshed on the opposite side of the yard.

She felt the pinch of hurt at his rejection of her offer. However, she smiled. She wasn't letting this get her down.

She'd make him the best lunch he'd ever had.

What was that about?

Caleb walked into the coolness of the toolshed, more to escape Bekah than to retrieve a tool. He leaned against the dusty workbench. The place needed a good cleaning, but he and Johnny hadn't had the time. It was another thing on a long list of unending chores that still needed to be done. But he didn't mind. After going through the nightmare of almost losing his herd, everything else seemed inconsequential.

Except for Bekah.

He took off his straw hat and tossed it on the bench. He'd managed to avoid her since their hug in the barn last week. And since he'd let his feelings overcome him. Fortunately she hadn't seemed to notice that he had whispered her name—and kissed her ear, of all the silly things.

But holding her like that . . . He looked down at his arms. They felt empty even now.

He had to get things back on an even keel, and the easiest way to do that was to stay away from her. That had proved harder than he thought since Katie had needed her help so much. For good reason. Although Johnny and Katie hadn't said anything, Caleb knew Katie was pregnant. Today they had taken great pains to hide the fact they were going to the doctor. But having two significantly younger brothers, Caleb knew the signs. Between Katie's energy slowing, her constant munching on saltine crackers, and frequent trips to the bathroom—though she had seemed a little better the last few days—it was hard not to see the obvious. If Bekah knew, she was keeping quiet about it. Caleb would do the same.

He plopped down on the bench. She was driving him crazy . . . in a good way. And a bad one. When had he become attracted to her? Was it seeing her devotion to Promise? How she cared for her sister? Her ability to be serious and capable when she needed to be?

Since that ordeal—and even before that, he had to admit—she'd helped Katie, working in the house and the kitchen without complaint. And while the few suppers she made weren't up to par with Katie's, they weren't *that* bad. But she'd changed in other ways since their experience with the horses, like now. She was *offering* to make him lunch? Why would she do that?

Unless she wanted something. His eyes widened. He knew what that was, and he was going to make sure she understood that he wouldn't allow it.

He grabbed his hat and went into the house. "Bekah?" he called as he headed for the kitchen. He walked into the room and saw her cutting dough for biscuits.

"*Ya*?"

"I know what you're doing."

"Making biscuits," she said, looking a bit confused. She lifted up her hands, which were coated with globs of dough. "I don't think they're supposed to be this sticky."

He glanced at the slightly misshapen biscuits on the baking tray. He loved biscuits, especially smothered with butter and honey. He moved toward her. "It's not going to work."

"They might turn out. I think I need more flour." She reached into the canister and pulled out a healthy pinch.

"Bekah, stop."

She looked up at him, frowning. "What's wrong, Caleb?"

"This." He gestured to the mess on the table before pointing at her. "You!"

Bekah stepped back, her bottom lip shaking a bit. "What did I do?"

"Oh, you know exactly what you're doing. Cleaning house, washing windows, making food from scratch. You detest all that."

"Caleb, I—"

"And besides helping Katie, there's only one reason you would do any of it. You want something." He stepped closer to her until they were almost touching. Anger rose within him, and an attraction he had to fight. He wouldn't be used . . . and he wouldn't be made a fool of. "You're not going to ride her."

"What are you talking about?"

"Promise. She's off-limits. All the horses are." He leaned over her. "Am I making myself clear? Don't *geh* anywhere near them. Ever."

Bekah didn't say anything for a long while. She just looked at him, her bottom lip quivering. Then she rushed out of the kitchen.

He turned in time to hear the back screen door slam shut. Where was the argument he'd expected? The denial? The excuses?

Caleb looked at the table, covered in flour and dough. Among the mess he saw a recipe card. Fried chicken. Another one of his favorites.

She sure was planning to butter him up good.

Dread mixed with a good dose of guilt gathered inside him. She'd never reacted like that before. And she'd never run off like a wounded animal. Bekah Yoder always stood her ground, even if she was wrong.

Caleb slammed his palm on the table. Flour flew up in a puff around him. He'd messed up. Somehow he'd have to fix it.

Bekah plopped on the bank of the pond, tears streaming down her face. What a fool she'd been. Caleb couldn't stand her. Worse, he thought she was underhanded. Which she had been, before. She had no one to blame but herself for his opinion of her.

The dough was drying and getting hard on her hands. She started to pick at it, then gave up. What was she going to do now? Her heart felt squeezed in her chest. The pain and rejection seeped into every fiber of her body. She'd never experienced this kind of heartache.

"Bekah?"

The sound of his low voice startled her, but she didn't turn around. Was he here to rub it in? To tell her to get back in the kitchen and clean up her mess? To make extra sure she knew exactly where she stood with him?

Rising from the grass, she kept her head down as she turned around, rubbing her eye with the back of her hand. "I'm sorry. I shouldn't have run out and left the kitchen a mess. I'll take care of it right now." But when she tried to move past him, Caleb blocked her way.

"Bekah."

She looked up at him. He'd left his hat at the house, and his hair was a wild mess. She longed to run her fingers through it, to try to tame the wayward strands. She shook her head. How could she be thinking such intimate thoughts about him right now? Yet she couldn't stop her mind—or her heart.

"I'm sorry," he said.

"It's okay. You had a right to say those things. I know sneaking off and riding the horse was wrong." Bekah looked up at him, straightening her shoulders a bit. "For the record, I wasn't trying to get you to let me ride Promise. I wouldn't want anything to happen to her, or any of the horses. I know how important they are to you now."

"You do?"

"*Ya*. And"—she swallowed—"I respect you for it." As she spoke, a weight she hadn't even known she'd been carrying seemed to lift, and tears came to her eyes. She wasn't crying out of hurt any-more, but because she was finally, after all these years, doing right by Caleb. He deserved her respect, not her scorn. "I promise from now on I'll stay out of your way. You don't have to worry about me bothering you, or causing trouble. That's the last thing I want to do." She didn't wait for his reaction, just stepped to the side of him and hurried back toward the house.

But he lightly caught her arm. "Bekah, wait."

She glanced at his hand. He wasn't hurting her, but he was making sure she didn't leave.

"I . . ." He licked his lips. "I shouldn't have assumed that you were trying to do something sneaky. I jumped to a conclusion and I shouldn't have. And I'm . . . I'm sorry."

She looked up at him as he let her go. The hard expression he'd worn for so long every time he was around her had softened, melting her heart. To hide any hint of those emotions, she looked down and focused on brushing the dried dough off her hands. But it stuck to her skin like a fly to flypaper. After she struggled for a few moments, Caleb took her by the hand and led her to the pond.

He didn't say anything as he gently pulled her down with him and kneeled against the edge. He cupped his hand and scooped up some water, then rubbed it over the dough on her hands.

"I can do this," she said, and started to pull away. He held on tighter.

"Let me."

As Caleb washed the dough off her hands, her skin tingled. When he was done, he sat back on the grass, placing his wrists on top of his bent knees and staring at the rippling pond water, seemingly unaffected by the intimate gesture they'd just shared.

"That's the nicest thing anyone's done for me," Bekah said.

Caleb glanced at her. "Then I need to start being a lot nicer to you." He started to get up. "I better head back. I've got a lot of chores left to do today."

She stood, wiping her damp hands on the skirt of her dress. She began to nod, then stopped. "We should *geh* fishing," she blurted.

Caleb arched a brow. "Fishing?"

"After supper tonight. We haven't done that in years." She smiled. "It will be fun."

He looked hesitant. "Maybe . . . if I get all my work done."

She moved closer to him. "Caleb, the work can wait. When have you taken time to relax? To live in the moment? To enjoy yourself?"

"It's been awhile."

"Then it's settled. I'll meet you right here at 6:30 p.m." She eyed him. "Don't be late." With that she turned and walked away.

"Sounds like I don't have a choice!" he hollered after her as she strolled back through the woods.

Bekah jumped over a thin-trunked fallen tree, grinning. She just hoped he wouldn't be too mad when she caught more fish than he did.

CHAPTER 18

Jeremiah stroked the back of the enormous Maine Coon cat who surprisingly seemed to enjoy the petting even though she was on the examination table. The cat moved closer to him, rubbing her face against his white lab coat. "She's friendly," he said to the Amish woman who had brought the cat in earlier. Her young daughter stood close beside her, glancing up at Jeremiah with round, hazel-colored eyes.

"*Ya*. She's always been that way."

"She's *mei* kitty," the girl piped up in *Deitsch*.

Jeremiah responded in kind. "She's a great cat. You must love her very much." The girl's eyes widened, and she tugged on her mother's dress. The woman leaned down as the young girl whispered in her ear. "Sorry about that," she said as she straightened. "Hannah is surprised you know *Deitsch*."

"I don't speak it very often anymore." He felt along the cat's belly, which was hidden by massive amounts of fur. He looked at the little girl. "Can you help me get your kitty to lie on her side?"

The girl nodded and stood by the examination table. It was low enough that she could reach up and scratch the cat's lower back. The cat immediately collapsed onto its side, facing the young girl. "She likes to be scratched."

"Then you keep scratching her while I look at her belly." He parted the hair and saw the problem that had made them bring the cat to the vet—a large, but not significant, papilloma. He combed back the fur with his fingers. "You can hold her now, Hannah."

Hannah picked up the huge cat and snuggled her close. "Is she going to be okay?"

"She'll be fine." He turned to the mother. "The bump is nothing to worry about. There's a few more of them on her skin, but unless they get irritated we'll just leave them alone."

He could see the relief on the woman's face. She turned to her daughter. "Can you take Buster out in the waiting room while I talk to Dr. Mullet?"

As the little girl left, Jeremiah turned to wash his hands at the small sink in the exam room. "Interesting name for a female cat," he remarked, smiling.

"Hannah named her before we had a chance to tell her she was a girl. She refused to name her anything else. *Mei dochder* can be very stubborn. She insisted we bring Buster in to be checked. She wouldn't stop fretting about her until we did." A worried expression came over her face. "How much do I owe you?"

He grabbed a paper towel and dried his hands. "Nothing."

"But I have to pay you something."

"Not this time. The first visit is free of charge."

She finally smiled. "*Danki*."

"You're welcome. Both of you have a great day."

"You, too, Dr. Mullet."

The mother had just walked out the door when Doc Miller came in from the back of the clinic. "First visit is free?" Doc said, peering at Jeremiah over his glasses.

"I know. Not your standard operating procedure."

"If it was I'd be in the poorhouse."

"I was going to pay for their visit." He looked at the closed door. "She seemed worried about the cost."

Doc slapped him on the back. "I've done that a time or two myself," he admitted. "Some things are more important than money."

Jeremiah nodded. When he'd arrived in Middlefield almost two weeks ago, he'd been worried about his bills, especially his loans. But since then he'd thought very little about them. God had provided him with enough money to pay for his room and board, the gas in his car, and one loan payment. He needed little else for now.

"Do you have some time to talk?" Doc said. "I checked with Amy and there aren't any appointments this afternoon."

"Sure. Let me wipe down the table and I'll meet

you in your office." Usually the veterinarian tech took care of that job, but Doc's tech had left the job soon after Jeremiah arrived. Amy had been filling in for the time being. Since she had enough work to do, it wasn't a big deal for him to clean the exam room himself.

A short time later he walked into Doc's office, which, as usual, looked like a windstorm had swirled through it. But Doc knew where every invoice, bill, and catalog was in the place. The mess drove his wife crazy, but Amy kept her own small space for the clinic's accounting in a corner behind the counter.

"Sit down," Doc said, leaning back in his rickety office chair.

Jeremiah lowered himself in another chair that had seen better days. Doc and Amy lived almost as simply as any Amish family he'd ever known. "Is everything okay?"

"Yes. It's great. Leg is feeling better every day." He tapped his cast. "I get this thing off in a couple of weeks, and I'm hoping to transition to a cane." His expression sobered. "Speaking of transitions, I have a business proposal I'd like to discuss with you."

"Oh?"

Doc folded his hands over his belly. "It's no secret I've been slowing down over the past couple of years. I hate admitting that out loud, but Amy's right. It's time I faced facts—I can't do this job for much longer. It's time for me to retire."

"I'm sorry to hear that."

"Hey, I'm not saying I won't practice a bit of it here and there. I just can't run the clinic anymore. Frankly, Amy's tired of it. She'd like to travel. And we both want to see our daughter more often. The grandkids aren't getting any younger, and Arizona is far away."

"I understand."

"I knew you would. Now that you've had a chance to work here in your own capacity, I thought you might be game for taking over the clinic yourself."

Jeremiah didn't answer. He'd thought that was what Doc would ask him when he started talking about retirement. "I don't know what to say."

"Yes would be nice." Doc chuckled, but his eyes remained serious. "I understand you need to think about it." He sat up and leaned forward. "If this helps, there isn't anyone else I'd rather have take over this business. I built it from the ground up over thirty years ago. Poured my heart and soul into it." Doc cleared his throat. "You're like a son to me, Jeremiah. Having you take over the clinic would be like it staying in the family. And I know I would be leaving it in good hands."

A little stunned by Doc's heartfelt admission, Jeremiah searched for the right words to say. Doc wasn't the sentimental type. Much like Jeremiah's father. The men had more in common than either of them knew. "I'm glad you have so much confi-dence in me."

"I'm not the only one. Johnny Mullet came by a few days ago to specifically sing your praises."

"I thought he came by to pay his bill."

"That too," Doc said wryly. "But he couldn't stop telling me how much he appreciated what you did for their herd and their business. Said you were the best vet he'd worked with. Next to me, of course." Doc grinned.

Jeremiah lifted a brow. "You realize Johnny and I are cousins, right? He was being nice to family."

"He was being honest." Doc shook his head. "You Amish and your humility. It's a great thing, but learn to take a compliment every once in a while."

"Some habits are hard to break." Jeremiah might not be Amish anymore, but there were many aspects to his faith and upbringing that he would never leave behind. They were as ingrained in him as the desire to eat and sleep.

"I want you to consider my offer," Doc continued. "Really think about it for a few days. Or a few weeks. It's a big decision, and there's no rush." He pushed up from the chair and grabbed his crutches. "I'll be glad to get rid of these things." He paused and looked at Jeremiah. "Why don't you take the afternoon off?"

Jeremiah shook his head. "I've got things to do around here. Inventory, for one thing."

"Amy and I can do that. It's a slow day, and you haven't had any time off since you got here. If there are any emergencies, I'll give you a call. "

"But—"

"Don't make me close the clinic, now. I'm still the boss, you know."

"All right." Jeremiah grinned. "I'll go."

"See you tomorrow, then."

Jeremiah left the clinic and walked to his car. He opened the door and let the hot air out of the interior. The day had started warm and was turning into sweltering. But the weather wasn't on his mind. Neither was taking over Doc's business. One phrase kept repeating in his mind.

You're like a son to me.

He stared at the windshield of his car. Jeremiah had a better relationship with his employer than with his own father. That's not how it was supposed to be. He and *Daed* had exchanged a handful of words over the past month. Their relationship was so broken . . . but he had no idea how to repair it.

One step at a time . . .

He nodded as the words appeared in his mind. Ignoring his father wasn't going to help anything. Jeremiah was in the wrong and he knew it. As he got in the car, he knew what the first step would be—an apology.

But there was another reason he was going to his father's house. Work had been so busy during the past few days, but Anna Mae hadn't been far from his mind. After he talked to his father, he would go next door and check on her. He had wanted to give her space after he dropped her off at Judith's last week, and he had prayed for her every day. Maybe by now she'd be ready to see him.

A short time later he was pulling into his father's driveway. Before he lost his courage, he got out of the car and went to the front door. Instead of knocking as he usually did, he walked inside.

He could hear voices coming from the kitchen. He went back there and entered the room. He stopped at the sight of not only his brother and father having lunch but Judith and Anna Mae joining them.

"Hi, Jeremiah!" Amos's smile filled his face. "You came for lunch today!"

Jeremiah looked at the cozy scene. An unexpected lump formed in his throat. Judith was seated at the opposite end of the table, where his mother used to sit. The table was laden with delicious-smelling food—potato salad, fried chicken, corn on the cob, thick slices of bread. Not the usual cobbled-together meals he and Amos had grown up with. For a moment he flashed back to his childhood, when he and Amos were little, before his mother left. When his father used to smile and laugh. When they were all a family.

His mother's face floated in front of him.

"You made another A in school?" *Mamm* rubbed his arm, her pretty smile lighting up her eyes. "That's *mei* smart *sohn*."

"I drew a picture," Amos said, shoving a piece of paper in front of her. The three of them were in the kitchen, with her seated at the table and the boys flanking her.

"What a wonderful daisy." His mother brought it close to her face. "It's so real looking I can almost smell it." She looked at Amos and cradled his cheek. "God has given you a gift, *lieb*."

"You mean like a present?" Amos said, his eyes growing wide. "I'm going to get presents?"

She laughed. "*Nee*. This gift is more special than any present I could give you." She turned to Jeremiah, her expression sobering. "God has blessed you, too, Jeremiah. No matter what happens, don't you forget that. He loves you both very much."

His vision cleared, revealing four pairs of eyes staring at him. He hadn't thought about that time in the kitchen in years. That happened only a couple of months before their mother left.

"I'm sorry I interrupted," Jeremiah said, backing away. "I should have . . . knocked . . . or something." The kitchen seemed to squeeze in on him. "I'll come back another time."

"Jeremiah?" Amos called out after him.

Covered in memories of the past, many of them

he had buried deep, he ignored his brother and stumbled onto the front porch, gulping in the hot summer air. The force of the past had blindsided him. But why?

He spun around at the sound of the screen door opening. Expecting Amos, he was surprised to see Anna Mae come outside. "Are you okay?" she asked, standing beside him.

Turning from her, he said, "I don't know."

Anna Mae touched Jeremiah's shoulder. She had never seen him so upset. All her trepidation about talking to him, about the kiss and the past, disappeared. His face was stark white, the stubble on his chin and cheeks standing out in little black dots. It was almost as if he'd seen a ghost.

She sucked in a breath. *Or the past.*

"Jeremiah." She moved closer to him, grasping his hand. "Let's go."

"Where?" he said, sounding numb.

"Anywhere but here."

Anna Mae led him to his car, still holding his hand. His breathing had slowed a bit. "Are you okay to drive?"

He nodded.

She opened the driver's side door. "Then get in."

He got behind the wheel, and she jumped into the passenger seat.

"Where . . . ?"

"I don't know. Just drive."

Jeremiah steered the car onto the road and drove. Anna Mae kept an eye on him to make sure he was still steady. The farther they got from the house, the more relaxed he seemed to get. When he had finally released his white-knuckled grip on the steering wheel, she spoke. "We can pull over somewhere," she said. "Whenever you're ready."

"I know where I'm going now." He didn't elaborate, and she didn't ask. But as soon as he turned onto an isolated dirt road, she knew exactly where he was headed.

He glanced at her, and she was glad to see the wild look in his eyes had disappeared.

Ten minutes later they stopped in front of a tiny *Amisch* cemetery. He pulled up the lever that put the car in park and looked at her. "I won't be long. I'll keep the engine on so the air conditioner will keep running."

She reached over and turned the key toward him, shutting off the car. "I'm going with you," she said. "We can visit both of them together."

He nodded, and they exited the car. When he reached for her hand, she didn't pull away. They walked among the simply marked graves until they stopped at one in the middle of the cemetery. Jeremiah let go of her hand and knelt down on the grass in front of his grandmother's gravestone.

Anna Mae kneeled beside him. "Were you thinking about her back at the house?"

"No," he sighed. "I was thinking about *Mamm*."

"Then what brought you here?"

Jeremiah reached out and touched the grass covering Ella's grave. "For so many years, she *was* my mom. She raised Amos and me after *Mamm* left." He paused. "I knew she would be buried next to *Grossvatter*," he said.

"It was her last request."

Jeremiah sat back on his knees. "I was so wrong not to come to her funeral." He looked at Anna Mae, his eyes dry but filled with sorrow. "She was so good to us. She supported me when I told Dad I wanted to be a vet. She made sure Amos had paper and pens and crayons so he could draw." He looked at her grave again. "And I didn't come back to tell her good-bye."

Anna Mae's heart went out to him. "I'm sure she understood."

"You didn't understand. *Daed* didn't." He looked at Anna Mae. "Don't you see? I'm a coward. Like my mother. She never said good-bye either."

She didn't know what to say. She'd never seen him so vulnerable, even after his mother left. He had been strong, even as a young boy. She realized he'd had to be, for both Amos's and his father's sakes.

"I know why she didn't," he said, running his fingers over the corner of the gravestone. His voice faltered. "It hurts to say good-bye. It's easier to leave, to put the past behind and forget about it. To pretend it never existed." He choked. "But it's always there, no matter how much you pack it down inside you."

"Jeremiah," she said with a choked whisper, realizing that he wasn't talking about leaving her or being here for *Grossmutter* Ella's funeral. "I'm so sorry she hurt you."

He sniffed. "And I turn around and do it to the people I care about." He angled his body toward her. "Anna Mae, I should have told you good-bye. But I needed to get out of here. Away from . . . everything."

"Including me?"

He shook his head. "No, not you. Not Amos. But I couldn't take you two with me. You belonged here." He paused. "At least that's what I thought. I didn't know you wanted to leave."

"I wasn't as sure as you were at the time. You were running toward something, Jeremiah. Not just escaping here."

"There's no escape, Anna Mae. The pain haunts you, no matter where you go or what you focus on. It's always hovering in the background, coloring everything." He took her hand in his. "I found her, you know."

"*Yer mamm*?"

"Right before I graduated. I wrote her. I thought she could come to the ceremony, and afterward we could talk. I'd tell her I understood—not why she left, but the way she did. I could tell her she was right about Amos's gift." He drew in a breath. "I could have told her lots of things."

"She didn't show up?"

"No." He let go of her hand. "She didn't. She wasn't that hard to track down, once I figured out she was in California. But all I had was an address, not her phone number. I thought she would have at least called me when I gave her mine. Sent a card . . . something."

At a loss, Anna Mae looked at the grave in front of her. What could she tell him that would lessen the blow of a mother's abandonment? Not once, but twice? What would dissolve the pain he'd tried so hard to flee?

"Funny thing is, I came over today to talk to my dad. Not about Mom, but to try to work things out between us. I've been avoiding him. I wanted to talk to him. Then I saw all of you at the table and all the memories came flooding back. I just had to get out of there." He looked at the gravestone. "Didn't realize I'd end up here." He stood and held out his hand. "We should visit Bertha too."

They crossed the graveyard to Anna Mae's grandmother's grave. She noticed he didn't let go of her hand, and she didn't want him to. They stood, the summer heat pounding on their heads, sweat dripping down Anna Mae's back. "I remember when I found her diary. I had *nee* idea Ella and she had ever been friends."

"They didn't act like it," Jeremiah said. "But they eventually forgave each other."

"And became inseparable." She swallowed. "She died a month after *yer grossmutter* did."

"I didn't know that."

She turned to him. "You're right about talking to *yer daed*. You two need to work out your problems."

He squeezed her hand. "You're doing it again."

"Doing what?"

His gaze locked with hers. "Saying the right thing. Being here for me. Just like when we were kids."

They looked at each other for a long time. She could see the perspiration on his forehead from the heat. He'd gotten another haircut since she'd last seen him. Short on the sides and the back and sticking up randomly on top. She remembered when she had been in his arms. He had comforted her. How she longed to be that close to him, only this time to comfort him.

"We should get back," he suddenly said, looking away. "I don't want my dad to think I kidnapped you." He let go of her hand and put his hands in his pockets. "He probably blames me for you deciding to leave the church."

"Why do you think so?"

He shrugged. "A gut feeling, I guess. Or it could be I just assume he blames me for everything."

They drove back to the house in silence. He

didn't say anything further about their discussion in the graveyard—or about when she had kissed him. They would have to talk about it eventually, because like everything else she and Jeremiah had tried to ignore and run away from in their lives, it would have a way of coming back at them.

Now wasn't the time. This was about Jeremiah's relationship with his father, not some desperate kiss he probably hadn't given a second thought about. Anna Mae prayed that he and his father could find some peace with the past—and with each other.

CHAPTER 19

Judith walked into her kitchen through the back door of her house. She'd left David's house shortly after Jeremiah and Anna Mae disappeared. Upset, Amos had gone out to the barn, his father close behind, leaving Judith alone in their kitchen. She cleaned up, praying for all three Mullet men and Anna Mae. She'd grown close to all of them, and their pain had become her own.

She went into the living room and looked at the bookcase against the wall, hoping to find something to read to take her mind off of everything. One bookshelf was filled solely with Bibles. Her Samuel had collected several of them over the years. He liked to compare the texts, often making notes in the margins as he studied. Her late husband could have easily been a scholar if he hadn't been *Amisch*. His personal Bible studies satisfied that yearning for knowledge that had never left him.

She turned away from the bookcase without selecting anything. Nothing appealed, and she was fooling herself if she thought reading would keep her from worrying over David and his family. At a loss, she got a dust cloth and started wiping down the furniture, even though she had dusted yesterday. She was straightening copies of *The Budget* on her coffee table when she heard a knock on the front door. "David?" she said as she opened the door.

He held his hat in his hands, a troubled, vulnerable look on his face. "Is that offer to talk still *gut*?"

"Of course."

After she'd fixed them both something to drink, she sat down next to him at the kitchen table. But she didn't say anything, waiting on him to talk when he was ready.

"I'm sorry about Jeremiah," he said.

"You don't need to apologize. Did he and Anna Mae come back?"

"Not yet. Amos is in the barn, keeping himself busy."

"It's *gut* you let him draw in there."

David looked at her. "It was *mei mutter*'s idea.

It keeps him busy. And happy." He took a drink of iced tea. "That's what I've always wanted for both of *mei buwe*. To be happy. At least one of them is."

"Jeremiah seems happy with his job."

"I guess." He put down the glass. "He's a lot like his *mutter*."

"Which is why you have trouble talking to him."

He didn't respond. She yearned to take his hand, to tell him everything would be all right. But that wasn't her place. She was here to listen.

"I've been keeping something from him," David said. "From both of them." He rubbed his wrinkled forehead with his work-roughened hand. "It's tearing me up inside."

"Then tell them. Whatever it is, they'll understand."

"It's not about understanding." He met Judith's gaze. "She's hurt them so much already."

Judith pulled back. "Marie."

David pulled three letters out of his pants pocket. They were folded in half. With slightly trembling hands he separated them. "I don't know what to do."

She looked at the envelopes, noting who they were addressed to and where they were from. There was no name in the left-hand corner, just a return address. "Are you sure they're from her?"

"I'd know her handwriting anywhere." He

picked up the letter addressed to him. "I haven't been able to bring myself to read it yet. Things weren't perfect between us. They hadn't been *gut* for a long time before she left. We could have worked it out, though. What made her leave is that she didn't want to be *Amisch*." He licked his lips. "She didn't want to stay." Pain pinched at Judith. Though she had prayed for years for a child, she had never been blessed with one. Yet this woman had left hers behind as if they were nothing more important than old furniture. But it wasn't her place to judge. "I'm sorry you had to *geh* through that."

"It was hard. When the *buwe* were older, I explained what I could to Jeremiah. He didn't say much and rarely brought up his *mamm* over the years. Amos didn't understand, and that's a blessing. *Mei mutter* moved in and took care of them. I wouldn't have been able to raise them without her help. When she passed away two years ago . . ." He looked down at the table.

Judith didn't say anything. She waited until he was able to collect his thoughts. He swallowed before he looked at her. "I've tried to do the best by *mei sohns*, Judith. I haven't always been the best *vatter*. But I love them."

"I know you do."

"And I knew I'd have to let Jeremiah *geh* someday. He was just like Marie. He looks like her. He's smart like she was. Some of the things he'd say . . . just the way he'd say them reminded me of her. It still does, even now."

"So you resented him for it. *Nee* one can blame you for that."

He shook his head. "*Nee*, that's not it. I liked seeing her in him. It was like a little piece of her was still around. I loved *mei* wife. I know she didn't love me as much, but I never stopped loving her."

Judith sat back, struggling with her own emotions. The depth of love this man possessed, that he would continue to love a woman who had abandoned him and his family . . . Did Marie have any idea how lucky she had been? Did she even give a thought to how much she'd hurt him? How she'd hurt her sons?

"When Jeremiah left, that part of her went with him. It was like losing her all over again. And losing him. I depended on him. He has *nee* idea how much I needed him. Not because of Amos. Amos will be fine. God is watching over him."

"*Ya*," she said, wiping a tear from her cheek. "He is."

"I needed Jeremiah for me. He was *mei* rock all those years." David stared out in front of him. "I never told him that. I never told him how . . . proud . . . I am of him." He met her gaze, his eyes heavy with hurt. "I've made so many mistakes."

"You've done the best you could."

He shook his head. "I should have done better."

She took a risk by putting her hand on his. To her surprise, he held on tight. "You've shown so much kindness to me and Amos, and you've asked so little in return." He gestured to the letters. "I thought about throwing them away. But that wouldn't be right." He picked up his letter again. "I don't want to read this alone," he whispered.

She clung to his hand, never wanting to let go. "You don't have to."

Carrying a fishing pole and a bucket of home-made bait, Bekah walked to the pond and sat down on the bank. She'd hoped Caleb would already be here. Katie had felt well enough to make dinner for them, which included the fried chicken and fluffy biscuits Bekah had planned to make for Caleb's lunch earlier in the day. Of course it was perfect and delicious, much better than Bekah would have managed. But that was okay with her. Cooking wasn't her gift.

But catching fish was.

She'd asked Katie to set aside some of the biscuit dough for bait. After adding some cheddar cheese, she had rolled it up into a few dozen balls. Even if they didn't use all the bait it would keep in the cooler for a couple of days.

Bekah laid the pole beside her, removed her shoes, and hugged her knees to her chest. She wouldn't start without him, but now he was late. He had almost inhaled his supper and quickly fled the kitchen, saying he had work to do. She hoped he was finishing up early so he could join her here at the appointed time.

Or maybe he was avoiding her again.

She sighed, glancing at the bait bucket. She should just go ahead. He wasn't going to come. She was fooling herself thinking he would. She lifted the lid off the container.

"Trying to get a head start?"

She looked to see Caleb striding toward her, carrying three fishing poles. "I wasn't sure you were coming."

"I had to find my lucky poles." He sat down next to her. "I still didn't find *mei* favorite one."

"Um, is this it?" She held up the pole she had grabbed out of the shed.

He nodded. "*Ya*. That's it."

"Here." She held it out to him.

He looked at it. "Nah. You use it. I'll be okay with these."

A few moments later Bekah had her line in the water while Caleb had set two of the poles down on the ground, the baited fishing wire hanging over the side of the bank. He held on to one pole, but could easily grab the others if they got a bite. She noticed he'd also brought a beat-up creel and put it in the water. "Feeling optimistic?" she asked.

"Very." He tugged on the line a little bit.

They sat there in near silence, the only sounds

the light chirping of birds and buzz of crickets. A couple of squirrels barked at each other in the woods. Bekah breathed in the scent of the pond water, the warm, fresh air surrounding them, and the cool, soft grass beneath her bare feet and legs.

"This is nice," he said. "I'm glad you suggested it."

Bekah curled her legs up underneath her skirt. "The fish don't seem to be biting, though."

"Give them time." Caleb glanced at her. "You may be *gut* at fishing, but you're a little too impatient."

"Me? I'm the ultimate example of patience." They both burst out laughing.

"Shh," he said. "We'll scare away the fish."

At that point she didn't care. It was just nice to be spending time with him without the oppressive tension and strain that had been between them for the past several years. She jerked her pole to the left a little, giving the fish something to chase after.

"When do you think they're going to tell us?" Caleb said suddenly.

"Who?"

"Katie and Johnny." He reeled in his line, then cast it out again.

"About the *boppli*?"

"You figured it out too."

She nodded. "It wasn't that hard." She smiled. "I'm going to be an *aenti*. Again."

291

"And I'll be an *onkel*." Caleb grinned. "Again."

"They're not fooling anyone, you know. I wouldn't be surprised if my mother suspects." Bekah felt something tug at her line. She pulled, then reeled it in. Or at least she tried. "I think it's stuck on something." She scrambled to her feet and tried again to reel in the line as she walked to the edge of the pond.

Caleb came up behind her. "Here, let me help."

"I've got it." She yanked on the pole. The tip of it bowed into an arch.

"Bekah, if you break *mei* favorite pole—"

"I'm not." She tugged again, without success. "Never mind. It's definitely stuck." She turned to Caleb and saw him tugging off one of his boots. "Oh no," she said, setting down the pole. "I got it stuck, so I'll get it out."

He yanked off the other boot and rolled up his pants leg. "Not if I get there first."

Bekah laughed and charged for the water, only to have Caleb's arm hook her around the waist and pull her back. She twisted in his arms to get free, but he slipped on the grass and they both fell to the ground.

They laughed, with her on top of him, their faces near each other. Then she saw his smile fade, his eyes darken. She felt his hand tighten at her waist. "Bekah," he whispered.

"I knew it," she said, placing her palms on his chest. "You did say *mei* name the other day."

"Bekah—"

"I bet you kissed me on the ear too. I thought I was just tired and imagining things but—"

He put his finger on her lips. "Will you be quiet for once?"

"Why?" she said, her words slightly muffled.

"So I can do this." He put his hand at the back of her head and guided her mouth to his. The kiss was quick, soft, sweet. And it took her breath away.

She felt the rise and fall of his chest underneath her. Then before she realized what was happening, he scooped her up and set her down beside him. She frowned. "What did I do wrong now?"

He shook his head. "*Nix*. I just think a little distance between us is a *gut* thing right now."

She looked at him for a moment. "Oh."

He lifted his head. "*Ya*."

She stared at the pond. "This wasn't what I had in mind when I invited you to *geh* fishing," she said.

"Me either."

"But . . . was it okay?"

He finally looked at her. "Better than okay."

She smiled, warmth traveling throughout her body. "What are we going to do now?"

He swung around and faced her. He looked so different, and it wasn't because he had grass sticking in his hair. The hardened expression she was so used to seeing on his face when they were together had softened, making him more appealing than ever before. "Things have been strange between us for a long time."

"I know," she admitted.

"I didn't think you paid much attention." He yanked out a piece of grass.

"That's true. I didn't pay attention. To your feelings or anyone else's. I should have been less selfish."

"You're not selfish." When she gave him a pointed look, he backtracked. "Well, sometimes. But we all are, at various times. None of us is perfect."

"Not even you?" she said, joking.

"Especially not me." He tossed the blade of grass to the side. "I haven't been a *gut* friend lately."

"Is that what we are?" She swallowed, her mouth growing dry. "Friends?" It seemed strange to ask him after that kiss, but she wasn't sure where they stood.

"*Nee*, Bekah. We're not friends. Not anymore."

"Ah." She thought about it for a moment. "Okay, what does that mean?"

He laughed. "You're definitely different."

"I'm painfully aware of that."

"*Nee*, I mean in a *gut* way. The things I said irritated me are actually the things I like about you. When I'm with you we have fun together.

Things are never boring. You remind me when I'm being a stick-in-the-mud."

"Which has been a lot lately, by the way."

"There was a reason for that, though." He reached for her hand. "I didn't want to fail Johnny. I didn't want to fail myself. So I had to be serious and focused and put everything I had into this farm."

"And it's been a great success." She entwined her fingers with his. It felt strange to be so intimate with him, yet it also felt so right.

"But it really wasn't up to me, you know? Though I acted like it was. I forgot who is truly in control. And I lost myself along the way." His gaze met hers. "I also couldn't see what was right in front of me."

"What's that?"

He tweaked her nose. "You."

"You know, Katie used to say you had a crush on me."

"Now, hold on—"

"And Anna Mae said you liked me."

"How would Anna Mae know?"

"Are they right?" She grew serious.

He nodded. "They are." He paused, then held up their joined hands. "This is the part where you tell me you care about me too." He frowned. "You do, right? I mean, you wouldn't have kissed me like that if—"

She leaned forward and pressed her lips against

his. When she drew away she said, "I think that's self-explanatory."

"Not that I'm complaining, but it would be nice to hear the words too."

Bekah pulled out of his grasp and stared at him. "Caleb, we need to get something straight right now, before this . . . whatever this is . . . goes any further."

"I'm listening."

"You said I'm different. I'm glad you're okay with that. But I'm not going to change. I have to be me. I have to be the person God created me to be. And that means I'll burn bread every once in a while. And I might forget a birthday occasionally, although my memory is a little sharper since I forgot *Mamm*'s last year."

"Please don't forget mine."

"I'll try. When is it again?" When he started to tell her, she laughed. "April 2."

"December 12 is yours."

She grinned, pleased. But she had to finish saying her piece. "I don't sew very well, I don't notice dust unless it's dancing in sunbeams, and I haven't made *mei* bed in a year."

"I don't care about that," he said. "None of that is important to me. As long as you're happy being you—and you don't burn down anything—I'm okay with that." He grinned. "Actually, I prefer it."

"You do?"

"It's tiring being a stick-in-the-mud all the time."

She took his hand again. "Caleb, since we're being completely honest . . ."

"What?" He rubbed her finger with his thumb.

"I, uh . . . well, I may have had a crush on you at one point. A small one. Long time ago."

He leaned back and grinned. "I knew it."

"You did not!"

"Of course I did. How could you resist me?" He winked.

She squeezed his hand. "Where do we *geh* from here? I've never . . ." She looked away.

"Dated anyone?"

She nodded. "Until now, I never wanted to."

"Just one more reason for me to like you." His gaze grew thoughtful. "When you date someone, you spend time getting to know them. But we know each other pretty well."

"Very well," she said.

"I guess we're past the dating part, then. We should move right on to being a couple."

"I agree," she said.

"But I don't want anyone to know. Not right away."

She nodded. "Katie and Johnny have their secret, and we'll have ours."

"*Ya.*"

"This could be fun," she said, rising to her feet.

He joined her. "It will definitely be fun. Now, *geh* get my fishing pole."

"I thought you said you were going to do it?"

"I changed *mei* mind." He put his hands at his waist. "Besides, I know you're dying to get your feet wet."

He was right. She'd been itching to dip her toes in the water since she'd gotten there. She went to the edge. "Don't you push me in," she said.

"Mr. Stick-in-the-Mud? Of course I wouldn't."

Bekah moved to put a foot in the pond—

Splash!

Johnny brought Katie a cup of herbal tea. He sat next to her on the small back deck of the house. "How are you feeling?"

"Still better. I'm tired, though. I'm glad the doctor said there was nothing to worry about." She rested her hand on her flat belly, still amazed she was going to have a baby. All these years of hoping and praying, it had finally happened. Although the morning sickness had been worrisome, now she felt more at ease since seeing the doctor.

"I'm sure Bekah won't mind sticking around a little longer to help you instead of finding another job. If you need her to." He took her hand. "Speaking of Bekah, she and Caleb have been gone for a while."

"Hopefully they've caught a lot of fish."

"Sure," he said. "Fish." Katie and Johnny looked at each other and started laughing.

It wasn't too long before Bekah and Caleb

appeared from the woods. Johnny pointed at Caleb. "The way he's carrying that creel, I think it's empty."

"I think you're right." She leaned forward in her chair, noticing that Bekah's *kapp* was sagging. "Does Bekah look wet to you?"

"So does Caleb."

They waited for the two of them to approach the deck. Katie hid a grin as she looked up at them, soaked from head to toe, Caleb carrying the creel, the bait bucket, and his shoes while Bekah held the poles and her shoes.

"How did the fishing turn out?" Johnny asked. How he spoke with a straight face Katie would never know.

"Fish weren't biting," Caleb said. He gestured to Bekah.

"So you went for a swim instead?"

"*Ya,*" Bekah said quickly. "That's what we did." She turned to Caleb and lifted her chin. "Caleb," she said curtly, her face pinched.

"Bekah."

Katie looked at Bekah, then at Caleb. "Is everything okay between you two?"

"Other than him being a complete jerk, everything's fine. I'm going to get a shower." She thrust the poles at Caleb, who had already set his belongings on the ground, and marched inside.

"She never could take a joke," he mumbled,

practically scowling. He turned away and headed to the shed to put up the poles.

Johnny rocked back and forth in the chair. "They're not fooling anyone," he said, winking at Katie.

She took a sip of her tea and smiled. "*Nee*. They're not."

CHAPTER 20

Jeremiah pulled into Judith's driveway to drop off Anna Mae. He put the car in park and looked at her, then looked at his father's house. "I better see Amos first," he said. "I'll have to explain why we took off like that. And we've been gone for hours."

"I'll talk to him," Anna Mae said. "You *geh* find *yer daed*."

He turned off the engine. "Might as well leave the car here," he muttered. "Dad doesn't like the eyesore in plain sight of the road."

He felt Anna Mae's hand slip into his. "It will be okay."

"What if he doesn't listen?"

"Then keep talking." She released his hand and smiled. "I'll find Amos. I'm sure he's in the barn." Anna Mae got out of the car and headed for the barn.

Jeremiah watched her go. His father wasn't the only person he needed to talk to. He and Anna

Mae had things between them that needed settling.

He looked inside the house and didn't find him there. Anna Mae hadn't come out of the barn, so he knew she was in there with Amos. There was only one other place his dad would be. Jeremiah went to the fenced-in pasture, and sure enough, his father was there, watching the cows as they grazed in the dusk of evening.

Jeremiah tried to collect his thoughts, to shore up his courage. His mind was a blank. There was so much to say, yet the words wouldn't come.

He went to stand beside his father, who didn't look at him. Didn't even acknowledge him. Jeremiah closed his eyes, praying for something to say. Then he opened them and saw his father staring at him, his eyes red-rimmed. As if he'd been crying.

"*Daed*," he said, alarmed. "What happened?"

"I'm sorry."

"For what?"

He thrust an envelope in Jeremiah's hand and walked away.

Confused, Jeremiah looked down at the crumpled paper. He smoothed it out so he could read what it said. He glanced at the return address . . . and felt the blood drain from his face.

"You sure you want me to read this to you?"

Anna Mae stared at the envelope in her hand.

She'd found Amos where she'd expected him to be, in the barn, drawing. What she hadn't expected was for him to give her a letter. Now they were sitting next to each other on a stack of hay bales, and she didn't know if she was doing the right thing.

"I don't read too *gut*," he said. "*Daed* told me it was from *Mamm*, but I don't understand what it says."

"You've read it?"

"Some of it." He pointed to the letter. "She's got really pretty handwriting. But I don't read too *gut*."

Anna Mae put her hand on Amos's knee. "I know," she said quietly. While to Amos it seemed that getting a letter from his mother after fifteen years wasn't a big deal, Anna Mae was practically in shock. She also felt like she was intruding.

He put his huge hands on his knees, looking at her expectantly. She carefully opened the letter and started reading.

My dearest Amos,

I know you are surprised to receive this letter from me. I should have written to you before. I should have sent more letters. I should have mailed you birthday cards. I should have sent you presents, like books and crayons, paints and paper. I should have been there when you were growing up. I should be there now to see the man you've become.

Saying I'm sorry isn't enough. I can't explain why I left—the reasons are too many and too complicated. Just know that I thought of you every day. That I missed you and Jeremiah. I can never forgive myself for what I did to both of you and your father. I can ask for forgiveness, but I don't expect it. I can hope that someday you will be able to forgive me.

Anna Mae paused, tears in her eyes.

"Why did you stop reading?" Amos asked. His expression hadn't changed. He didn't look sad or angry. But she knew the words she read next would break his heart.

She swiped a finger across the top of her cheek. "I had something in my eye."

"Okay," he said. "Is that the end of the letter?"

"*Nee.*" She took a deep breath and continued.

I'm very sick, Amos. I have what's called pancreatic cancer. The doctors can't help me. The end is near, and by the time you read this, I will be gone.

"Gone where, Anna Mae?"

She took his hand and continued reading.

Know that I loved you, my sweet Amos. I loved both you and your brother more than anything else in my life. You are very special.

Use your gifts to make other people happy, the way you made me happy from the day you were born.

Love,
Mammi

She looked at him, still holding his hand. He didn't say anything, just stared at the barn floor. Then he stood.

"Amos?" Anna Mae rose and walked over to him. "Are you okay?"

"*Ya.*" He looked at the walls around the barn, as if he were searching for something.

Jeremiah came rushing inside the barn. From the paleness of his face, she could tell he had received a letter too. As Amos continued to stare at the barn walls, she went to Jeremiah.

"Is he all right?" Jeremiah asked. He looked at her, glanced down, and saw the letter in her hand.

"I'm so sorry," she said, folding the letter in half. "He asked me to read it to him."

"It's okay." He watched Amos walk around the barn. "What did he say?"

"*Nix,* so far." She moved closer to him. "Are you okay?"

"I'm fine."

But the hoarse tone of his voice said otherwise. Anna Mae looked from one brother to the next. Both lost, and both needing each other. She put Amos's letter in Jeremiah's hand before slipping out of the barn, leaving them to find their way together.

Instead of going to Judith's house, Anna Mae found herself walking along the road, thinking about the letter. About Jeremiah and Amos's mother. Her letter was filled with regrets and unanswered questions. Did Marie regret leaving her husband and sons? Or was it only when she had to face death that she realized she'd made a mistake? She'd had the chance to see Jeremiah when he contacted her, but chose not to. Yet in Amos's letter she said she loved him. Maybe she hadn't been sick at the time and thought she would have another opportunity to see him.

Or maybe she simply didn't want to.

Anna Mae continued walking until she found herself in front of her parents' house. A week had passed since she left. Being away from her parents had been painful, but the separation had also brought her clarity. She knew what she wanted to do now, and felt that God was leading her in that direction.

But he'd also led her here. And she knew why. Saying a short prayer for strength, she walked up the porch steps and knocked on the front door.

"Amos?" Jeremiah said, approaching his brother carefully. He gripped the letter in his hand. He assumed it said the same thing his did—that their mother was dead. He was grateful Anna

Mae had been with Amos when he got the news. But there was no reaction on his face, only a lost look in his eyes as he kept walking the perimeter of the barn, staring at his drawings.

"Help me find room, Jeremiah," Amos finally said. He turned to him. "Help me find room, okay?"

"Room for what?"

The tiniest tremble of Amos's bottom lip was Jeremiah's only clue to his brother's pain. "For *Mammi*," he said, turning away and looking at the wall in front of him.

Jeremiah understood. He looked around, searching for any spare space on the barn walls. But they seemed to be full. He thought about painting over one of the existing drawings, but which one? They were all special, all part of Amos's life.

"Here."

Jeremiah turned and saw Amos pointing to a small space near *Grossmammi* Ella's portrait. He nodded, and Amos crossed to the other side of the barn to his wooden box of pastel chalks. He opened the box, pushed a few pieces out of the way, and selected what he needed. He then went to Jeremiah.

"Will you help me?" he asked.

Shaking his head, Jeremiah said, "I don't want to mess up your picture."

Amos smiled. "You won't mess it up. We should do this together."

Jeremiah looked at the chalk in Amos's out-stretched hand. Brown, the color of his mother's hair and eyes. He took it. "Before we do this, I need to know . . . you understand what happened to Mom, right?"

"She died. Cancer." He smiled. "But she's okay now."

"How do you know?"

Amos didn't answer. Instead he turned and started sketching his mother's face. Young. Beautiful. The way she had looked when they were little.

When Amos was ready, Jeremiah started coloring his mother's hair. He wiped the tears that fell down his cheeks. He had no idea how he had any left. His mother had basically been dead to him for fifteen years. But knowing she was physically dead, knowing he would never see her again . . .

"She's very pretty, isn't she?" Amos said as he outlined her round eyes.

"*Ya*," Jeremiah said thickly. "She is."

When no one answered the door, Anna Mae walked around to the back of the house. Her parents' buggy wasn't parked in front of the barn. She must have missed them. She turned to leave.

"Anna Mae."

She looked over at her father, who was rising from the wooden swing in the yard. She hurried toward him, and they met in the middle. She looked up at him, seeing the worry in his eyes, and the sadness. "I'm sorry," she whispered.

He took her in his arms. "You don't need to apologize." He leaned his cheek against her *kapp*. "I wish I would have been here."

She pulled away with a small smile. "And miss your trip to Canada?"

"You're more important than a fishing trip. You know that."

"Is *Mamm* here?"

"You just missed her. She didn't say where she was going." He led her to the swing, and they sat down, much like they had done when she was younger. "She's having a tough time of it, Anna Mae."

"I know. So am I." She looked at her father. "I miss you both so much."

"Then come home."

"I can't."

He leaned forward on the swing, resting his arms on his knees, his head down. "I should have suspected this. I saw the signs."

"You did?"

"*Ya*. I knew you were unhappy. I knew Caroline was worried. I told her God would sort it out." He sat back up. "Guess he did, just not the way she and I wanted." He looked at her. "You feel this is God's doing, telling you to leave the *Amisch*?"

"I do. I'm sorry I'm disappointing you."

Her father took her hand. "I'm glad you haven't turned your back on God and that you're listening to him and obeying. That's the important thing." He sighed. "It doesn't make it any easier, though. What are you going to do now?"

"Stay with Judith until I get my GED. Then college, hopefully nursing."

"And that's really what you want?"

"It is."

"Do you have to stay with Judith? You could live here and study."

She squeezed his hand and let go. "I think it's better this way. For all of us."

He nodded. Pushed the toe of his boot against the ground and made the swing rock back and forth. "You'll have to tell *yer mamm*."

"I know. Is it okay if I wait here for her?"

"Sure." He smiled. "Wanna hear about *mei* fishing trip?"

She grinned. "*Ya*. Tell me every detail."

Judith had forced herself not to go over to David's after he left. Knowing what was in the letter . . . seeing him break down and cry over Marie's death . . . She pressed her hands against her heart, praying with every breath for him and Jeremiah and Amos. She felt so helpless. A plate of oatmeal cookies or a fresh apple pie wouldn't soothe them. There was nothing she could do but pray.

She puttered around the kitchen, the house eerily quiet. Anna Mae hadn't returned since leaving with Jeremiah. Maybe she would be with him when he found out the news. That gave Judith a little bit of comfort.

A knock sounded on the front door. Had David returned? She hurried to open it and was shocked to see Caroline Shetler on her front porch.

"Is Anna Mae here?" she said through the screen door.

Judith shook her head. *"Nee."* She gripped the side of the door, bracing for the harsh words she knew would come.

Instead, Caroline rubbed her hands together. She looked to the side, then back at Judith. "Can I come in?"

Surprised, Judith opened the door. Caroline stepped inside, but didn't go very far. "Do you know when she'll be back?"

"I'm sorry, I don't. The last time I saw her she was with Jeremiah."

Caroline's closed lips tightened, and Judith knew she'd said the wrong thing. "Is this his doing?" Caroline asked. "She was perfectly fine until he came back."

"Was she?"

Caroline's eyes narrowed. Then she let out a breath. *"Nee.* She wasn't."

"Kumm," Judith said. "Sit down. You can wait for her here."

After hesitating a moment, Caroline perched on the edge of the couch.

"Would you like something to drink?" Judith asked.

"I'm fine."

But Judith could see she was anything but fine. She sat down across from her. "Anna Mae is doing well," she said, trying to find something encouraging to say.

"She would be better at home." She looked at Judith. "But that's not going to happen, is it?"

"I don't know. God has plans for Anna Mae. I know she's been praying about her future."

"I'm glad to hear that." Caroline folded her hands on her lap. "I . . . I appreciate you giving her a place to stay. I shouldn't have asked her to leave. But I know now that she would have left anyway. In her own time."

"Maybe this was the right time," Judith said. "She misses you and her family. This has been hard on her."

"You don't think it's been hard on us?"

"I know it has." Judith rubbed her forehead, trying to keep her voice on an even keel. Between David and his family and Anna Mae and her family, she was having a hard time keeping it together.

Caroline stood. "I should *geh*. When Anna Mae returns, will you tell her I stopped by?"

Judith nodded. "I will."

"I can see myself out."

Judith didn't bother to protest as Caroline walked out the door. She leaned back against her chair, her heart heavy with the pain of her friends, who along the way she had started to consider family. They were all at the point where only God could bring them together and heal them. She prayed that he would do just that.

CHAPTER 21

Jeremiah and Amos finished the last touches on their mother's portrait. They both stood back and looked at it. A decent likeness of her, thanks to Amos's expert eye and Jeremiah's acceptable coloring skills. Amos had even shown him how to do shadows and shading, although it was nowhere near his level of expertise.

"Looks *gut*," Jeremiah said, glancing at Amos.

"It needs a little more work." Amos took the chalk out of Jeremiah's hand. "I'll fix it."

Jeremiah smiled slightly. "You going to be okay out here?"

Amos nodded. "You need to find *Daed, ya*?"

"Yes. I'm worried about him."

"Are you gonna fight again?"

He reached up and rubbed Amos's hair. "Not if I can help it." Then he drew his brother into a hug. "I love you, Amos."

Amos didn't respond but embraced Jeremiah tightly. He let go, then went back to his drawing.

Jeremiah left the barn and checked the pasture, but his father wasn't there. He went into the house and called his name. No response. He took the steps two at a time and checked the bedrooms. His *daed* was standing at the window of his bedroom, staring out into the front yard.

"Did you hear me calling you?" Jeremiah asked.

His father nodded.

"Why didn't you answer?"

"I wanted to be alone."

Jeremiah took a step back, about to grant him his wish. But he couldn't keep running. Instead he moved to stand by his father. They looked out the window in silence, both of them consumed with memories. With pain.

Finally his father spoke. "Did you read the letter?"

"Yes. Amos read his as well."

Dad turned to him. "Is he okay?"

"He's fine." Jeremiah swallowed. "Are you all right?"

His father shook his head and walked to the bed. "*Nee*, I'm not." He sat down on the ratty blue-and-red quilt he'd had on his bed ever since Jeremiah could remember.

Jeremiah leaned against the windowsill and crossed his arms. "Did you know she was sick?"

His father shook his head. "That's the first I'd

heard from her since she left." He sighed. "California. That's about as far away as she could *geh*." A tear slipped from one eye.

Jeremiah uncrossed his arms. He'd never seen his *daed* cry before, not even after *Mamm* left.

"I've done so many things wrong, Jeremiah. I let *mei* anger at *yer mamm* eat at me for so many years. I've pushed you and everyone else away. I've done the exact opposite of what God wanted me to do. And I thought I was justified in doing it." He turned to Jeremiah. "Resentment and anger. That's the legacy I've given you."

The threat of tears clogged Jeremiah's throat. Why hadn't he tried harder to see his father's side of things? To understand the burden he was under? "*Nee, Daed*. You always did the best you could."

"That's what people told me. It's what I kept telling myself." He ran his hand over the quilt. "I could have done better. If I had done more . . . maybe she wouldn't have left. If I'd been a better husband, she might have stayed." He looked up at Jeremiah. "If I'd been a better *vatter*, maybe you would have stayed."

Jeremiah turned to his father. "Don't blame yourself—"

"Oh, but I do." *Daed* wiped his eyes with the back of his hand. "I handled it wrong. I kept you and Amos isolated. I wanted to protect you from the world. You'd both been hurt enough. In the end, it was the world that took you—and her—away from me."

"*Daed*, listen. It wasn't the world. It was my career. My calling. If there had been a way I could become a vet and still be here, I would have."

His father looked surprised. "You would?"

He nodded. "I learned a lot while I was gone. Not just school stuff, but a lot about what I don't want. The world . . . it doesn't appeal to me. Not like you think." He sat down next to his father. "Not like it did to *Mamm*. I should have visited. I should have written letters. I should have come back when *Grossmutter* Ella died. I'm the one who was wrong . . . not you."

"We were both wrong." He suddenly clenched his hands into fists. "She was wrong."

"Why did she leave?" Jeremiah asked.

"She didn't tell you in the letter?"

"No. All she said was that she had her reasons. That she was sick and dying." He found his resentment rising. "That she hoped I could forgive her someday." He looked away. "She wouldn't even come to my graduation."

"You talked to her?"

"I tracked her down. Wrote to her." He shrugged. "She didn't care, apparently."

"She loved you," his father said. "That never changed. But her love for me did. Her commitment to being *Amisch*. We might have been able to save our marriage, but not when her heart and

315

soul was in the Yankee world." He paused. "She asked me to *geh* with her. She wanted all of us to leave." He lowered his head. "But I couldn't do it. And she wouldn't take my *sohns* away from me. She promised me she would stay away. She kept that promise."

Jeremiah's jaw dropped. "Why didn't you tell me?"

"I didn't know how. Amos never would have understood. You wouldn't have either, until you were an adult." He ran his palms over his thighs. "And part of me was so angry with her. She hurt me. I wanted her to hurt too. I ended up hurting everyone." He looked at Jeremiah. "Can you forgive me, *sohn*? Can you ever forgive me for this?"

Jeremiah's anger drained away, like a plug had been pulled out of a tub filled with filthy water. He looked at his father, his heart filling with love and respect. He hadn't known until this moment how deeply his father's love for him and Amos ran—or how much pain both his mother and Jeremiah had caused him. If only he hadn't been so quick to judge his father, had tried to understand his feelings more.

"Can you forgive me?" Jeremiah said through tears. He fell into his father's embrace.

Daed squeezed him tight. "Jeremiah . . . there's nothing to forgive."

Anna Mae walked with her father to the end of her parents' driveway. The sun had already dipped below the horizon, and she wanted to get back to Judith's before dark. "I'm sorry I missed *Mamm*," she said.

"Me too. But you can always come back and talk to her." Her father looked down at her. "Your decision hasn't changed the fact that we love you."

She smiled, glad her father had accepted her choice, even if he did not entirely understand it. Now if only her mother would as well. She prayed she would.

Anna Mae started for Judith's house. She saw a buggy coming on the opposite side of the road and recognized it. Her mother. Fortunately, there was no traffic, and Anna Mae flagged her down. Her mother stopped the buggy, and Anna Mae ran across the road.

"I was just at the house," Anna Mae said. "I wanted to talk to you."

Her mother gave her a half smile. "I was at Judith's, waiting to talk to you." She paused. "Do you want a ride back to her *haus*?"

Anna Mae nodded and got in. Her mother turned the buggy around, and they were on their way. For a few minutes an awkward silence hung between them. Then her mother spoke.

"Did you talk to *yer daed*?"

"*Ya.*"

"What did he say?"

"That he misses me. That you miss me too."

"I do." She tugged on the reins. "I suppose you haven't changed your mind about not joining the church?"

"*Nee.*"

"What about going to school?"

"I plan to do that. I still want to be a nurse."

Her mother lifted her chin. "That's an important profession."

"I think so."

She pulled into Judith's driveway and halted the horse. She turned to Anna Mae. "Is Jeremiah a part of this plan too?"

"I don't know, *Mamm.* That's up to the Lord."

Her features softened. "Isn't everything?"

Anna Mae reached for her mother's hand, knowing that while she didn't say the words out loud, she did accept that she had made her decision. "I have faith that it is."

Her mother held on to Anna Mae's hand. "I'm sorry," she whispered. "I shouldn't have told you to leave." She took a deep breath. "I should have tried to be more . . . understanding."

"It's okay," Anna Mae said.

"Your father was so angry with me when he got home." She shook her head. "He wanted to come get you and drag you back home."

She arched a brow. "He did?"

"*Ya.* I convinced him to sleep on it, at least. The next morning he went to work. He didn't say anything else about what happened. But that's your father. He's not much for talking . . . unless it's about fishing."

Anna Mae chuckled. "I heard about his trip."

"He had fun." *Mamm* smiled, but it faded quickly. "I need you to be honest with me," she said.

"I will be."

"I need to ask you again. Is Jeremiah a part of this?"

Her guard up again, Anna Mae opened her mouth to deny him being in her life at all. But she had promised to be honest with her mother, and with herself. "I don't know."

"What does that mean?"

"It means I'm not leaving because of him. That's all I know."

Her mother squeezed her hand. "Anna Mae, your father and I want you to be happy. That's all we've ever wanted." Tears slipped down her cheeks. "If this is what you have to do—"

"It is, *Mamm*." Anna Mae reached over and hugged her mother.

Her mother tightened her arms around Anna Mae. "Just know that we love you," she whispered.

Anna Mae smiled through her own tears. "I do."

Plink. Plink.

Anna Mae's eyes flew open at the sound at her window. Silvery moonlight streamed through the glass. She waited. Silence. Maybe she was hearing things. She closed her eyes and started to fall back asleep. After the day she and everyone else had had, she was exhausted.

Plink.

She opened her eyes again. There was definitely something there. She got out of bed and went to the window, looking through the screen. She saw a tall, slim figure standing beneath her window. "Jeremiah?"

"Meet me outside," he said in a loud whisper.

"Why?"

"Please, Anna Mae."

She stepped back from the window, put a kerchief over her hair, and slipped on a dress. She crept downstairs in the darkness, barefoot. Judith had already gone to bed too. They had talked a little bit about what had happened with the letters and with her parents, but both of them had been too exhausted to stay up any later.

With careful and quiet movements she opened and closed the front door. The moon was nearly full, casting the night in a silvery glow. She had just stepped foot on the cool grass when Jeremiah appeared. He grabbed her hand and took her to the back edge of Judith's backyard, as far away from the house as they could be.

"Jeremiah, what's going on?"

He let go of her hand and took a step back. "I'm sorry to wake you up. But we need to talk."

"Now?"

"Yes. Now."

She looked at him, noticing his white T-shirt, shorts, and bare feet. "Where are your shoes?"

"At the house. I spent the night."

"You talked to *yer daed*?"

"We worked a few things out. We still have a ways to go."

She nodded. "I'm sorry about *yer mamm*."

"Thanks. We're all going to be okay. Amos said something about having a little service for her. Me, *Daed*, you, and Judith." He paused. "I think it's a good idea."

"Just tell me when and I'll be there." Confused, she added, "But, Jeremiah, you could have told me this tomorrow."

"That's not what I wanted to talk about." Jeremiah took her hand and pulled her down to sit on the grass with him. A warm breeze stirred the night air. "Doc Miller wants me to take over his practice."

"Is that a *gut* thing?"

"It could be."

He held on to her hand, the warmth of his touch triggering her feelings for him. Did he have any idea how his nearness affected her? She doubted it, or they wouldn't be talking about Doc Miller right now. His face was silhouetted in the dim moonlight, and she couldn't see his expression clearly. "I don't understand," she said, which was probably the biggest understatement she'd ever uttered.

"Have you decided what you're going to do?" he asked. "We haven't talked about it." He turned his head. "I probably don't have the right to ask."

"Jeremiah," she said, making him turn toward her again. "You have every right to ask." She explained to him about wanting to be a nurse. About studying for her GED and possibly going to college. As she spoke, he nodded and rubbed his thumb over the back of her hand. She wondered if he realized he was even doing it.

"Judith said I can stay with her until I get my GED," she continued.

"Have you told your parents?"

"*Ya.* I'll still visit *Mamm* and *Daed,* but it would be best for me to stay with Judith."

He nodded. "I understand."

"Once I've gotten the GED, then I'll have to apply to colleges. I'll need to get a job and figure out a way to pay for it. Plus live on *mei* own." She drew in a breath. "Although I don't have to tell you all that."

"It's all right. I want to hear it."

She leaned forward, smiling. "It's scary and exciting at the same time." Then she sat back. "What if I can't do it?"

"What? The schooling?"

"Any of it." Doubts crept in, making huge chinks in her confidence.

"Anna Mae, you're smart. You're determined. And if this is what God wants for you, he'll make it happen." He looked down at their hands. "I have to be honest. It won't be easy."

"I know. But you did it." The clouds that partly covered the full moon started to drift. "With God's help, I can handle it."

He looked at her again. "So you're sure this is what you want to do?"

"Definitely." She pulled her hand out of Jeremiah's and glanced over her shoulder. "I should get back to the *haus*."

"Wait," he said, grabbing her hand again. "We're not finished."

"What?"

"I want to talk about that kiss."

She froze, unsure what to say.

"You remember it, *ya*?" He spoke *Deitsch*, his words soft, like a whisper floating on a moonbeam.

"*Ya*," she said, moving out of his grasp. "And I shouldn't have done it." She looked down at her lap, tucking her skirt more tightly underneath her legs.

"You're right. You shouldn't have."

Shame filled her, along with a little bit of anger. "If I remember right, you kissed me back."

"I did. I shouldn't have done that either."

This was becoming painful. "I don't think we need to discuss this anymore." She moved to get up, but he stopped her, taking both her hands in his.

"Don't leave, Anna Mae." He dropped one hand, but held the other one as he moved to sit next to her. "Just because we shouldn't have kissed doesn't mean it wasn't right." He traced his finger along her jaw. She was tempted to pull away, but she couldn't. "I've lived with a lot of regrets these past few years. I don't want to live like that any-more."

"What do you mean?"

"I'm finished running. I'm finished being a coward when it comes to my family . . . and my feelings for you."

Her breath hitched.

"I care about you." He turned her face toward his and kissed her. When he ended the kiss, he asked, "Did that feel wrong?"

"*Nee*," she whispered. It felt anything but wrong.

"Remember what you told me when we were kids? That I needed to follow my dream? You need to follow yours too. I want to help you do that. You don't have to do it alone."

"Like you did." She touched his face.

"I can help you study for the GED. We'll look at colleges together." He snapped his fingers. "I'll take over Doc's clinic, and you can work for me as a tech. Or do the office work. I'll help you find an apartment—"

"*Nee*."

"What?"

She looked down at their joined hands, her heart slamming in her chest. How easy it would be to choose Jeremiah's way. How simple to lean on him, to accept the help he was so willing to give. But as much as the kiss they had shared felt right, agreeing to his offer felt wrong.

Must I leave everyone I love behind?

She knew the answer. She wouldn't be following God, she'd be following Jeremiah. And like him, she couldn't stay in Middlefield. The still, urgent voice in her heart told her that she needed to follow a different path.

Anna Mae stood up. "I'm sorry."

He shot up from the grass. "Sorry? I don't underst—"

"You're right. I don't have to do this alone." She pressed her lips to his, tasting the tears rolling down her cheeks . . . and his. "But I need to."

"What are you saying?"

She stepped away, saw the pain in his eyes illumined by the night sky. "I'm saying good-bye, Jeremiah."

"Wait." He reached out to her, only to pull back before he touched her arm. "What about us?" Now he stepped forward.

Every part of her being wanted to reach out to him. But if she did, she would never let go. "I love you," she whispered, her voice breaking.

"Then stay."

She shook her head. Wiping the tears from her cheeks, she said, "You know I can't." Unable to be near him without her heart smashing into pieces, she turned and walked toward Judith's house.

He didn't move. He didn't chase after her. But he did call out her name, his voice halting and haunting at the same time. She turned and faced him.

"I'll wait," he said in a thick voice. "I'll be here . . . and I'll wait."

Anna Mae nodded. It was all she could do, not sure he could even see it in the dark. She turned and left, hoping he would keep his word . . . and knowing she was selfish to want him to.

CHAPTER 22

Bekah sat at Katie's kitchen table, scrutinizing the drawing in front of her. She smiled. Finally she'd gotten it right. This would be the perfect green-house for Johnny and Katie. It had taken her few days, but she was pleased. In tiny letters she signed her name at the base of the bushes she'd drawn. Perhaps it was a little prideful, but she couldn't help herself, and she made sure it was hidden enough that no one would see the signature unless they searched for it.

She started picking up wads of discarded paper

around the trash can in the corner of the kitchen. She really had to work on her aim. As she tossed the last paper ball into the container, Caleb came into the kitchen, smelling of sweat, horse, and hard work.

Could she possibly love him more?

He went to the sink and filled a glass with water. He drained it before looking at her. "Where's Katie?"

"At *Mamm*'s. She said she needed to get out of this *haus*. I think she was going stir-crazy. She took *yer* buggy. Hope you don't mind."

"Nope. She's welcome to it anytime." He gazed at her. "So are you."

Bekah felt her cheeks redden. "Better be careful. Johnny might walk in."

"He's gone too." Caleb moved closer to her. He let his finger trail down her forearm. "Can you meet me at the barn in a few minutes?"

"Sure. Why?"

"You'll see." He walked out of the kitchen, a slight smile on his face.

She leaned against the counter, tapping her chin with her finger. What could he be up to? She watched the clock. He said a few minutes. After five passed she dashed outside, unable to stand waiting anymore.

"Caleb?" she called as she walked into the barn. She passed by the stalls, checking on the horses. She hadn't been out here very often.

Although Caleb had told her to stay away from the horses out of anger, she wanted to respect her boundaries when it came to the farm. But she couldn't resist touching the velvety nose of a pale-blond horse.

She stopped at Promise's stall. Strange, it was empty. Maybe Caleb had taken her to the corral. She noticed he seemed to favor her in particular.

Bekah walked into the corral. Sure enough, Caleb was there with Promise, holding her bridle. She hung back until he gestured for her to come over.

Smiling, she crossed the short distance and stood by Promise's head. She looked at the horse, so vibrant and healthy now that the toxic lead was out of her system. But like the other horses, she would be sold in the near future. The thought filled her with sadness, causing her smile to fade. She pushed thoughts of Promise's sale out of her mind and forced another smile, putting her hands behind her back. "So, what is it you wanted to show me?"

"You're looking at it."

Bekah glanced around the corral. Nothing was different. "What am I supposed to be seeing, exactly?"

Caleb took Bekah's hand and put Promise's reins in her palm. "She's yours, Bekah."

Her mouth dropped open. "What?"

"Promise belongs to you."

"But I thought you were going to sell her."

Caleb moved closer to her and to Promise. "I was. But she belongs here, on our farm. She belongs to you."

As if the horse had understood what Caleb said, Promise nuzzled Bekah's shoulder. Bekah reached up and stroked her nose. "I don't understand."

"Think of her as an engagement gift," he said.

Her eyes widened. "Did I hear you right?"

"If you heard 'engagement gift,'" he said, smiling, "then *ya*, you heard me right."

"You're asking me to marry you? But we've only been dating for—"

"Nope," he said, taking her hand so they were both holding Promise's reins. "Remember, we skipped that whole part?" His gaze grew serious. "I love you, Bekah."

She looked up at him, and she knew she wanted to spend the rest of her life with this man. "I love you too. And I'd be thrilled to marry you."

He opened his arms as if he were going to give her a hug, but held back. "Are we still keeping it a secret?"

"Like it's been a secret to anyone?"

They both looked to see Johnny and Katie standing nearby, laughing. "We were wondering when you two were going to make it official," Katie said.

"What about you?" Bekah retorted, stepping

away from Caleb. "When were you going to tell us about the *boppli*?"

Johnny and Katie looked at each other and shrugged. "Guess we don't have to."

Bekah went to her sister and hugged her. "I'm so happy for you," she said.

"I'm happy for you too." They separated, and then both of them said together, "It's about time!"

Jeremiah flipped open the trunk and pulled out a cardboard box. The flaps were tucked underneath each other. He shut the trunk and went inside his father's house.

"Amos!" he called as he walked into the living room. No answer. He headed for the kitchen, stopping when he heard Judith and his father talking.

"I miss her," Judith said. "The *haus* is so lonely without her."

Jeremiah shifted the box on his hip and stood close to the kitchen door, straining to hear.

"I miss her too," his father said. "She was like a *dochder* to me."

"Me too. But she had to leave. She had to follow her own path."

Jeremiah's throat closed. Three days had passed since he'd talked to Anna Mae. Since she'd told him good-bye. It still hurt when he remembered how she had walked away, so beautiful in the moonlight, so strong in her conviction. He'd realized at that moment he had fallen in love with her. But he didn't go after her. He couldn't. He had to let her go. He understood more than anyone the choice she was making.

"I talked to Caroline yesterday," Judith continued. "She said Anna Mae went to Sugarcreek. Elijah has a cousin who left the *Amisch*. She's staying with their family."

The kitchen had grown silent. Jeremiah peeked through the doorway and saw his father reach for Judith's hand. They didn't say anything, just sat there and comforted each other.

Jeremiah stepped back and walked out the front door, his emotions mixed. He ached for Anna Mae, but was happy that his father was finally finding the peace and love he deserved.

He wondered if he'd ever find that for himself.

Pushing Anna Mae out of his mind, he went to the barn and found Amos there, working this time, mucking out a stall. "You got a minute, Amos?"

"*Ya.*" He walked out of the stall and wiped his hands on his pants legs. "You weren't at breakfast this morning."

"I had a few things to take care of."

"Does this mean you're not staying here anymore?"

Jeremiah shook his head. "Amos, I can't stay here forever. I have to get my own place eventually. But I'll be here for a little while. Until I find an apartment." He grinned. "In Middlefield."

Amos tilted his head, confusion in his eyes. Then he smiled. "You're not leaving us?"

"Nope."

His brother hugged Jeremiah, making him drop the box. "Oof," Jeremiah said, caught off guard.

"I thought you would *geh* find Anna Mae," Amos said as he let go.

"I don't need to find her, Amos. She's right where she's supposed to be."

Amos frowned. "But don't you miss her? I miss her a lot."

"Me too."

"Then why did she have to leave?"

Jeremiah sighed. How could he explain it to Amos? Or to his father, or to Judith? Then he realized he didn't have to. "What did Anna Mae tell you when she said good-bye?"

"That she would write. A lot."

"Anything else?"

He paused. "She said that she wanted to be a nurse. That she had to leave to be a nurse. Like you had to leave to be a vet." He looked at Jeremiah and smiled. "I get it now."

Jeremiah grinned. "*Gut.*" He picked up the box. "I brought you something."

Amos took the box and sat down on the pile of hay bales. "What is it?"

"Open it and find out."

He pulled out four small art canvases, oil pastels, watercolors, pencils, and regular paints.

"I didn't know which ones you wanted to use," Jeremiah said, "so I just bought different kinds of supplies."

Amos held up the canvas, which was stretched on a board. "What is this for?"

Jeremiah hunkered down in front of him. "I was hoping you could make some pictures for the clinic." He paused. "My clinic."

"I don't understand."

"I took Doc Miller's offer to take over his vet clinic. He'll still be around for a while as we transition . . ." He paused at the confusion on Amos's face. There was no need to go into details about the transaction with Doc. He'd explain it to his father later. "I just wanted some new artwork for the walls. Some animal pictures, if you don't mind."

"But people will see them."

"That's the idea."

Amos shook his head. "I don't want to get into trouble."

"You won't. No one will know you painted them but me." He touched Amos's knee. "Okay?"

Amos grinned. "Okay. I'll paint after *mei* chores are done."

Jeremiah started to leave, but Amos's voice stopped him.

"She'll be back, you know."

Jeremiah turned and looked at him. "How can you be so sure?"

Amos stood up and walked over to Jeremiah. He put his hand on Jeremiah's shoulder and squeezed. The look in his brother's eyes gave Jeremiah a chill. For a split moment Amos wasn't the childlike man he'd always been. He was stern. Confident. His voice and words and expression were laced with a wisdom and depth Jeremiah had never seen before.

"I just know." He removed his hand from Jeremiah, turned, and went back to the stall.

Jeremiah watched him, still reeling, and for the first time since Anna Mae had said good-bye, he was filled with hope for the future.

He left Amos in the barn with the art supplies and walked away, leaving his father and Judith back at the house. His family was finally finding peace.

Now he would have to find his own.

He headed to the car. He'd stay with his father and Amos for another week or so, then find his own place nearby.

As he opened the door to the car, his cell phone rang. He fished it out of his pocket and looked at the screen. The number wasn't familiar. "Hello?"

A long pause.

"Hello?" he said again.

"Jeremiah?"

He leaned forward and put his hand on the hood of the car. "Anna Mae."

"Hi."

His heart pounded in his chest at the sound of her sweet voice. "Hi," he said softly.

"I . . . I hope it's okay that I called. Doc Miller gave me your number."

He half-smiled. "Of course."

She told him about her father's cousin in Sugarcreek. How she would be staying there until the near future. "I got a cell phone," she said. "But I guess you already knew that."

He could hear the strain in her voice. "Is everything all right?"

"*Ya*. It is . . . it really is. I know I'm doing the right thing. I feel a peace about being here."

He shut the car door and leaned against it. "Good. That's important."

"But . . ."

He held his breath. "But what?"

"I . . . I miss you, Jeremiah."

"I miss you too."

"Would you mind if I called you every once in a while? So we can keep in touch?"

His heart flipped. "That would be great."

"Okay. I have to *geh. Mei* cousin is taking me to an adult education center to find out about the GED test."

"Good luck."

"Thanks. I'll talk to you later."

"Anna Mae?" He couldn't let her go just yet.

"What?"

"I'm praying for you."

She paused. "Thank you."

When she hung up he stared at the phone for a moment. Hearing her voice stirred up both pain and joy. More than anything he wanted to jump in his car and head to Sugarcreek. He ached to be near her. But instead he put her number in his contacts and pocketed his phone.

He'd respect her decision. He understood it, despite how difficult it was to accept the choice she'd made. But at least they would have phone contact. And maybe at some point he could visit her.

Unless she found someone else . . .

His fingers clenched around the phone. He wouldn't let his mind go there. He had to put his relationship with Anna Mae in God's hands. He glanced at his phone again, remembering what she'd told him the night she said good-bye.

I love you.

Jeremiah believed her. And because he loved her, he would do whatever she asked . . . even though it was killing him inside.

EPILOGUE

Four Years Later

Anna Mae pulled her car into the circular drive in front of Doc Miller's clinic. The sign in front still bore his name, but underneath was the name *Jeremiah Mullet, DVM.*

She stopped the car and turned off the engine. Her pulse throbbed in her temples. This was the first time she'd been back to Middlefield since leaving to pursue her nursing degree. She was nearly finished; she'd completed her clinicals last week, and once she took her test she would be an RN. Then she would start applying to hospitals and hopefully would soon be working at a job she loved.

But before then, she had to return home. She had to see Jeremiah.

They hadn't lost contact the past four years. If anything, distance had brought them closer. She looked forward to their frequent conversations on the phone. He had even visited Akron a few times, where she had ended up going to school. But they made sure to keep things light between them. Friendly.

It had been the hardest four years of her life.

The summer sun beat down through the windshield of her car. Was this how he'd felt when he came back? Like his nerves were all misfiring at once? She looked down at her crisp, flowered, capped-sleeved shirt, white capris, and sandals. Maybe she should have worn a dress. She touched her hair, wishing she had waited awhile longer to get it cut. The last time she'd seen him her hair had been shoulder length. What would he think of her pixie?

What would he think of her once she told him what was on her heart?

She got out of the car. They hadn't talked in a few weeks. She'd been busy finishing school, and he had left the country to go on a mission trip to Haiti with his church. It was the longest they hadn't spoken to each other, and as each day passed, she ached to hear his voice. Ached to see him. Ached to be near him.

She went to the door, lifted her hand to knock, then changed her mind. What a dumb idea, knocking on the door of an open clinic. She walked in, a tiny bell tinkling above the door. An elderly man with a Yorkie in his lap looked at her, and a cat in a crate sitting next to a young girl meowed.

"May I help you?" a young woman called from behind the counter. A *pretty* young woman, she noticed. Anna Mae went to her. "I'm here to see Dr. Mullet."

"He's not here." The woman checked a logbook. "Do you have an appointment?"

"No . . . I was just hoping I'd catch him when he wasn't busy."

"He's out for the afternoon. Did you want to talk to Dr. Smith?"

Dr. Smith must be the new vet Jeremiah had hired a few months ago. The business had flourished since he'd taken over Doc Miller's practice. She shook her head. "That's okay."

The receptionist put the appointment book back on the desk. "Dr. Mullet will be here tomorrow. Do you want me to leave him a message?"

"No message." Anna Mae backed away and turned around, only to stop when she saw four small paintings on the wall in the waiting room. She inspected them more closely. One was a beautiful pastel drawing of a herd of horses grazing in the pasture. Another was a winter scene, a buggy and horse trotting on a powdery white road. Her heart warmed as she gazed at the third one, a Labrador retriever playing with a calico cat next to a wishing well.

The fourth one made her breath catch. Painted in exquisite watercolor, there was a calf, taking her first steps. Belle's heart on her forehead was prominently displayed as she stood by her mother, who nudged her with her nose.

Anna Mae smiled. There was no signature on the paintings. But she knew who had created them.

She hurried to her car, got inside, and turned

the key. Maybe she should have called. Maybe she should call him now. Or maybe she should just wait until the end of the workday. She could go see her parents in the meantime—

A knock sounded on her car door, surprising her. She pressed the button to roll down the window. The receptionist stood there, shading her eyes in the sun.

"I'm not sure why I'm telling you this—or if I'm even supposed to." She sighed. "You can find Dr. Mullet at his cousins' farm. I'll give you directions—"

"I know where it is." Anna Mae smiled at the woman. "Thank you."

She nodded, returning the smile. "It seems important that you see him."

"It is."

A short time later she pulled into Johnny and Caleb's driveway. Before she got out of the car she sat back and took in all the changes. Instead of one farmhouse, there were now two. There were two barns, and the driveway was covered in asphalt instead of gravel. As she got out of the car, a little girl about three years old appeared from the back of the house. She didn't approach Anna Mae, but looked at her with wide-eyed curiosity, the skirt of her tiny blue dress lifting in the breeze.

Anna Mae smiled and moved closer to her. She knelt down in front of the little girl. "What's your name?"

The girl didn't respond, putting her finger in her mouth instead.

"Ella!" Bekah Yoder—Mullet, Anna Mae had to remind herself—appeared. "I told you to stop running off—" She stopped and smiled. "Anna Mae?"

Anna Mae went to her and hugged her. "It's *gut* to see you, Bekah." She stepped back. "*Mamm* told me you and Caleb got married the fall after I left." She glanced at Ella, who was looking up at both of them, her blue eyes still wide. "Is she yours?"

"Katie and Johnny's. They went to town for the day and I'm watching her." She looked down at Ella sternly. "She's a wanderer who doesn't like to listen to her *aenti*."

Ella glanced away as Bekah knelt in front of her. "Ella, say hello to your cousin Anna Mae."

She gave Anna Mae a short wave. "Can I play in the sandbox?"

Bekah nodded. She stood, and the two of them followed Ella into the backyard. "Have you been back long?"

"Just drove in."

"You'll have to tell me everything," Bekah said, turning to her. "Later."

"Later?"

"*Ya*. After you see Jeremiah. He's here."

"I know."

Bekah smirked. "So you didn't come here to see me, then?"

"I did, but—"

"I'm teasing. He's in the barn with Caleb." Bekah pointed to the barn Anna Mae remembered.

But Anna Mae didn't move. Bekah frowned. "What's wrong?"

"Nothing, I'm just . . . I don't know." She glanced over her shoulder. "I'm nervous."

Bekah put her hand on Anna Mae's arm. "Don't be."

Anna Mae nodded and walked toward the barn. Before she reached it Caleb came out, alone, looking a bit different now that he had a beard. He paused as if he didn't recognize her, then gave her a wave but didn't approach her. Instead he headed toward the house, where Bekah now stood waiting. Everyone seemed to know she needed to speak to Jeremiah alone.

She walked into the barn and saw him putting his stethoscope in his bag as he looked up.

"Anna Mae?"

Their gazes met, his eyes lighting up as he looked at her. Her heart thrummed, as it always did when she saw him. Suddenly her breath caught, nearly knocking her off her feet. The last of the emotional clouds that had hovered over her the past few years finally cleared. Their separation had been painful for her, but necessary for them both. God's timing had been perfect—as it always was.

"Is everything okay?" he said, his smile suddenly turning to a frown.

"Everything is perfect."

"Good," he said, nodding. But he tilted his head, concern and hesitation showing on his face.

"I know I should have called first. And I'm sorry I'm interrupting your work."

"Don't be. I'm glad you're here." He didn't move. He held back, the way he always had when they were together over the past four years. The longing for each other hung in the air between them, creating an invisible barrier that neither of them had dared to cross.

Until now.

She drew in a breath as she walked to him, took his hand, and led him to a short stack of square hay bales near the back of the barn. The earthy scents of hay and horses surrounded them, tickling the memory of them working together to save Johnny and Caleb's horses. She released his hand and sat down. He did the same.

"I needed to talk to you, Jeremiah. Not over the phone. Face-to-face."

He angled his body toward her. "Okay, I'm here."

She smiled, her heart swelling with love for him. "You always have been." Unable to stop herself, she reached for his hand again. "Thank you. For everything."

"What's going on, Anna Mae?" He pulled out of

343

her grasp, worry furrowing his brow. "This isn't . . ." He swallowed.

"Isn't what?"

"Good-bye?"

The pain in that one word propelled her toward him. She touched his cheek, the texture of his day-old beard rough against her fingers. "No," she whispered. "Not good-bye."

Before she could catch her breath, he took her in his arms and kissed her. She didn't hold back, not caring that anyone could walk into the barn at any moment.

He broke the kiss, his gaze still locked with hers. "I've waited so long." His voice sounded as breathless as she felt.

Guilt made her squirm in his embrace. She stopped when his arm tightened around the small of her back. "I'm sorry," she said.

"No apologies." He ran his hand over her short hair. "I like it."

"The haircut?"

"Everything." His finger trailed down her cheek. "You don't know how many times I've wanted to do this," he said. "All those visits to Akron, knowing I had to keep my distance."

"Which is why we always went *out* to dinner," she added.

"Or lunch. Or coffee." He dropped his hand. "It's been a long four years."

Anna Mae nodded. "For both of us."

He lifted her hand, tracing the top of her knuckles with his thumb. "I need to know something."

"What?" She tightened her fingers around his.

"Why are you here? What's changed?"

"I have. I don't have to be alone anymore. I don't *want* to be." She fought back the tears threatening to fall.

He didn't move, his eyes continuing to lock onto hers. "I'm not leaving Middlefield," he said. "This is my home. It always has been, even when I was away. I want to keep working here. To raise my family here."

She nodded. Even though she didn't regret for a minute going off on her own, she'd always felt the pull of the place where she grew up. She moved off the hay bales and knelt in front of him, her heart slamming so hard in her chest she thought it would burst. They'd never talked about this, never made such a deep, verbal commitment. But it seemed right to tell him how she felt. She didn't have to hold back anymore. "I need you, Jeremiah. I'll stay in Middlefield. Or I'll go somewhere else, as long as I'm with you. I can't stand being apart anymore."

"What are you saying?"

She took his hands. "That I love you. I want to marry you."

He tilted his head, not saying anything for a moment. Behind her a horse whinnied. Jeremiah kept staring at her. Then he stood, bringing her up with him. He took her in his arms and kissed her so sweetly the tears she'd been holding back slipped down her cheeks.

"I love you too." He wiped her tears with his hands and touched his forehead to hers. "Does this mean you're ready to come home?"

She leaned her head on his shoulder and closed her eyes. For the first time, everything was right. She was where she was supposed to be, with the man she loved. "I'm already here."

ACKNOWLEDGMENTS

Writing is never a solitary endeavor, and I had the privilege to work with amazing people who helped me bring this story to life. Thank you to Becky Monds, Jean Bloom, and Sue Brower for your valuable editing and feedback. It was a treat to work with you on this book together. Thank you, Kelly Long—you got me through this book! Thank you also, Brooke Frensley, for helping with Bekah—you know what I mean :)—and to Sue Laitinen for your horse expertise. And a special thanks to you, dear reader, for coming with me on another Middlefield journey.

READING GROUP GUIDE

1. During Anna Mae's struggle in deciding whether or not to leave the Amish, she isolated herself from family and almost all her friends. Do you think this was wise?

2. Would Anna Mae have been better off confiding in the community about her indecision? Why or why not?

3. Early in the story, do you think Caleb was being unfair to Bekah? Why or why not? How could Caleb and Bekah have handled themselves differently?

4. Do you think Jeremiah was selfish for leaving his family, especially his brother, behind? What, if anything, should he have done differently?

5. Did Judith do the right thing by allowing Anna Mae to stay with her?

6. If you were in Anna Mae's shoes, how would you have handled her decision to leave the Amish?

7. Have you ever had to leave a community (family, church, neighborhood, etc.) behind? How did God help you through it?

8. Now that Anna Mae has returned to Middlefield, do you think she'll become close to her family again?

ABOUT THE AUTHOR

Kathleen Fuller is the author of several best-selling novels, including *A Man of His Word* and *Treasuring Emma*, as well as a middle-grade Amish series, The Mysteries of Middlefield. Visit her website at www.kathleenfuller.com.

Twitter: @TheKatJam
Facebook: Author Kathleen Fuller

Center Point Large Print
600 Brooks Road / PO Box 1
Thorndike, ME 04986-0001 USA

(207) 568-3717

US & Canada:
1 800 929-9108
www.centerpointlargeprint.com